MY GREAT EX-SCAPE

PORTIA MACINTOSH

Boldwood

First published in Great Britain in 2020 by Boldwood Books Ltd.

Copyright © Portia MacIntosh, 2020

Cover Design by Debbie Clement Design

Cover Photography: Shutterstock

A CIP catalogue record for this book is available from the British Library.

Paperback ISBN 978-1-83889-081-0

Ebook ISBN 978-1-83889-082-7

Kindle ISBN 978-1-83889-083-4

Audio CD ISBN 978-1-83889-079-7

MP3 CD ISBN 978-1-83889-426-9

Digital audio download ISBN 978-1-83889-080-3

Boldwood Books Ltd
23 Bowerdean Street
London SW6 3TN
www.boldwoodbooks.com

For Joe —The future Mr MacIntosh

1

'How would you like £50,000?'

I never expected to hear those words this evening. Who am I kidding? I never expected to hear those words ever.

I always try to look on the bright side of life, searching high and low for the positive in every negative situation. My mum calls this The Rosie Outlook – an obvious pun combining my name, Rosie, and my ability to always try and find the good, even when it seems impossible.

For example, not beating around the bush, I hate my job. I realise that hate is a strong word and not the kind of chat you would usually expect to hear from someone who prides herself on being positive, but I do, I absolutely hate my job.

When I was a kid, all I wanted was to be a detective. Not a police detective though, a private detective, the kind you see in film noir. You know the sort, the cigarette-toting, low-key sexist, wisecracking type in the long, plain coat with a fedora on top of their head – the only kind I saw on TV growing up. As I matured into my teens and this no longer seemed like a viable job (if it even seemed like a real job at all), I realised that a job did exist that involved exposing the truth. I wanted to be an investigative journalist, and this actually seemed like a goal I could achieve.

Flash-forward to me, here today, thirty-one years old, and I am a journalist... just not the kind I wanted to be. I work for the *Salford News*, just outside central Manchester. It's only a small, local paper though, so not only is there not much room for an investigative journalist, but every page of the weekly paper is pretty much an advert. I spend most of my days writing paid advertorials – which is basically an advert hiding inside a news article – and given that the clients are paying for exactly what they want these pieces to say, it's not exactly a challenge.

I don't just hate my job, I resent it. I'm kind of trapped in it, until I can find something better – well, trapped by my finances at least, I'm technically a freelancer, so I'm not exactly bound by a contract. Unless I just want to stop paying my bills – but I've heard that doesn't go down very well.

I did say there was a plus side though, and that plus side is Sam, my boss. I hate my job, but I love my boss. Sam is my editor and I can tell that she tries her best to give me the good jobs and, of the very few perks you get being a local faux journalist, she'll often toss a few my way. She's great when I need time off, she lets me off the hook when I arrive late – she even buys the office pizza on Fridays. Sam really is a wonderful boss.

Money isn't great... I know, it's not really great for anyone right now, is it? But I live within my means. My apartment is small (which means my rent is too), but at least it's close enough to work for me to walk. I just keep doing what I'm doing and hoping things will get better.

I was a little down in the dumps today because David, my boyfriend of four months, cancelled our plans this evening because he needs to work late. He's a lecturer at the university, teaching Palaeobiology (I didn't know what it was either). I wrote my dissertation on yellow journalism and the paparazzi. David gets more excited about things like mass extinction. We might not have much in common, but we still get on really well. Sometimes opposites just attract, don't they?

So David was going to be teaching young adults studying for their master's degree all about macroevolution (I don't know what it is either, I just remember seeing his lesson plan over his shoulder and feeling like a bit of a dummy) tonight and I was going home to my tiny apartment to watch *Hollyoaks*... or so I thought.

I was just about to leave work, after a particularly gruelling day writing an 'article' about a local window cleaning company, when Sam called me into her office. She had two tickets for the live filming on a new TV quiz show, but it was her husband's birthday, so she wasn't going to go. She offered them to me and Gemma, the other girl who does the same job as I do, so with nothing better planned I made the short trip to MediaCityUK – the development in Salford where all the big TV studios are based.

I didn't think anything of it when they told us we had to download an app so we could play along, nor did I expect anything eventful to happen to me when I found out contestants would be plucked from the studio audience. But then I sat down and, as the filming started, I couldn't believe it when my phone started ringing. Mine. *I* had been selected at random to play the game. Gemma was fuming, she's not happy unless she's the centre of attention. I was just a combination of embarrassed and terrified. I've never been on TV before – well, how many people have? – but I'm not really the kind of person who likes to be the centre of attention and I couldn't even begin to imagine how many eyes would be on me – and not just here in the studio.

The show is called *One Big Question*. I'm guessing it's aiming itself at millennials because the app seems to be at the heart of it. It can be used by people to play along at home, but here, in the studio, it's what I can use to ask the public or the audience for help with answers.

I can't actually believe my luck, but I'm on the final question – the titular one big question – and if I answer it correctly, I'll win the money I've banked so far. A whopping £50,000.

'I said, how would you like £50,000?' Mike King, the host, asks again.

'I'd love £50,000,' I admit, my voice wobbling almost as much as I am on this tall chair.

If I'd known I was going to be chosen to take part today, I probably would have turned the opportunity down, even with the knowledge that I could win some serious money. I don't think I would've thought I had it in me to get this far...

I'm somehow too hot and too cold. I want to say the studio lights are hot, but there's cool air con to offset the warmth. I am sitting opposite the host in the centre of a brightly lit circle, in an otherwise dimly lit room. I can't see the audience – I can't even see the camera, not really. I only know they're there now because of the little red LED lights I keep spotting. Even without them, I don't think I'd be able to forget I was on TV. On live TV, no less.

'This is your final question,' Mike explains. 'Who said blondes were dumb, huh?'

I smile politely. I have had to contend with the dumb blonde thing my entire life. First, when I was younger, when I had naturally blonde hair, and then more recently from all the highlights, because for some reason my hair gets darker as I get older.

'Your only remaining lifeline is to make a call from your speed dial numbers,' Mike reminds me.

When we started, I was allowed to select three numbers from my phone in the event of choosing the 'make a call' option. Without many friends or people who I even believed would answer, I chose my dad, Tim, Sam, and David. I don't suppose any of them would know all that much about anything based in pop culture, but I think I have that covered myself. Anything on the life and works of Alan Titchmarsh, unscrupulous news practices, or bones, and one of them might be some use to me. I doubt my boss would appreciate me calling her on her husband's birthday, so here's hoping for the Chelsea Flower Show or cavemen. At least if it's the latter, David's lecture will be over and he'll be able to take the call. My dad probably won't even hear his phone ring.

'Ready for it?' Mike asks.

I nod unconvincingly.

'OK, here we go... Which dinosaur had fifteen horns?'

An impossibly big grin stretches all the way across my face. This has to be a joke. I might be optimistic, but I am under no illusions – I am not a lucky person. I don't get picked for TV shows, I don't have many people to call for help, and I definitely don't get questions that are going to be easy... and yet here we are.

'You know this one?' the host asks in disbelief.

I know I might be blonde, but that doesn't mean I don't

know anything about dinosaurs. I mean, I don't know anything about dinosaurs, but what gives him the right, huh?

'I know a man who does,' I say as my grin inches even wider. 'I'd like to call my boyfriend please.'

'Your boyfriend knows a lot about dinosaurs?'

I nod, only semi-smugly.

'I'm sorry to hear that,' the host jokes. 'What's your boyfriend's name? What does he do?'

'His name is David and he's a lecturer.'

'What does he teach, dinosaurs?'

'Palaeobiology,' I reply.

'Is that dinosaurs?'

'Yes.'

The audience laugh wildly. Mike is a sort of cheeky-chappy host. A thirty-something former musician who has somehow made it as a TV presenter. I suppose it's his charm – the audience clearly love him.

'OK, let's get Dinosaur Dave on the phone,' Mike says.

I wince as he says 'Dave' – David hates being called Dave.

'So all you have to do is, when Dinosaur Dave answers, just tell him you have one big question to ask him. If he gets it right, you'll be £50k richer!'

'Sounds good,' I say.

It doesn't just sound good, it sounds great. David knows everything there is to know about dinosaurs, there's no way he's getting this one wrong. I just hope he answers – can you imagine if he didn't?

'Quiet in the studio,' Mike says, hushing the audience as the phone rings.

'Hello,' David says when he answers the phone.

'Hey David, it's Rosie,' I say, in a suspiciously formal

manner. 'I... erm... I have One Big Question I need to ask you...' I try to hide the nerves in my voice, but it's impossible. I'm on TV – calling up my boyfriend on live TV – to ask him a question about dinosaurs so that I can win £50,000! I cannot stress enough that this is not a typical day for me.

'Let me stop you there,' he says. 'Because I think I know what you're going to say.'

'David...'

'No, let me speak,' he insists, as though he's talking to one of his students. 'For a while now I have suspected you're far more serious about this relationship than I am, and I was happy to let it slide because no one was getting hurt, but now I suspect you're calling me to ask me to move in with you perhaps – maybe even marry you, you can be quite full-on... Anyway, I just don't want you to make a fool of yourself so, the time has come – we need to break up. I didn't want to do this on the phone but... it's not you, it's absolutely not you. It's me. I'm just not that into you and you're getting way too serious too quickly...'

I sit on my chair in stunned silence. The host is in silence. The audience is in silence. I imagine everyone watching at home is sitting in silence. If the cast of *Gogglebox* were watching this show, it would be one of the quietest episodes of *Gogglebox* ever. No one knows what to say or do.

'Rosie, say something,' David prompts.

I look over at Mike who has his hand raised over his mouth. He looks shocked, he's cringing, but I can also see something hidden deep in his eyes that makes me think he knows this is TV gold, and he's just leaving things to see how they play out. So I do the only thing I can think of doing...

'Which dinosaur had 15 horns?' I ask.

'The kosmoceratops...'

I tap the button on the player dashboard in front of me.

'Kosmoceratops, final answer,' I say blankly.

'I... erm...' Mike blusters.

'Kosmoceratops,' I say again.

I don't know if you can use willpower to stop yourself from blushing, but I am trying my hardest not to show how absolutely mortified I am. It's taking all my strength – and even more not to burst into tears.

'Kosmoceratops,' I insist for a third time.

'Erm... OK...,' Mike tries to push on. 'Is that the right answer?'

I have to endure one of those painfully long, uncomfortable pauses they do on quiz shows to build suspense while you wait to see if you've got the right answer. Every second is absolute agony as I try to keep a lid on my embarrassment. If this had happened under any other circumstances, I probably would have burst into tears.

The screen flashes up that this is the right answer, as it has done with all the other questions, only this time, as this is the final question, it is accompanied by a rainstorm of gold glitter. As it cascades down over me, Mike hands me a comically large cheque for £50,000.

This feels like one of those nightmares where everything seems fine before events take a horrible turn, like you're giving your Oscars acceptance speech but then you look down and realise you've forgotten to put on your dress. It is somehow one of the best and one of the worst days of my life. I can't even begin to figure out how I should be feeling right now.

'Sorry,' he whispers into my ear, giving my shoulder a

squeeze, before turning back to the camera to finish the show for the evening.

As he wishes the audience and the viewers goodbye, instructing them to tune in tomorrow for another live show, I look at my cheque.

Of all the things I expected to happen today, the events of the last few hours were certainly not on that list.

2

Last night I got dumped. Last night I got dumped in front of an audience. Last night I got dumped on live TV.

However you look at it, it's bad, but the more you think about it, the worse it gets.

I'm trying to use my Rosie Outlook to remind myself that I am £50,000 better off than I was yesterday, but even that is proving challenging today.

I may be £50,000 richer, but I'm also one boyfriend poorer – albeit one terrible boyfriend who I'm better off without. I mean, come on, seriously, he thought I was trying to take our relationship to the next level, so he dumps me over the phone? And, I have to stress, I have shown no signs of wanting to level-up our relationship – none at all. I've just been a good, normal girlfriend. I haven't expected much, I haven't stopped him going out with his friends. I've just given myself to him with blind optimism and he's tossed me away like an old dinosaur bone. Well, I don't suppose he'd throw an old bone away, would he? He'd salivate over it and write a book about it. I guess that one doesn't really work... He's thrown me away like [insert cool thing here] because David hates cool things. His mum bought him a snapback cap for his holidays and he threw that away. He hates avocados with a fiery passion (not because he doesn't like the taste, but because they're a hip thing to eat) and he always looks at my iPhone with all the disgust you'd give a dog turd, so I guess he's thrown me away like any of those things instead.

I sigh to myself. I really, really don't want to get out of bed, but I need to leave for work in forty-five minutes. I know, I've just won £50k, but it's not exactly quit-your-job money, is it? At least not overnight.

I roll over in my small double bed and grab my phone from my bedside table. The stupid One Big Question app drained my battery last night and by the time I got home and plugged it in, I was asleep before it had turned back on. I just wanted the day to be over with and, to be honest, I didn't want to make any more phone calls anyway.

My screen looks like a whole mess of stuff that I can't quite make sense of, so I grab my glasses. I don't need them for reading so I don't usually wear them in bed. I generally wear contact lenses through the day because I think my glasses make me look dorky, but my eyes feel all funny so I grab my glasses to wear for now.

Does that say... No? It can't. Apparently I have over 100 notifications. I don't think I've ever had 100 notifications on my phone, not even when I downloaded Tinder – *especially* when I downloaded Tinder.

Missed calls, iMessages, emails, Twitter, Facebook, Instagram – they're all blowing up. I wonder if the One Big Question app has caused something to malfunction in my phone... until I notice a notification for a suggested YouTube video called 'Woman dumped on live TV by dinosaur nerd'.

I click it, as though there might be some small chance that this isn't a video of me, but of course it is, and it's had over three million views so far.

Oh boy...

I click Twitter and see that my mentions and DMs have erupted with messages from strangers. I keep my DMs open for work, which I seriously regret right now. Some people feel sorry for me, some find it all absolutely hilarious... and then there are the comments that are especially hard to take, the ones calling me a bunny boiler, laughing at me but in a mean-spirited way, saying David did right to dump me. No doubt from the idiotic incels of the internet who delight in seeing a young woman being made a fool of. As I get into the tweets where people start insulting the way I look, I realise there is only one thing for it. I need to deactivate my social media accounts. All of them. At least until all of this blows over.

I toss my phone to one side and get out of bed. As if this situation wasn't bad enough, I just had to go viral, didn't I? And not just in the UK, oh no, worldwide! Absolutely fantastic!

I wander into the kitchen and put the kettle on. I take a mug from the cupboard and toss in a teabag. I watch as the kettle boils, only to abandon it the second it does. What am I doing? Why am I carrying on like nothing has happened? My life is over. I'm humiliated.

I wonder if £50k can buy me a new identity. I wonder what I can actually do with it... I could go on holiday. I could quit the job I hate, using the cash as a buffer while I find another one. It is such a soul-destroying gig; I'd love nothing more than to leave. I'm an adult though, so I won't. I might call in sick today, but I need to make sure I keep going to work and acting like everything is fine – things will catch up eventually, right? And at least I'll be around allies of sorts, rather than reliving my mortification.

I grab my phone and call Sam.

'Rosie, oh my God, are you OK?' she asks, answering after one ring.

'Oh, you know,' I say as casually as I can, though of course she knows – *everyone* knows. 'I'm just ringing to call in sick. I'm dying of embarrassment. Hoping I'll feel better tomorrow.'

She laughs sympathetically. There aren't many bosses who would accept embarrassment as a legitimate reason for a sick day.

'I've been trying to call you,' she says. 'Gemma wants to write a news piece about the local girl who works for the paper who went viral overnight. I didn't think it was a good idea, but the powers that be have signed off on it... so...'

'Oh, OK,' I say. Typical Gemma, that backstabbing snake. I'll bet she's over the moon that this has happened to me – and in front of her too. She was smiling like the cat that got the cream all the way home in the taxi last night. 'I guess I quit then.'

'You quit?' Sam replies.

'Yeah... I quit.' The words leave my lips so effortlessly, so softly, they tickle. It's one of the easiest things I have ever done. That's money for you, it makes everything easier. Anyone who insists that money doesn't bring happiness has obviously never been trapped in a dead-end job that sucks the life out of them.

'Well, I understand,' she says. 'And I know you've just come into money, so I doubt I can say anything to change your mind. You know I'll give you a glowing reference, right?'

'Thanks,' I say. 'I suppose I haven't been happy for a while and this money has just given me the push I needed. I thought all this was going to blow over but... meh.'

'I'll make sure the article is sympathetic, it's the least I can do,' she replies.

I hang up the phone, wondering what I am the most annoyed about – that Gemma is going to write this article about me, or that Gemma is getting to write articles. Real ones, not adverts pretending to be articles.

I'm about to discard my phone when it buzzes again. Since I deactivated my social media accounts, the barrage of notifications have stopped. Anything that comes through now can only be from people who have my number – and that's a pretty short list these days.

When I see it's from David, I stare at my phone suspiciously as I wonder what he wants. With that obviously getting me nowhere, I give in and open the message. He wants to see me. He's asked me if I'll go over. Why does he want to see me? He can't be mad at me for not telling him we were live on TV when I called him because he didn't even give me the chance... Even if he was going to break up with me anyway, David is an introvert. He'd never want to do it on TV, he's not that hurtful. Perhaps he wants to apologise? I suppose I just gave him a scare, making him think I wanted to move in together or whatever... Hmm.

I hurry on a tracksuit and pull my long blonde hair into a bun on the top of my head. I put on a little foundation, but that's it. Now that spring is starting to edge closer to summer, it's quite bright out on a morning, so I'll just hide behind my sunglasses. I want to keep things incognito anyway. I'll just low-key slink over to David's place, hear what he has to say for himself, and then work out what the hell I'm supposed to do with myself now that I'm internet famous and unemployed. I swear to God, this is how most people get into the porn business. I'm yet to receive an offer, as far as I can tell, but I'm not sure I'd accept anyway. My boobs are nowhere near big enough, my arse is covered in cellulite and I don't even have a washing machine in my diddy apartment, so no chance of it breaking down.

I'm about to head for the door when someone knocks on it. I instinctively drop behind my sofa – a pointless move, living in a first-floor apartment, but still. I'm terrified of who might be behind it. They knock again, but I remain in cover. I allow them a few minutes before slowly getting up and looking through the spyhole. Confident there is no one there, I open the door to leave. I'm about to step through the door when I stop myself just in time. There's a flower arrangement sitting on my doormat.

I pick it up and take it into the kitchen. It's a beautiful bouquet, with white oriental lilies, creamy white chrysanthemums and baby pink roses. I remove the card to see who they are from.

'I love you. I should never have let you go. I want you back.'

Oh my gosh, they must be from David. This must be why he wants to see me.

I grab the only vase I own (which is empty and just waiting to be used, but that's because no one ever buys me flowers, not because I'm super tidy or organised) and place my flowers in water before heading back into my bedroom to get changed.

If David and I are getting back together, I don't want to be dressed like a shamed TV star hiding from the paparazzi... even if I do kind of feel like one right now.

3

What kind of apartment do you expect a university lecturer to live in? Something stylish and studious? Books – lots and lots of books – but neatly and sensibly organised? Browns and greens and maybe, just maybe, the occasional bit of red? I always imagined David's apartment being like that. A bit like Sherlock Holmes's office, I suppose... but David's apartment isn't like that at all.

For starters, while he does have a lot of books, he has even more magazines. Piles and piles of them everywhere. On the coffee table, on the kitchen worktop – he's even using an especially tall pile as a table for his keys to live on by his front door.

And then there's all the dinosaur junk – not that I'd ever refer to it as that in front of him. I suppose it's good that he's passionate about his work, but it's two kinds of creepy, in my opinion. It's creepy to have bits of real bones and replica skulls and whatnot lying around, but it's potentially even weirder that he has dinosaur toys all over the place. Yes, kids' toys, stationery – he's even just handed me a cup of tea in a dinosaur mug. I glance down at it. It features a cartoon image of an especially sad-looking diplodocus, his head hanging low with a little frown and heavy eyes, accompanied by the caption 'All my friends are dead'. I can't help but smile to myself.

'So, you wanted to talk,' I say, getting the conversation going.

If he wants me back, he's crazy if he thinks I'm going to give him an easy time of it. Well, how can I just take him back after what he put me through last night. I know that he didn't know we were live on TV, and that I scared him with my choice of words, but he's going to have to show me that he's serious about me, that he made a mistake last night, and that he's really sorry.

'Yes,' he says, placing his own dinosaur mug on a coaster in front of him. His mug features a T-Rex along with the caption 'Tea Rex', which is about what I've come to expect from dinosaur mugs. They don't get much better than that.

'I know you never meant to embarrass me,' I say, immediately kicking myself for making this easier for him.

'Of course I didn't,' he replies. 'I would never do that to you – I'd never do that to anyone. I panicked. When you said you had a big question for me, I thought you were trying to propose or something...'

'Yeah, you said,' I reply, trying to laugh that wild assumption off. It was too soon for us to even think about marriage. 'But the show is called *One Big Question*, and when you call someone to ask them this One Big Question, you have to say "I've got One Big Question"...'

'It makes sense now,' he says with an awkward smile. 'How's the fallout?'

'Nuclear,' I reply. 'I've had to deactivate my social media

accounts, people won't stop messaging me, some of them are being actually really quite mean – even I was shocked – and then there's the fact I quit my job.'

'You quit your job?' he says. His tone of voice would suggest that he doesn't think that was a smart move.

'I did. I hated it. And I'm too embarrassed to go in at the moment anyway. And now I have this money, I can use some of it to keep me going while I find myself a new job. I suppose I'll wait a few days, for this "gone viral" business to calm down, I don't want job interviewers bringing it up, but then, yeah, I'm sure I'll find something.'

I'm hoping that's true.

'Not the smartest move,' he replies. 'But I'm sure you've thought this through.'

It was more of a go-with-your-gut reaction, if I'm being honest. But even now, after I've had a little time to think about it, and seen David's reaction to it, I still feel like it was the right thing to do.

'Of course I have,' I reply. 'Don't worry, I don't expect you to start paying for everything.'

'I mean, why would I?' he says. 'We broke up.'

I look at him with a raised eyebrow.

'Rosie, I broke up with you last night,' he says clearly, in a way you would speak if you were trying to explain something to someone who was completely delusional. 'You know that, right?'

'Well, yes...'

'You come over here all dressed up, talking about me looking after you now you've quit your job—'

'Whoa, that's not exactly true,' I insist. 'And I'm here because you said you needed to talk to me.'

'Yes, I want to talk to you about the money,' he says. 'The prize money.'

'OK...'

'I think I deserve a share – potentially half of it.'

I laugh, until I realise he's serious.

'Are you kidding me?'

'You don't know what a Kosmoceratops is,' he says.

'I do,' I reply confidently. 'It's a dinosaur with fifteen horns.'

'You didn't know until I told you,' he clarifies, as though that might make me change my mind.

'David, are you joking? You humiliated me on TV.'

'You don't think it was embarrassing for me?' he replies. 'My students are calling me Dinosaur Dave; they've lost all respect for me. It's all over the uni intranet.'

'Embarrassing for you? Embarrassing for you?' I plonk my dinosaur mug down on his table – without a coaster – and pace in front of him angrily. 'If you hadn't been so quick to dump me...'

'Well, that's the thing,' he starts. 'I dumped you. Have you even stopped to think about why or are you too busy having a pity party and counting your money that you didn't earn?'

'OK, wow, that's it,' I say, grabbing my coat from the hook next to the door. 'Well, I'm not sharing the money with you and there's no way I'm taking you back. You can stick your flowers where the sun doesn't shine.'

'What flowers?' he asks.

'The flowers... the ones you sent me.'

'I didn't send you any flowers.'

Of course he didn't. He dumped me on TV, he's not going to want me back. He just wants a share of the prize money – well, he can think again.

Ergh, I am so annoyed at myself for coming over. I'm not even sure what I ever saw in him now. I feel like girls are always willing to date guys, to give them time to come out of their shell, to see how things go, even if they're not quite working. And guys just cut and run.

I pop my sunglasses on and storm out. I'm outraged at his request – of course I am – but that's not really on my mind right now. The only thing going through my head right now is a question: if Dinosaur Dave didn't send those flowers, then who did?

4

It isn't a long train journey to my parents' house just outside Manchester, but it certainly feels like it is today.

It doesn't matter how old you get in life, when the shit hits the fan you can always go running home to your mummy and your daddy, with tears in your eyes and your tail between your legs, and no matter what you've done, they'll probably forgive you. I say probably because I'm sure there are some things even the most forgiving parents couldn't overlook... I'm not quite there yet, so here I am with a packed bag and a racing mind, hurrying to their house to hide out. I can sleep in my childhood bedroom (even if they have turned it into an office) and watch TV with my dad, help my mum peel potatoes – it will be just like Christmas, but without the presents and with my life completely coming apart at the seams.

I arrived home from David's place to a voicemail from Sam, saying that the team from *This Morning* had reached out to her in the hope of getting in touch with me. Apparently they want me to go on the show and talk about what happened. As much as I'd love to meet Phil and Holly, I never

ever want to be on TV again, and I certainly don't want to relive the single most embarrassing moment of my life.

It was that, combined with those bloody flowers sitting on my worktop, that drove me out of my own home.

Without a name on the card, I am left wondering where they might have come from. Yes, I tried calling the florists, but, as per the data protection act, they can't tell me who sent them. I tried to explain my particular circumstances to the lady on the phone, but she wasn't very sympathetic to my cause. She mumbled something about 'bloody GDPR' and how busy she was before hanging up, so that wasn't much use.

Fortunately, because the card said 'I want you back', that means it must have come from one of my ex-boyfriends. I say fortunately because I have only had, including David, five ex-boyfriends. The reason I am so puzzled though, is because, of these five boyfriends, I have been dumped four and a half times. We'll get to what constitutes a half dumping in a minute.

I know what you're probably thinking because I'm thinking it too. If every single one of my boyfriends has dumped me, is it me who is the problem? Am I just so unlovable – or at least easily dumpable – to the point where all my relationships end in (my) tears?

Kevin was my first real boyfriend – well, as real as you can get when you're fourteen years old. We met across a crowded, smoky food-tech room in year 9. Some pranksters thought it might be funny to put a wooden spoon in the oven, and it was – at least it was at the time. Everything is funny when you're fourteen and don't want to make scones. I look back at it now and just feel so, so sorry for the teacher. Anyone who teaches in a secondary school is a hero because I remember most of the kids being absolutely horrible.

After that day, with the almost fire, we were split from our friendship pairings and made to work with a pupil of the opposite sex. I've never really been sure of the boy-girl system. How or why does it work? Seems like an archaic, sexist system to me, that is heavily reliant on the two genders not being friends.

Anyway, I wound up working with Kevin. He was my next-door neighbour, so we'd been all the way through school together, but I honestly don't think we'd ever said more than two words to each other up to that point, and it took us a while to have a proper conversation. At first we were both so shy and awkward, too scared to take the lead with our weekly cooking challenge. We'd edge around each other carefully, speaking as little to each other as possible, until one day our hands met over a slightly overcooked ham and pineapple pizza and we just hit it off. We became friends, then boyfriend and girlfriend. We stayed together all the way through school, but I stayed at school to do my A Levels while Kevin went to college. Not exactly a long-distance relationship, but we were definitely moving in different directions.

After Kevin, there was Eli. We had a reasonably brief relationship, lasting from towards the end of year 13 until not long after I started university. Eli worked at his dad's mechanic workshop in town so, when I went to study English at uni in Bangor, we were far enough apart for it to cause a strain on our short-lived relationship.

There was no one else, not who I had anything serious with, until after university, when I met super sexy Simon. I was doing an internship at a lifestyle magazine in

Manchester where he was a photographer. He was forever going off to fancy places and snapping beautiful people. I always felt like I was punching above my weight with Simon, and it didn't help seeing models constantly buzzing around him like excitable little wasps, desperate for him to catch their good side. Let's just say that Simon and I had some... trust issues.

My last ex, before Dinosaur Dave, was Josh. I feel like I did a lot of growing with Josh, but then we started growing apart. Unlucky for me, Josh realised the relationship wasn't going to work within minutes of me realising the same, and it just so happened that he broke up with me before I could break up with him. Yes, I realise it's not a competition, but when every boyfriend you've ever had has broken up with you, you start to worry that it's a thing, and now that David has dumped me too, I am petrified that it's a thing.

There is a hint of good news in all of this though... You don't have to be a detective (or an investigative journalist) to realise that, given what it said on the card that accompanied the flowers, while all of them may have dumped me, at least one of them regrets it. But which one? That's the question. It's definitely giving me pause, that's for sure. It's making me wonder... could my future be hiding somewhere in my past?

My past is definitely my future today, as I walk up the driveway to my parents' front door. A beautiful suburban detached down a cute little cul-de-sac. I reach for the perfectly polished handle, but it's a waste of energy. My mum bursts through the door to greet me.

'Rosie, Rosie, Rosie,' she says. 'Oh, Rosie.'

'Hello, Mum,' I say as she squeezes the life out of me.

'Oh, Rosie.'

She starts crying.

'Are you crying because I'm home, because I got dumped, or because I was embarrassing on TV?' I ask.

'I think it's all of them,' she mumbles into my body.

My mum is adorably petite. Sneaking in at just over 5ft, she's small and skinny. I'm a bit more like my dad, who is broad-shouldered and towers over my mum at 5'10. I'm 5'8, so I dwarf my mum too.

I'm starting to regret telling them the full extent of what happened when I called them earlier to say I was on my way over for a few nights. Thankfully they missed it, and can't work their TV to get it on demand. I'd rather they didn't see it.

'Hello,' my dad says with a nod of acknowledgement.

I wiggle free from my mum's grip to give him a hug.

'Oh... love...'

'Mum, let's not talk about it,' I insist. 'Tell me how you guys are doing.'

'Oh, we're fine, we're just cleaning out the shed,' she replies.

'Oh, God, I'm not sleeping in it, am I?'

'Course not,' my dad says. 'I'm making room for tomato plants.'

'Fab,' I reply.

'And you're helping,' he adds.

'What?'

'Did you think you could just hide in our living room, watching TV all day?'

I absolutely did, without a moment's hesitation. I even looked into what constitutes daytime TV now because it's changed so much since the last time I was knocking around during the day. I couldn't think of anything better. It sounds like they've got other plans for me though.

Outside, it doesn't look like they've been working on the shed for long, so I guess I've got my work cut out: shifting tools, moving boxes of God knows what, sweeping, trying to ignore the spiders...

I thought coming here was going to be a nice break... I was absolutely wrong.

5

After hours of dragging dusty boxes around, dodging creepy-crawlies, and listening to my dad's views on who should be the next prime minister, I finally find a moment to sneak into the kitchen for a breather and a glass of lemonade.

I can't decide how right my parents were when they said that a bit of hard work was just what I needed right now, in my 'situation' as they're calling it... I sincerely don't think their reaction would've been different if I were a pregnant fourteen-year-old, like maybe they think I've got myself into this mess that has potentially ruined my life as I know it... maybe I have.

The hard graft in the shed is certainly keeping me busy, but my mind is all over the place. I'll forget about recent events for a moment, distracted by the discovery of potential antiques or magazines that, at a quick glance looked like weird porn but upon closer inspection are just really graphic angling magazines of my dad's. But despite the pictures of dead fish, my mind goes back to my life and, well, what I'm going to do with it.

'Rosie,' my mum cries out. 'Rosie, where are you?'

I put down my lemonade and leg it outside, convinced my mum's screams spell out disaster, but rather than finding my dad on the ground with a pair of secateurs sticking out of his temple – either through a ridiculous accident of his own, or via the hands of my mother when she inevitably snaps – they're both just standing there, absolutely fine, with green bin bags full of rubbish in their hands.

'I thought it was an emergency,' I say, just a little annoyed.

'It is, we can't move for rubbish. You're supposed to be putting it in the gardening bin for us,' she replies.

My parents, Timothy and Evelyn Jones, are the caricature couple you see in cartoons about relationships – usually the ones that accompany agony aunt pages. Timothy – or Tim, to his equally blunt friends – is your classic northern bloke. Firm but fair, stoically silent until you find a topic he'll talk your ear off about, like fishing for example.

Evelyn – or Evie as she's more warmly known – is the exact opposite. She is outgoing, chatty, friendly... she's so warm, it starts to burn a little. All up in your space, all up in your business, but always with the best of intentions. She and my dad are both recently retired (my mum was a teacher and my dad was a builder) and I'm pretty sure she spends her day chasing my dad around with a rolling pin because he keeps drinking milk from the bottle every time he passes the fridge.

His latest thing, which, since arriving back home, I have only recently learned he has been doing, is pinching sugar from the jar – just to eat. I saw him do it earlier, just dip his hand in, grab a pinch of sugar and pop it in his mouth. He says it satisfies his sweet tooth (he's on a diet, apparently, and missing eating cakes and biscuits and the like, so he's taken to having a cheeky dip in the sugar to stop him breaking his diet), but I just think it makes him look like Manchester's answer to Scarface.

My parents do drive each other mad, but you can't deny that they're still head over heels in love.

Since I moved out, I'm not sure I could live with either of them. Even just staying with them for a few days is probably going to drive me mad, but it's better than hiding out in my flat.

I grab a couple of bin bags and head for the front garden, where the bin store lives.

'Green bin,' my mum calls after me.

'Got it, Mum,' I call back.

This isn't my first trip to the bins with bags full of shed crap. I know that the green bin is for the garden stuff. Then there's the black and the brown and blah, blah, blah. I suppose that's one good thing about living in a tiny apartment, I don't have a million different bins with a million different rules for each.

I toss the bags in an attempt to squash them down in anticipation of the bags that will follow. I try with my hands, but I'm not exactly Abbye 'Pudgy' Stockton (she was a bodybuilding strongwoman – I learned this watching repeats of *The Chase* with my dad over our lunch break earlier), so I hop up onto the bin next to it and swing my legs into the gardening rubbish bin, using my body weight to jump up and down on it, squashing it down into the bottom.

'Are you OK?' I hear a man's voice ask.

I jolt my gaze from my feet to next-door's garden, staring like a rabbit caught in the headlights.

At first I'm embarrassed to be caught, you know, in the bin (although it's hardly my most embarrassing moment in the last twenty-four hours), but as I realise it is a familiar face I'm looking at, I cock my head curiously.

'Kevin?'

'Hello, Rosie,' he replies.

Kevin tosses a bag into his parents' wheelie bin, like a normal person, rather than getting in it, before making his way over to the fence that separates the gardens. I clamber out of the wheelie bin and meet him there.

'Oh my gosh, it's been years,' I say as I hug him over the fence. 'How are you?'

'I'm great,' he says. 'How are you? Were you... were you trying to get in the bin?'

'Oh, no, no, no,' I insist. 'No. I'm helping my parents clean out their shed, I was just trying to make room in the bin for all the junk they're throwing away.'

'That makes more sense,' he says with a laugh. 'I'm just here for dinner with my parents.'

I look my first boyfriend from secondary school up and down. He looks great. Older, but I haven't seen him in like fifteen years and time will do that to you. So he's looking a bit crinkly around his eyes and his hairline is creeping back – I've got a few wiry grey hairs hiding in my blonde locks and I need to wear two bras when I exercise now.

'How are they?' I ask him.

'Yeah, they're great. How are yours?'

'Probably dead in the shed after some kind of weird standoff with gardening tools used as projectiles,' I reply, very matter-of-factly. 'But otherwise fine.'

'Oh, I'll bet,' he laughs. 'Well, how about I let you get back to them, but, if you're around tomorrow we could go for lunch? Have a proper catch-up. It's wild, that we never see each other.'

I am taken aback by his invitation. So much so I just stare at him.

'Don't worry if you're busy,' he backtracks.

'No, no, I'm not busy at all. Never busy,' I add, although I probably shouldn't have.

Kevin just laughs at me. 'OK, well, meet you at Sally's in town tomorrow – midday?'

'Sounds great,' I reply. 'See you then.'

'See you then,' he says. 'Don't wear the gardening waste bin.'

'The black is more my colour,' I joke after him.

Gosh, is that weird, him asking me to lunch? I haven't seen the guy in years. Our parents live next door to each other and suddenly he's right here in front of me, asking me for a catch up.

Could it be Kevin who sent me the flowers? I suppose I'll have to have lunch with him tomorrow and find out.

6

I've claimed a table by the window in Sally's Tearoom. It's an impossibly cute place – older than I am. I've been coming here since I was a kid.

It's 12:04 now (I've been here for about twenty minutes because I wanted to make sure I wasn't late) and there's no sign of Kevin... he did say midday-ish though, didn't he? Or did he just say midday? Either way, I'm not going to worry.

I felt bad, hogging a table in such a busy tearoom, so I ordered myself a cup of tea and one of their signature white chocolate blondies. Remembering my manners, I haven't touched either yet, although the blondie is practically screaming my name.

'Hello,' a young woman standing at my table says.

'Hi,' I reply.

She's a twenty-something brunette who I've never seen before in my life. She doesn't work here; I can tell that by her lack of the cute little uniform they wear here with the adorable white pinny.

I purse my lips and raise my eyebrows expectantly, waiting for her to say something.

'I saw you on TV,' she says.

Oh God.

'Me?' I reply, hoping she'll think she's made a mistake.

'Yeah,' she says. 'You got dumped on the quiz show.'

Christ, is this how it's going to be from now on? When I walked in here today, Jon Bon shitting Jovi could've been sitting at one of the tables and I wouldn't have said a word to him, I would've let him enjoy his coffee and his cake in peace, and he's a real celebrity, not a viral epic fail like I am.

'Erm, yeah,' I reply.

'OK, bye,' she says before wandering off.

Oh, brilliant, she just came over to point it out – to remind me, in case I forgot.

'Who was that?' Kevin asks. I hadn't realised he'd walked in.

'Oh, no one,' I say.

'OK, well I'll grab a coffee and join you,' he says.

I watch Kevin as he orders his drink. He's looking really good, in a pair of jeans and a plaid shirt. He's still in great shape – he was always really sporty at school. I was never all that sporty, but he played for the school rugby team and I loved to watch his games, even if I didn't really know what was going on. It was just nice to go along and support him, cheer for him on the sidelines, be proud of him when he won.

Our very first date – and our first interaction outside the food-tech room – was at a McDonald's. We had cheeseburgers and milkshakes while we chatted about school and Blink-182. We shared our first kiss in a McDonald's booth (the old-style cream plastic ones, before they all got funky new makeovers) while Celine Dion's 'My Heart Will Go On' blared out of the speaker above it. It was like something out of a corny movie.

Coincidentally, we also broke up in a McDonald's, just after he left school. After a high tackle that saw Kevin break his jaw – although supposedly this happened because I was distracting him by watching him play, according to his dad – Kevin decided that it had to be me or rugby, and rugby won. That time we didn't stay long, and I definitely don't remember what music was playing. He dumped me over ice cream – I'm pretty sure it was one of those hot fudge sundaes they used to sell, or did they discontinue them sooner than that? Either way, the fact that they don't sell them any more is the only real tragic takeaway. I'm only now, for the first time in years, recalling just how angry I was, to be dumped for a sport. Oh, I was great (that's what he told me), but not as great as bloody rugby, it turns out.

I left McDonald's that day wishing I had dumped my ice cream on his head and I swore to myself that, if I ever saw him again, I would launch the nearest dairy product at him. As he sits down next to me, suddenly nothing on the table seems worth sacrificing. I'd rather drink my tea and eat my blondie and, anyway, we're both adults now. It would be crazy to be mad at him some fifteen years later.

'So, how are you?' he asks. 'We can do more than scratch the surface today.'

'Yeah, I'm doing good,' I say, being mostly honest, but as for more than scratching the surface, I don't know what to tell him, so instead I ask: 'Still playing rugby?'

'I am,' he replies. 'But only for fun. I'm actually an estate agent.'

'Oh wow,' I blurt. 'That's different.'

'Yeah... I don't know, after my injury, I started looking at things differently. I started to worry about hurting people, or getting hurt again. Having a broken jaw really sucked. The thought I might put someone else in that position... so... yeah, I sell houses now. What do you do?'

I smile. He always did seem a little too sensitive to play such a violent sport.

'I'm a journalist,' I say, semi-proudly.

'Oh, cool, who do you write for?' he asks, sipping his coffee.

'I'm actually between jobs right now,' I admit. 'But only as of this week. I didn't like the scruples of the paper I was writing for so I'm venturing out in search of something a little more rewarding.'

'A journalist with scruples is about as useful as a rugby player who is too scared to hurt anyone, surely?' he says with a chuckle.

'Perhaps,' I reply. 'But I'm going to see what I can find, take a bit of a break...'

He nods thoughtfully.

'That's the thing with us,' he starts. 'We're too pure. We don't want to hurt people – whether it's with a high tackle or a few careless words in the paper.'

I smile at him. He still seems like that awkward kid who silently measured flour with me in year 9, but it's hidden deep down inside. He's got that confidence that comes with nothing other than growing up and leaving school. He has no trouble talking to women or... or sending them flowers? Is that why he's brought me here today? To try and get back with me after seeing me on TV and realising I'm his one that got away? Perhaps he is still a little shy after all, I mean, whoever sent the flowers didn't put a name on the card – was that intentional? Has he invited me to lunch to test the water and see if I'm interested? Am I interested? Maybe I should show him that I am, just a little... Just interested in seeing what he has to say, and if he really is the person I wasn't supposed to let go.

With the flowers coming from someone in my past, I am growing increasingly convinced that my future might be in their hands. It's just simple course correction. One of my ex-boyfriends has clearly realised he was not supposed to depart my life when he did, and I'm starting to think it might be Kevin.

'I always thought we'd get married,' I say. No, I'm not being too full-on, before you go all Dinosaur Dave on me, I was a teenager when we got together, remember. 'I suppose, just because you were my first boyfriend, and you always think you're in love with your first and that you're going to stay together forever, don't you?'

'I know what you mean,' he replies, pausing briefly to bite his Chorley cake – a choice that hasn't impressed me, it has to be said. You can tell a lot about people by what kind of baked goods they eat. 'But I really do think that, when you know, you know. I knew. You just know, deep down, in your heart of hearts, if you should marry someone.'

'You knew?'

'I did,' he says. 'I knew 100 per cent.'

Wow, and Dinosaur Dave thought I was full-on.

'I, erm—'

'I think that's why I asked so soon into our relationship,' he says as he rummages around in his pocket.

Wait, what? He can't be talking about me...

Kevin pulls out his phone and taps the screen a few times before holding it up in front of me. It's a photo of a stunning blonde woman sitting on the grass with two beautiful small blonde children.

I glance between the phone and his left hand. He's been wearing a wedding ring this whole time. I really need to start looking for wedding rings now that I'm in my thirties.

'Oh, wow,' I blurt. 'Is that your wife and kids?'

It clearly is, I don't exactly need confirmation. I don't know what else to say while my brain processes this new information.

'Yep,' he says proudly. 'June, my wife, and those two little angles are Annie and Bethany.'

'They're all gorgeous,' I say. They really are.

'What about you, do you have any kids?'

'None that I know of,' I joke awkwardly... I'm not sure that joke works when you're a woman... unless that's what makes it funny? Kevin isn't laughing though.

'Married?' he asks.

'No, I'm—' I'm interrupted by a voice behind me.

'That's her,' the girl from earlier says. 'The one who got dumped on TV.'

'I got dumped on TV,' I tell Kevin. Well, he clearly didn't watch it, and the brunette has let the cat out of the bag.

'Oh...' He pauses for a moment. 'Were you on *Catfish* or *The Undateables* or something?'

'Was I on *The Undateables*?' I squeak. I don't think he's ever watched *The Undateables* – at least I hope he hasn't. 'No, I wasn't.'

'Oh, OK, well... I'm sorry.'

'Thanks,' I reply.

'You've always had such a colourful life,' he points out.

I raise my eyebrows. I really haven't. Suddenly, Kevin

seems like a stranger. Someone who knew me when I was kid, but as an adult there's just no connection there.

OK, so maybe it wasn't Kevin who sent the flowers. And after today, I'm not sure I'll be hearing from him again – not even when he hits his midlife crisis and fancies an affair with an old flame.

I suppose there is a silver lining here, hidden away in all the continued embarrassment: if David didn't send the flowers, and Kevin didn't send the flowers, then there are only three possible people who could have. Only problem is, I have no idea where they are.

7

After an awkward encounter with Kevin I decide to talk a walk to clear my head.

I stroll down the local high street. Well, what's left of it, anyway. A few of the shops I grew up with have stood the test of time – Argos, Poundland, New Look. But the hole where Woolworths used to be tugs at my heartstrings. I used to bloody love going to Woolworths when I was little, picking out toys (or CD singles when I got a little older). For a while, when I was a kid, I would swear that the happiest day of my life was when my mum took me to Woolies to buy a VHS copy of the *Spice World* movie. I remember it came in a limited-edition tin (which I'll hazard a guess is in storage somewhere with the rest of my childhood stuff) and my mum took me for chicken nuggets after. I felt so grown-up.

It's kind of chilly but really sunny, so I'm wearing an over-sized padded coat with my aviator sunglasses. The sun is behind me now, but I'll keep the glasses on. I like to hide behind them, they give me a self-confidence I absolutely don't deserve.

I'm also trying to put my awkward lunch not-date with Kevin behind me. I can't believe I thought, for a second, that he might have sent those flowers. It really was just coincidence that I bumped into him. Still, I wish I'd noticed his wedding ring before I let my imagination run away with me. This flower business has really rattled me, I feel so off the ball.

Amidst all the mobile phone shops, pawn shops and empty units, an old-fashioned sweet shop shines like a diamond in the rough. I pop in and buy myself a bag of jelly-beans for my stroll home. I could get the bus, but I'm in no hurry to get back. Well, Mum and Dad will only start giving me jobs to do again and all this hard work is tiring me out. I'm not used to any physical work or activity at all – unless you count the few stairs at my old office that I'd sometimes have to carry bundles of newspapers up and down.

I rank the different flavours of jellybeans as I walk. Popcorn is obviously up there as one of the best, whereas the root beer one is like pure poison. This is important work that I'm doing right now, a definitive ranking is needed.

I am snapped from my hardcore time-wasting as I realise where I am. I'm outside Wilson's mechanics, where my ex-boyfriend Eli worked – he probably still works here actually, it's his family business and it was always the plan that he would take over from his dad.

Kevin might not have been fate – and this might not be fate, as such, but I must have walked this way on autopilot at least?

I hover outside for a moment. Do I really want to embarrass myself in front of another ex? Why not, eh?

I walk into the waiting room – it's a lot different than it used to be. Before, it was an empty shell of a room with a couple of foldout chairs and a calendar of topless women straddling tyres on the wall. Now it has carpet, a comfortable sofa, magazines without a breast in sight – there's even a plant, for crying out loud. A real, living, plant. It's nothing like the macho chauvinistic hellhole I used to hate waiting in when I was meeting Eli, it's positively modern.

The receptionist is a woman, which I'm not sure is progress or not. On the one hand, they didn't used to have any women working here, but now that they do, she has the obvious job.

'Hello,' I say brightly. 'I'm looking for Eli Wilson, I think he works here.'

'Eli Wilson?' she repeats back to me.

'Erm, yes...' I reply cautiously. 'He works here? He did when I knew him...'

'Just a second,' she says.

She disappears into the workshop for a moment before returning with two men. Big, burly blokes in blue overalls covered in oil. Well, I say oil, I don't know cars. I don't know what oil looks like. I don't know what other liquids cars can leak. I am a thirty-one-year-old baby who has always been a little too scared to learn to drive. Scared of the massive responsibility that comes with driving around in a heavy, fast, metal death machine, but also kind of scared of the financial burden too. Cars are expensive. Parking is expensive. Petrol is expensive. Insurance and tax and MOTs and repairs are all oh-so expensive. It's a commitment I'm just not ready for yet – mentally or financially.

'She's looking for Eli,' the woman practically bursts. 'She thinks he works here.'

'He used to,' one man chuckles. 'You looking for him for something specific?'

'Just a catch-up,' I say. 'He was my boyfriend when I was eighteen, he—'

Fantastic, all three of them are laughing now. How wonderful, an in-joke. An in-joke everyone is in on but me.

'He lives not far from here; do you want his address?' the man asks.

'Please,' I say through gritted teeth.

I take the company-branded post-it note with Eli's address on and leave as quickly as possible. It might be positively progressive now, but it's still uncomfortable in there.

I punch the address into my phone and see that, wherever it is, it's only five minutes away. I've come this far, I may as well drop in on him.

I know you shouldn't have favourites, but Eli is maybe my favourite ex. I'm not saying my feelings were stronger for him than they were for the others and we weren't even together that long, but I just had so much fun with him whenever we were together. Unfortunately, because I was at uni for most of that time, we didn't get to see each other all that much.

All of a sudden, I happen upon the apartment building where he lives. It's a tall building with big windows and balconies all the way to the top, where the penthouse sits, entirely made of glass.

I punch Eli's flat number into the intercom. Eventually someone answers.

At first there are a few seconds of silence and then...

'Is that... Rosie Jones is that you?'

'Hey Eli,' I say awkwardly. I didn't realise he could see me.

'What the hell are you doing here? Come in! Get in the lift, I'll bring you up.'

He'll bring me up? What is he going to do, step outside

his apartment and call the lift? Does he not think I can handle being told a floor number?

The door pops open in front of me.

'OK, see you in a sec,' I say nervously and head into the waiting lift.

I feel like I'm at a weird disadvantage because he's seen me but I haven't seen him. As the lift doors open after the ascent, I'm about to step out when I notice something strange. Straight opposite me is a bathroom. The door is ajar, but that's a bathroom for sure, I can see the heated towel rail on the wall. Stranger still, the hallway is full of ornaments – plants, vases, art.

'Rosie!' I hear Eli call out.

I glance to my left to see him emerge from a huge open-plan living room.

'Hey,' I say, a little taken aback. 'Am I... in your flat?'

'Yep, penthouse, baby,' he replies, grabbing me for a hug, squeezing me tight. 'Look at you, you look amazing.'

'I look amazing?' I reply as he finally releases me from his tight embrace. 'Look at you, you look like a statue.'

Eli is ripped. I can see his muscles rippling underneath his perfect white shirt. He's wearing a suit and tie that absolutely doesn't look like it's from Primark, and his hair is perfectly coiffed. He has a light dusting of stubble that looks both careless and intentional and he smells simply incredible. There isn't a pair of overalls or an oil stain in sight.

'Did you just sniff me?' he asks.

'Yeah, you smell amazing,' I blurt.

'Creed Aventus,' he says, for my information.

Perhaps he's telling me this in case I genuinely do want to know what that incredible scent radiating from his perfectly gorgeous person, or maybe he's casually dropping into the sentence that he wears aftershave that costs over £200, because everyone knows it's pricey, right?

'You don't work at your dad's garage any more, do you?' I say.

'I don't,' he laughs. 'Well, I do occasionally, but I gave up on being a mechanic, that was never for me.'

'I always felt like you were destined for bigger things,' I point out. At the time, I never would have said anything, if he wanted to keep the family business going and follow in his dad's footsteps, I wasn't going to tell him not to. But Eli has just always had so much about him and so much ambition.

'Come in, sit down,' he insists, taking me by the hand, leading me into his living room.

'Eli, this place is incredible,' I say, twirling around like a kid at Disneyland. 'What do you do?'

'I'm an image consultant,' he says.

'Who for?'

'For anyone – for anything. I run my own consulting business from here, I have an office in the back. My first project was my dad's garage.'

'Oh my gosh, I just stopped by there, it's so different – it's better, so much better. More female-friendly.'

'Well, exactly,' he says as he runs a hand through his hair, almost victoriously. 'I just had to convince my dad that half the people in this town are female, and females drive cars too. Well, that's not strictly true... I waited until he and my mum went on holiday and then I just went in and pretended he'd commissioned me to sort the place out.'

'Oh God... how did that go down?'

'Initially, not well,' he laughs. 'But it worked and I just went onwards and upwards from there. I work with businesses, individuals – lots of unruly Manchester footballers who need a kick up the arse, image-wise.'

'Wow, Eli, that's just amazing.'

'I know,' he says with an immodest but completely charming nod. 'What do you do?'

'Oh, I'm just a journalist,' I say. 'One probably in desperate need of an image consultant but one that absolutely could not afford you – are your sofa cushions Versace?' I don't know why I'm asking; they blatantly are. They're a light gold colour with a massive Medusa logo embossed on the front.

'Are you OK?' he asks me.

I look at him, wondering if people aren't usually impressed by his cushions (or at least have the good grace to be inwardly impressed) before realising he's referring to my image consultant comment.

'Oh, yeah, I'll be fine,' I insist.

'Let me make you a coffee,' he says. He removes his jacket and rolls up his shirtsleeves before heading into the kitchen area. I'd say he fiddles with his big, complicated-looking coffee machine, but he masters it. Pushing buttons, twisting knobs – he knows exactly what he's doing.

For a moment I just look around again. His penthouse is gorgeous. So, so gorgeous. The view out of his floor-to-ceiling windows is breathtaking, even if we aren't in a city centre. This is easily one of the tallest buildings around. He's like the king in the castle up here.

'I can't believe this apartment exists,' I say. 'How long have the flats been here?'

'Since I built them,' he says.

My eyes widen – I didn't think I had any room left on my

face for them to widen any more, but I've made some for that reply.

'What?'

'Yeah, I've had a really good run over the last decade,' he says. 'The business took off, I made some good investments, which led to these apartments... So many people don't want to live in the city, or can't afford to, so I give them a city life in the suburbs, for much less money per square foot.'

'You're brilliant,' I tell him. 'I always knew you'd do amazing things.'

I glance at Eli's coffee table, where a bouquet of fresh flowers sits – not unlike the ones I received.

Could Eli have sent me the flowers?

I remember when we went on our first date. It was the start of the summer holidays, before I went to university. We met at a gig, at a pub in town – awful local band, way too loud, the kind of act that leaves you so disappointed with their performance that the tinnitus you have from the music being too loud for days after is actually a welcome sound. We struck up a conversation at the bar, bonded over alcopops and a mutual dislike for the trumpet player. By the end of the night we were a little more than tipsy and snogging outside in the car park. I didn't think I'd hear from him again, but the next day he called me up and asked if I wanted to go on a date with him. He turned up looking dapper as hell, with a huge bunch of flowers for me – no one had ever given me flowers before. Come to think of it, no one has given me flowers since. All signs are pointing to Eli now.

'Here you go,' he says, placing two lattes down on the table in front of me. 'One is caramel, the other is hazelnut. I didn't want to give you choices because I know you always struggled to decide what you wanted. I also remember that you'd always wind up wishing you had what the other person was having, so I made one of each. You can have first pick.'

I smile.

'Gosh, why did we ever break up?' I joke. 'You're a dream.'

'If I remember correctly, I broke up with you because you went to university and we didn't see each other much. I had all these big ideas of what I wanted to do and I thought a long-distance girlfriend would get in the way of that... and, you know, I'm gay, so there's that.'

'What?'

'OK, sure, I know wherever it was in Wales wasn't that far away, but I did throw myself into my work ideas and look at me now.'

'Not that bit,' I squeak. 'You're gay now?'

'Yes, well, I mean, that's not quite how things play out, I've always been gay... it just took me a while to realise. You helped me realise.'

'Oh OK, just, give me a second,' I babble. Oh God, is that why everyone at the garage was laughing at me? 'I know that people don't turn people gay, but it sounds kind of like you're saying being with me was the thing that made you realise you didn't like women...'

'Oh, shit, no, sorry,' he says. Eli grabs my little paper bag of jellybeans from next to me, empties them out onto his coffee table and hands me the bag. 'Breathe into this,' he insists. 'Get your breath while I explain. Rosie, I loved you so much – I still do. I loved being with you and hanging out with you. I suspected I was gay long before we met, but I wasn't exactly brought up in the most tolerant family – everyone is fine with it now, but I wasn't brought up thinking everyone would be chill with me dancing my way out of the closet in a pink leotard to Liza Minnelli or whatever...'

I cock my head. 'Are you making this up to spare my feelings?' I ask. 'Because it kind of sounds like you're just spitting out gay stereotypes.'

Eli laughs. 'I don't know what to tell you. People always expect me to very camp – I'm not very camp. I am very gay though.'

Eli seems almost amused by the situation, but for me, it's a lot to take in.

I feel my phone vibrating in my pocket. I pull it out and see that it's my mum.

'Oh, God, not now,' I say to myself. 'It's my mum.'

'I'll talk to her,' Eli says, snatching my phone from me. 'Evie! Hello! ... It's me, Eli! ... Oh, I know, it's been forever...' There's an extra-long gap while my mum talks his ear off. 'She hasn't told me that yet, no. I'm sure she was getting round to it, we were just catching up... Will she be in for dinner?'

I shake my head.

'Yes, she will,' he says. 'Oh, Evie, I would love to... see you then... OK, bye.'

I glare at him.

'Your mum has invited me round for dinner.'

'I gathered,' I reply. 'I'm guessing she told you... stuff?'

'Oh, she did,' he says. 'Live TV? Really?'

'I told you I needed an image consultant,' I say.

'OK, well, let me go and get changed.' Eli jumps to his feet. 'We can talk about it on the way to your parents' place.'

'You're actually coming for dinner?' I laugh.

'Of course,' he replies. 'Rosie, I would love it if we could go back to being friends, like we used to be?'

'I mean, I didn't realise we used to be friends,' I point out. 'The sex really threw me off.'

Eli laughs. 'You have always been sexy,' he points out. 'I'm only human. Just, you know, a gay human, who would rather have sex with men.'

'I understand how gay works,' I say. 'Friends would be great. I could certainly use one right now.'

'Great,' he says. 'You drink both of those coffees; it sounds like Evie is in full Evie mode. I think you're going to need them.'

I just smile at him. 'I'm so happy I looked you up,' I tell him. 'Thank you.'

He might not have been the person who sent the flowers but I'm so glad that they led me to his door.

'You're welcome,' he replies. 'But don't thank me yet, I want to hear all about your TV fail and I can't promise I won't find it funny.'

I see 'gay besties' in movies and TV shows all the time. They usually come in the form of a camp, bitchy gossip of a man – someone who isn't afraid to speak their mind or say outrageous things. The on-screen stereotype isn't really accurate though, is it? Eli might not be the kind of man who will bitch about boys with me over a bottle of rosé, but it's good to have someone to chat with who knows me.

It will be nice, having him over for dinner with my parents like old times, but if Eli didn't send those bloody flowers, then who the hell did?!

8

'So lovely to have you here, Eli,' my mum stresses for, oh, I don't know, the billionth time.

'It's lovely to be here, Evie,' he replies. 'Your cooking never fails to impress.'

I look down at my lasagne. It is really nice, but my mum isn't going to be winning *MasterChef* anytime soon. Eli has just always had this amazing way with my parents – he's always had the gift of the gab. Of course, the effect he has on my mum has been amplified now that he isn't an average-bodied young man any more, now he's all grown up and, like, *Love Island* levels of buff. My mum is a big fan of the new look – there was a really uncomfortable four minutes when we arrived where she just brazenly felt his biceps. I mean, I don't blame her, they're a sight to behold, but still...

'Would you like some more?' my mum asks him from the edge of her seat, ready to get Eli whatever he wants.

'Oh, I'd better not,' he says politely. 'I'm watching my weight.'

'I'll certainly watch your figure,' my mum says. 'If Rosie doesn't want to.'

I break out my confused face.

'Mum, we're just friends.'

'I know, I know... but you did make a gorgeous couple.'

'Mum, Eli is gay,' I tell her plainly, hoping she'll get the message and let it go. I feel like she's trying to push us back together.

She raises her eyebrows at me. My dad doesn't even look up from his dinner.

'Well, we know that,' she says.

'You do?' Eli chimes in.

'We've always known dear, haven't we, Tim?'

My dad nods casually.

'Erm, how?' I ask in disbelief.

'You've always been so clean,' my mum tells Eli. 'So clean and neat and tidy. Straight men are never so clean.'

'Hang on a minute,' my dad says.

'Tim,' my mum claps back. 'You leave little lines of white powder wherever you go.'

'Don't ask,' I whisper to Eli. 'Wow, I really wish someone had told me,' I say pointlessly.

'Me too,' Eli laughs.

'Speaking of your exes,' my mum starts. 'I saw lovely Kevin this afternoon, he said he'd been for coffee with you.'

'Yep,' I reply, hoping we can leave it at that.

'So, come on,' Eli prompts. 'Why are you visiting all your ex-boyfriends?'

'What?' I reply, feigning a blatantly exaggerated level of shock. 'I'm not, it's just...'

'Two down, two to go?' my mum says. 'That we know of, anyway.'

Christ, how depressing, that my mum knows every inch of my mediocre love life like the back of her hand.

'Well, OK, I wasn't purposefully visiting my exes... but, after I was on TV, I got these flowers from someone – obviously an ex – saying that they wanted me back. I have been wondering who they were from...'

'My money is on Sexy Simon,' my mum says. 'He was always flashy like that.'

'Sexy Simon,' Eli echoes. 'Not historically a sexy name. Who are some famous Simons?'

'Cowell, Pegg,' my dad chimes off from the top of his head.

'Ooh, Gregson. Simon Gregson from Corrie,' my mum adds.

'Right, so not your classically sexy guys,' Eli reiterates.

'Will you take Paul Simon?' my dad asks him.

'In neither sense,' he insists. 'Not technically a Simon, nor all that sexy.'

'Well, this Simon was sexy,' I insist, nipping their weird game in the bud. 'I suppose he could have sent them... but Josh was always quite romantic too...'

'Josh,' Eli says, almost excitedly. 'Josh is a sexy name. Lots of sexy men called Josh. Josh Jackson, Josh Holloway, Josh Hartnett.'

'Josh Groben,' my mum says. Such a mum pick.

'Josh Brolin,' my dad adds.

'I can't believe I'm playing "Name Sexy Joshes" over lasagne with my mum, dad and gay ex-boyfriend,' I laugh in disbelief. 'I also can't believe no one has mentioned Josh Charles from *The Good Wife*.'

'Objection,' Eli bellows, banging his hand on the table.

'Oh, I agree – just in case my objection was confusing – I just love that show.'

'Anyway,' I start, getting us back on track. 'I don't know where either of them are or what they're doing – I lost touch with them years ago – in fact, we never stayed in touch.'

'Well, Sexy Simon is still a photographer,' Mum says.

I snap my attention back to my mum. 'Wait, how do you know what he's doing these days?'

'I'm still friends with his mum on Facebook,' she says matter-of-factly.

'You never even met his mum,' I point out, so amazed by the concept my voice is about three times higher than usual.

My mum bats this away with her hand. 'He's a photographer for a fancy magazine – he lives in New York,' she tells me.

'Oh,' I say, immediately dismissing him as the phantom flower sender.

'But you did go viral worldwide,' Eli reminds me. He confessed to searching the internet for videos, comments and even memes while he was getting changed.

'Yeah, OK, well I'll just nip over to New York and see him,' I say sarcastically. 'And, wherever Josh is, I'll bob there on the way home, make an around-the-world trip of it.'

When Josh broke up with me, it was so that he could travel. He was signing with an agency who provided singers for events, and Josh wanted more than anything to be a professional singer. He didn't think he could realise his dream in Manchester and this seemed like too good an opportunity to turn down so... bye bye, girlfriend. Of course, when he said he was planning on going off to do a summer at a resort in Australia, I knew that things were coming to an end for us. No way would I be able to maintain a long-distance relationship like that – especially not with all the issues I was left with after dating Simon. When Josh broke up with me I wasn't at all surprised, I knew it had to happen... I was still gutted though, I really thought we had a good thing.

'I know where Josh is too,' my mum says between mouthfuls of her dinner. She says it so casually – like, of course she knows where he is.

'Oh?' I say. 'Dare I ask how?'

'I have his mum on Facebook too,' she replies.

'Of course you do,' I say with a laugh. At least she met Josh's mum a few times while we were together. 'Go on then, which country is he working in?'

'None of them, I suppose,' she replies. Again, this is said in such a casual manner, for something that makes so little sense.

'Is he dead?' Eli asks, his fork hovering in front of his face. My mum's comment has seemingly frozen him in time.

'What? No, don't be silly,' she says.

'Because him not being in any country isn't silly,' I point out.

'He works on a cruise ship,' she says, as if we're stupid for not figuring that out.

'Ohhh,' I say. Wow, I definitely thought he'd be working in the music industry by now, given how he, you know, bailed on our relationship to follow his dream. I feel almost annoyed that he hasn't. Our break-up had to be for something. Perhaps he just wanted rid of me... I feel like everyone just wants rid of me. Now, more than ever, I really want to talk to them both and just try and find out what was so wrong with me. I'll never be able to move forward, if I can't figure out what it is about me that's just so unlovable.

'Imagine working on a cruise ship,' Eli says, nudging me with his elbow. 'Must be awful.'

I smile at him. I appreciate him trying to cheer me up, I was slipping into a moody mindset then.

'Oh, no, it sounds like a fabulous ship,' my mum informs us. 'His mum has just got back, she sent me and your dad a voucher code to get a discount on the suites they offer. It's very sophisticated and exclusive. Silverline Cruises. Ultra five-star. We'd love to go.'

'You should go,' Eli tells them. 'Treat yourselves.'

'I do fancy the trip,' my dad chimes in. 'I've never been to New York.'

'It goes to New York?' Eli asks in disbelief.

'Yes,' my mum confirms. 'Liverpool to New York.'

'Rosie, come on, do you think this is a coincidence?' Eli asks me.

'What?'

Is he seriously suggesting I travel halfway around the world to chase down two ex-boyfriends?

'You're trying to track down your exes, and now, one you want to see is in New York and the other is literally your way there...'

'I know, it's a big coincidence, but I can't just go to New York—'

'Why not? You said yourself, you've got time off work, a big fat lump of prize money burning a hole in your pocket... I'd definitely be up for a vacation. Perks of being your own boss.'

I laugh his comments off.

'Rosie, I'm serious,' he says. 'Let's take this cruise to New York.'

'We can't just... Can we?'

'Sounds like a great idea to me,' my dad says. It's not like him to offer advice, especially not on my love life. 'And we've got the discount code, you can use that...'

I smile at Eli. I can't believe I'm considering this. 'You'd really go with me?'

'Of course,' he says. 'What are friends for? We can hang out, catch up, I can interfere with your life. Plus, I fancy a holiday.'

'Will the voucher work for two suites?' I ask my dad.

'Yeah,' he says. 'Doesn't say it can only be used for one.'

'Will you book it for us please?' I ask.

'I'll do it right now,' he says excitedly.

Wow, my dad is really into this. I can't believe he's humouring my quarter-midlife crisis.

I fetch my handbag and take out my card.

'Thanks, Dad,' I say as I hand it to him.

He hurries off to book the next available trip.

'I'll send you the money for my half,' Eli says. 'I'm really looking forward to it, it's been so long since I had a break.'

'I don't remember the last time I went on holiday,' I point out. 'Gosh, I'll need to go shopping.'

'I'll take you,' Eli says. 'We can have a day out in Manchester, have lunch, shop... maybe I can give you a little unsolicited image consulting when it comes to dressing.'

I look down at my T-shirt dress.

'What's wrong with how I dress?' I ask, just a little offended.

'Oh, nothing. It's the perfect outfit for smuggling snacks into the cinema,' he replies.

I gasp. 'Eli!'

'Rosie!' he responds in a similar tone. 'That dress is a shapeless, baggy sack – it's not even your size.'

'It's oversized,' I reply. 'Purposefully oversized.'

'Yes, I've noticed,' he says. 'The oversized coat I liked, but you can't wear it with oversized clothes. Christ, Rosie, you'll look like Kanye West in that "I Love It" music video if you keep this up. We need to get you in some outfits that show off your curves – I've seen you naked, remember, I know what's going on under there.'

I look at my mum, partially out of embarrassment but also for support. I know she's not going to let a man talk to her daughter like that.

'He's got a point, Rosie,' she says.

My eyes widen with horror. 'Thanks, guys.'

Maybe Eli is right though, perhaps my look is a problem. I've never been all that good at flaunting my body, I feel so self-conscious about so many things. There are the stretchmarks on my boobs that appeared seemingly overnight when I was a teenager – both the stretchmarks and the boobs appeared all at once. I don't suppose one would've happened without the other. Eli might say I should flaunt my curves, but some of them are a little... overdeveloped, shall we say. There's a reason I'm wearing this baggy dress, it's hiding my tummy. After taking down this large plate of lasagne, the last thing I want to be doing is shopping for bodycon dresses tomorrow. I'm also much paler than I ought to be – everyone seems to have such a great tan, but I never go on holiday, I'm too scared to use sunbeds and, as for fake tan, let's just say there was an incident that involved leaving an unfortunate stain on a friend's cream sofa that I'm never going to live down. All of the above, coupled with my inability to keep a boyfriend, have left me feeling a little subpar. Why wouldn't I hide away?

'All booked,' my dad says. 'Few details that need sorting

out, but, in four days' time, the Silverline Cruise will be departing Liverpool. Seven days at sea, a few days in New York, return flight home – first-class, no less. You're lucky, you got the last two suites.'

'So soon? That's great,' I say. 'We need to get our things ready, figure out the best way to get to Liverpool.'

'We'll drive,' my dad says.

Wow, I don't remember the last time I heard him say so many words about something other than Brexit or fly-fishing. It's all working out so well. And I'm actually really excited to take the trip now – catch-ups with ex-boyfriends aside – it sounds like it's going to be amazing.

I just need to get everything ready. Thanks to my prize money, I can buy all new stuff too – I don't need to worry about anything. Well, expect maybe tracking down Simon in New York, and facing Josh on the ship, but I'll cross that ocean when I come to it...

After a whirlwind few of days of shopping and packing for my cruise, I think I finally have everything I might need. I have various outfits, for various activities. Apparently there are lots of different things going on, on the ship, and supposedly dinner is quite a formal occasion. I think I have something for every eventuality.

After an especially awkward yet empowering conversation in Victoria's Secret, I managed to let Eli talk me into buying bikinis – only bikinis – so if I plan on swimming in the pool on board, I'm going to need to make peace with this ASAP.

'Your boyfriend can pop in and have a look if you like,' the fitting-room attendant said after earwigging our conversation.

People assuming Eli was my boyfriend became a common theme of the day – and the woman in the restaurant where we had lunch didn't just think we were together, she clearly thought I was punching above my weight. That's fair though, Eli is a solid 10/10 now. I can probably scrape a 6 with the right Instagram filter.

As well as bikinis, I have all the toiletries I'll possibly need, warm clothes in case it's chilly in New York, cool clothes in case their spring is better than ours, and I've even bought myself a couple of books and some new headphones so that I can have some chill time.

It's fair to say that I've been in my own little world since booking my holiday, and when I haven't been in my world, I've been in Eli's. I've been staying in his massive spare room, which is much better than sleeping on the sofa bed in my parents' office, so I haven't seen all that much of them. That is until today, when they picked us up from Eli's flat to drive us to Liverpool.

Yep, everything was going suspiciously well until just now.

'I hope I don't get seasick,' my mum says. 'Had a bout of it once on a boat on Loch Lomond. Terrible time. I had to throw up over the side of the boat.'

'You don't get seasick,' my dad insists. 'It was that deep-fried Mars Bar dessert you had in the hotel restaurant.'

Eli shudders at the thought, but, rather than weigh up the pros and cons of such a dessert (I love any and all chocolate, but that has to be a step too far?), I'm wondering why my mum thinks a trip to the dock car park is going to make her seasick.

I glance behind me, into the large boot of my parents' car. Mine and Eli's suitcases are there, but there are two other suitcases too...

'Does it sound like my mum and dad are coming with us?' I whisper to Eli while my mum and dad reminisce about their trip to Loch Lomond.

'What?' he whispers back. 'I don't think so?'

'Their cases are in the back.'

Eli looks behind us and then looks at me. 'Yeah, they're coming with us. I guess... did your dad think you were inviting them?'

I shrug my shoulders.

'So, this cruise is going to be great,' I say.

'Sure is,' my dad replies, not really confirming whether or not they're coming with us or going somewhere else.

I cast my mind back to when I asked my dad to book the cruise for us... did he think 'us' included them? It's not that I don't want them around, I just had no idea they were coming with me!

'It's years since we've been on a family holiday,' I muse.

'Long overdue,' he replies.

I shrug my shoulders at Eli. He just laughs.

It's hardly your classic family holiday, stalking your ex-boyfriends with your parents and your new gay best friend. I'm sure it will be fine though – it'll be nice to spend some time with them and I'm sure they'll be doing their own thing.

When we get to the dock and park up, it turns out we're a touch on the late side – that or everyone else was super early. This means that we hop on to the tail end of the queue and breeze through the process of: checking in, having our photos taken to go on the system, being given our own cruise-ship ID cards.

My dad takes the lead, checking us in. I suppose it's nice to have a real adult around for the boring stuff like that.

We're ushered from the check-in area to the bottom of a ramp that leads up to the enormous ship. The bright white beast of a cruise liner is even bigger than I thought it was going to be. I'd seen photos of it, but you just can't imagine how impossibly huge it is when you're standing next to it.

'Here you go,' my dad says, handing us a pile of papers. 'Your cards and all your room info are in here. We're going to go and get settled in. We can meet you after?'

'OK, sure,' I say. 'See you in a bit.'

The lobby of the ship doesn't seem all that different to a hotel lobby. You could actually be forgiven for forgetting you were on a ship at all – I wonder if that will change when we start moving.

'Sorry about my mum and dad tagging along,' I tell Eli. 'I had no idea.'

'Don't worry,' he insists, laughing it off. 'Always lovely to spend time with them.'

I search through the papers in my hand. 'OK, so that's my suite number, I just need to work out where it is...'

Eli takes the piece of paper from me. 'There's a map on the other side, I'll help you find it.'

We walk along a corridor, weaving in and out of other people looking for their cabins. I don't pay much attention unless we pass a staff member – if they are male, I glare at them while I work out if they are Josh or not. As soon as I realise they are not, I go on my way.

We approach the lift, to go up to our floor. There's something about a lift on a ship that I find really unnerving. Although it looks nothing like it, I can't get the lift scenes from *Titanic* out of my head. The scenes with the stairs are way better in that movie, so I think from now on I'll take those. Not that I'm likening my transatlantic crossing to that of the Titanic. As anxious as I can be at times, I can honestly say that I haven't floated the idea of sinking.

'I've just thought of something,' Eli says as he riffles through the papers.

'What's that?' I ask before stopping outside a door. 'Oh, look, this is my suite.'

'Actually... this is *our* suite.'

'What?'

'You only asked your dad to book two suites.'

'Yeah. One for me, one for you.'

'Except he thought you were inviting him and your mum along... so I think he's assumed you wanted one suite for them and one for us...'

'Oh... Ohhh, yeah.... We could book another?'

Listen to me, I think I'm made of money now.

'We could... but didn't your dad say he booked the last two? And is it not a bit late now we're on board and checked in?'

'Yes...'

'Well, you've proven yourself to be a completely fine roommate over the last couple of days,' he jokes. 'We'll be fine.'

'I think our bed-sharing days might be behind us,' I remind him.

'Perhaps, but we do have a sofa, apparently... You just might have to tie me to it, if the sea gets a little rough.'

'Stop flirting with me,' I joke. 'But yeah, I'm sure we'll be fine.'

Eli does the honours, letting us into our room. Our shared room. I can't believe my dad thought I invited them along, and that I was planning on sharing a room with Eli. When we were dating, Eli wasn't even allowed to be upstairs at the same time as me. I don't even just mean to sleep over, I mean that if I were upstairs getting ready, Eli wasn't even allowed to come up to use the toilet.

We walk into our suite and, again, I had imagined what I thought it was going to be like and this is not it. It's a large room with a super-king bed in the middle. There's a desk, a decent-sized TV, an inviting-looking sofa. The decor is nice. Subtle. Most of the soft furnishings are taupe. I worried about pokey little windows with water splashing against them, but we're so high up and we've got our own balcony.

'Ooh, we've got an aft balcony,' Eli says.

'A what now?' I reply.

'Basically we're at the back of the ship.'

'That's good?'

'Yeah, these ones are bigger – I looked it up – and when you're at the back, there's less wind.'

I walk over to the large glass door and peer through it. We aren't just at the back end of the ship, we're right at the back, looking out behind the ship. This means that, when we set off, we'll be able to watch as the UK gets smaller and smaller until it disappears.

'This is really, really nice,' Eli says.

He sits down on the sofa and bounces a little to test its firmness.

'Are you sure you want to sleep on it?' I ask.

'Yeah, it's really comfortable, come here,' he insists.

I sit down next to Eli, who wraps an arm round me.

'Thanks for bringing me along,' he says. 'Unless I assumed I was invited...'

I laugh. 'Thanks for coming.'

'I've been working so hard recently and swearing I would take a break soon but... well, it's no fun being single sometimes, is it?'

'That it ain't.'

'I'm glad this has forced me to take a little time off. So thank you.'

I rest my head on his shoulder for a moment before an announcement plays over the speaker that apparently neither of us realised was in our suite.

Our captain speaks, introducing himself to us before advising us on when and where to attend our lifeboat drill.

'Lifeboat drill?' I squeak at Eli.

'Yeah, I guess they always do them.'

'I mean, it makes sense but... still... makes me a bit uneasy...'

He just laughs at me. 'Come on, grab your life vest, let's go get it over with.'

As instructed, we remove our life vests from the wardrobe and head to the dining room, where we're all supposed to meet.

My mum and dad, who it turns out are staying in the room next to ours (they just got there much faster), are already there, sitting at the dining table, wearing their life vests.

'I'm pretty sure you don't have to put them on,' I say, laughing at them sitting at the perfectly laid dining table, all suited up to abandon ship.

'No need to go overboard,' Eli quips.

We high-five each other with our eyes until we're interrupted by a steward.

'If everyone could put their life vests on please.'

Oh, OK, I guess we do have to wear them.

I put mine on, but it doesn't quite sit right. I glance round at everyone else, who looks just fine in theirs. Dorky as hell, without a doubt, but they fit.

'Erm... Why is mine sticking out like this?'

'It's your boobs,' Eli laughs.

'OK, but I'm not the only person with boobs,' I say in as hushed a tone as possible.

'It's that bra you're wearing, it's got 'em up under your chin,' he informs me.

I glance down at the life vest, the bottom of which stands about 20cm off my body.

'God,' I say. 'It had better still work.'

'You've got your own buoyancy aids,' he reminds me.

I give him a playful nudge into his life-vest-covered ribs. I'm not even sure he feels it.

We are given a boring yet vital talk on health and safety and what to do in an emergency before we are led outside to our lifeboat. I think I expected them to be more sophisticated – and less over crowded than they'll be if the throng I'm standing in all piled in it at once. Still, if it's survival of the fittest, I'll bet on myself. I might not be very fit, but I'm one of the youngest people here. In fact, there aren't many young people on the ship at all now that I think about it.

'We're so much younger than everyone,' I whisper to Eli.

'We are... Imagine if we all got shipwrecked on an island, it would be up to us to repopulate it!'

'Nobody wants that,' I joke. 'It's weird that the suites are all older people.'

'Skint millennials can't afford suites,' he replies. 'We're the exception.'

'I'm barely an exception, I'll burn through my money in no time. You're the property-owning image consultant. I am a skint millennial.'

'Only because of this bunch of tax dodgers,' Eli replies.

An old woman coughs loudly behind us. 'You might be

young, but you're not very smart,' she tells Eli, not sounding at all impressed with what she just heard. 'You're on a Silverline Cruise – they're for pensioners.'

'Excuse me?' Eli asks.

'Most of the people on this cruise are retired,' she says. 'And we've paid tax for years, thank you very much.'

Just as the safety drill comes to an end, and Eli and I exchange a shared look of 'we have to get off this ship' – I feel something funny. An unsteadiness beneath my feet. We're moving. I am officially stuck on this boat for a week, no getting off, no turning back.

'Well... this is going to be interesting...' Eli says.

'It sure is.'

10

'Breathe, Rosie. Breathe,' Eli instructs me. 'You need to exhale.'

No, I'm not having a panic attack, I'm just wearing a dress. A long, red, clingy thing that Eli talked me into on our shopping trip. He talked me into quite a lot of items of clothing I wouldn't usually choose for myself, and these items can be divided into two piles: items Eli talked me into and items Eli talked me into after we drank too many cocktails at lunch. This dress is absolutely from that second pile. The sexy pile. The absolutely not me pile. The so tight I'm too scared to breathe out in case I burst the zip pile.

I didn't spend too much money on clothes. Well, I'm only on this ship for a week before it's back to unemployed reality. I heard dinner was always a formal affair aboard cruise ships so I bought a couple of fancy dresses, hoping I could alternate them without anyone realising - although now I'm here, that feels impossible. But this dress, this sexy, gorgeous, clingy, red, not me, silky, floor-length gown, was a gift from Eli. A gift that drunk Rosie accepted.

Eli suggested I wear it tonight and not wanting to throw his lovely gesture back in his face (and forgetting just how tight it was), I said yes.

So, here we are, casually strolling along to the dining room for dinner, except not all that casually because I'm mostly holding my breath.

'I am breathing, just... in stages,' I explain.

I'm hoping that, once we get to our table and I'm able to sit down, I can let my tummy poke out, safely hidden below table level. They say good posture is good for you, don't they? I can't see how. I'm at my most comfiest with my belly sticking out, hunched over just a little, my knees doing that weird thing where I let them relax so much they actually start to bend the other way. Whether I'm sitting on the sofa or lying on my side in bed, I'll just let my pizza-dough body go where it likes. It's no wonder I'm single, undressing me is like a mid-level escape room.

There are multiple dining rooms on board the ship, but this one is ours – the Alexander, named after blah blah blah... I absolutely wasn't listening when Eli read the bit in the guest information book about the dining room to me.

We flash our ID cards before being promptly shown to our table, except it's not our table, it's a shared table. My mum and dad I recognise from my life to date, but there are two other couples too. Two women and two men.

'Rosie, hello,' my dad says brightly. My dad rarely says anything, let alone says it brightly.

'He's in holiday mode,' my mum says. 'You both look fantastic. Did you pick this dress, Eli?'

'I certainly did,' he replies before taking my mum's hand and kissing it. 'And you look incredible too.'

We have all actually scrubbed up quite nicely. My mum is

wearing a lovely navy blue dress with little silver sparkles and my dad has made an alarming effort, in a matching navy blue suit.

Eli looks pretty damn good on my arm – a regular Jack Dawson, or should that be a stinking rich one?

'Hello,' I say to everyone else, suddenly aware all eyes are on us.

'Looks like someone booked the wrong cruise,' one of the women says with a chuckle.

Like I'm not living an embarrassing enough life at the moment. I decide to own it.

'Oh, no, not at all. My friend works on the ship, and we thought it might be nice to join my parents on a trip.'

'Married?' one of the men asks.

'Not yet,' I reply, baffled by his prying question.

'Been together long?'

Oh, he's talking about me and Eli.

'Since we were teenagers,' Eli replies. Well, I suppose it's better than explaining.

As I juggle all of my recent embarrassing incidents in my head, something occurs to me... *One Big Question* was a TV show aimed at younger people, the social media generation. No one at this table recognises me – I'll be surprised if anyone on this ship does. At least there's that.

'I used to work on cruise ships,' one of the women says. 'Mostly on the Med – have you cruised the Med?'

I shake my head.

'We have,' one of the men says. 'Best waters, without a doubt. Lovely weather.'

'I took a mini cruise to Dublin once,' Eli offers. 'The weather was really bad, we got bashed all over the place.'

'That's maybe the worst sea you can go on,' the woman says.

'Have you seen *The Poseidon Adventure*?' the older of the two men asks. 'When the wave washes over them and the ship turns upside down and everyone is screaming and hanging from the floor?'

'Colin!' his male companion ticks him off.

Colin recalls this scene from the film with all the humour and belly laughs you would afford a *Carry On* movie.

'What?' Colin replies. 'It could happen.'

'This is Colin and Clive,' my mum tells me. 'They're friends who go on holidays together.'

'A couple of eligible bachelors,' Colin says. 'We met working in the oil industry.'

'How fancy,' one of the women says.

'Licence to drill,' Clive jokes.

Oh, what a couple of likely lads. Clive must be pushing sixty. He's quite brown and wrinkly, like he's spent a lot of time in the sun. His hair is suspiciously dark brown and is the same colour all over his head, which makes me think it has come out of a bottle. Colin is a little older – or at least he looks it, with his grey hair and his handlebar moustache. I don't know how to describe their accents other than sounding like the old men in suits at the bank in *Mary Poppins*.

'Nice to meet you both,' I say.

'And then we have Karen and Linda, who are also here together,' my mum continues.

'Hi,' I say.

Karen is the one who was talking about working on cruise ships and Linda is her friend. They both have the exact same shade of blonde hair, it's incredible how identical it is. Once again, given that these ladies must be in their sixties, I'd hazard a guess their colour has come from the same bottle.

There are menus in front of us with three courses on them, with four or five options for each one. Servers walk around the tables taking everyone's orders. To start, I am having three cheese Gougères, followed by salmon en croûte for my main course. For dessert, I have chosen the hazelnut dacquoise and, if I'm being honest, that is the bit I am looking forward to the most.

Our first courses arrive and the presentation is impossibly fancy. A few mouthfuls of savoury choux pastry sit in the centre of my plate, surrounded by an elaborate garnish and some kind of reddish brown drizzled sauce that I can't identify by sight or taste, but I could eat it until I died, it's so delicious.

'We've has a lovely time learning all about your parents,' Colin says. 'But what do you two do?'

'I'm an image consultant,' Eli tells him.

Colin looks baffled. 'Oh, right,' he says, narrowing his eyes. 'What does one of those do?'

'I sort people's lives out,' Eli says, putting it simply. 'Say, if someone isn't doing as well as they could, or if they make a mistake.'

'Hey, you could do with his help, Rosie,' my dad offers through a mouthful of his food.

I shoot him daggers.

'Ooh, what have you done?' Linda asks nosily, lighting up at the hint of gossip. I think she and Karen have been a little bored throughout the work-based small talk.

'Oh, nothing,' I insist.

As the conversation dies down, Collin takes it upon himself to liven it up again, talking to Eli about his job.

'We had some business with some oil at work – slippery stuff, you know, can't always contain it. So, you know, people get upset and... we had one of your lot clean it up. Metaphorically, of course. Oil itself is much harder to clean up.'

There's so much to dislike about Colin, it's hard to know where to begin.

'What do you two do?' Eli asks Karen and Linda.

'We're retired now,' Linda says. 'We both worked on cruise ships. Amazing, that my daughter followed in my footsteps. We're a cruise family.'

'That's nice,' I say politely.

'She's been dragging me on them for so many years, it was bound to happen,' Karen adds.

Oh my God, they're mother and daughter. I thought they looked a little bit alike, but I also thought they looked the same age. Either Linda was really young when she had Karen, or ship life is a cruel mistress.

'Mother and daughter,' Colin says. 'How lovely.'

It seems like he's leering over both of them, but he can't be, can he?

'What do you do?' Clive asks me politely.

'I'm a journalist,' I tell him.

This gets Colin's attention.

'Argh,' he screams theatrically. 'Don't hack my voicemails!'

I laugh politely through my fake smile.

'I mean, didn't that stuff happen in the early noughties?' I say. 'I was probably only just into my teens, so not guilty.'

'Still, I'll keep an eye on you,' he says. 'Just in case.'

As the conversation grinds to an awkward halt and our plates are taken away, it isn't long before our fellow diners start chatting amongst themselves about all the different cruises they have been on in their lifetime. With a little time for just me, Eli and my parents to chat, we discuss our plan of action for our time on the ship. I didn't realise we were going to have a plan of action – then again, I didn't realise my mum and dad were going to be here with me. My plan of action was to relax, drink too many cocktails with Eli and maybe seek Josh out for a quick chat, just to see if he has any helpful little nuggets about our time together. Then I'll sail off into the sunset, find Simon in New York and just see what happens. The more I think about it, the more I convince myself that it must have been Simon who sent the flowers. If that's true, Josh will probably be too busy to spend much time with me anyway.

Oh, and I do realise that finding someone in New York sounds like a ridiculous thing to expect to be able to do. I am aware that New York is much bigger than Manchester. However, Simon is actually a pretty well-known photographer now, and it didn't take me much searching online to find out where he works. I suppose I'm just going to turn up at his office and ask for him... that's not weird, is it? I mean, once I rule out that it was Josh who sent the flowers, Simon is the only one left, so he'll probably be waiting for me to reach out, right?

God, now that I'm here, on the ship to New York, I really hope that I'm not making a mistake. I haven't really thought this through, have I? I got a little bit of money and I let myself get swept away – not even swept away, propelled away (or whatever it is that makes cruise ships move).

'There's so much to do on this ship,' my dad enthuses – my dad never enthuses. 'I'm putting our names down for everything.'

'Everything?' my mum asks.

'Everything,' he confirms. 'Up and at 'em first thing, have a lovely breakfast together, start making our way through all the activities.'

Oh, lord. My dad is usually so subdued and serious. A simple man who knows what he likes and likes what he knows and rarely gets the urge to talk about it, but now that he's in holiday mode...

'What kind of activities does the ship have to offer?' I ask. 'You know, with it being... erm... erm...' Desperate not to offend, I wrack my brains for a careful approach.

'Mature,' Eli tactfully interjects.

'Yes, mature, that's it,' I say. 'What are mature activities?'

'I hope you're not suggesting we're old, young lady,' Karen says, sounding kind of old just for saying it. Oh, yey, they're back in our conversation already. 'There are plenty of fun activities. Aerobics, dance classes – there's even a gym.'

'Don't forget the shuffleboard court,' Clive says.

I mean, how can I forget something if I have no idea what it is?

'Is that the game with triangles on the board and the black and white counters?' Eli asks.

'That's backgammon,' Collin snaps. 'The board games are in a completely different area of the ship.'

'How foolish of me,' Eli says, otherwise biting his tongue.

'There are some things up your street,' my mum tells me. 'Spa treatments, a pool, a cinema.'

'Wow, it really is going to be a laid-back trip,' I say.

'I suppose you young ones want to get wild,' Karen says. 'We can get wild. We do get wild.'

She's drank half a bottle of wine already, I absolutely believe her.

'Cool,' Eli says with a level of sarcasm detected only by me.

'There's entertainment every night – singers, cabaret nights, one time we had a magician,' she continues.

'On this boat?'

'On this *ship*, yes,' she says. 'We've been on it a few times.'

'Sounds wonderful,' my dad says. Wonderful! My dad just described cabaret as wonderful!

'Clive and I are taking these two lovely young ladies for a drink after dinner. Have a few cocktails, maybe a little dancing to the live music,' Colin starts.

'Oh God, they're all going to shag after,' Eli whispers to me.

'You four must join us,' he insists.

'Marvellous,' my dad says. 'We'd love to.'

'And now they've got your mum and dad involved in their weird OAP sexcapades,' Eli whispers again.

I shudder at the thought.

'You two can stop whispering, you're coming too,' my dad insists.

'Yes you are,' my mum says, before leaning in to whisper into my other ear. 'Don't leave me alone with your dad and strangers.'

'Lovely,' I say. 'Can't wait.'

As smaller conversations take place around the table and our mains are placed in front of us, I glance around the room at the different servers, looking to see if Josh might be one of them. It is a huge ship though, what are the chances he's going to be the guy who brings us our bread? He could be anywhere, doing anything... I'll just have to keep my eyes open.

I reassure Eli that we'll just go for one drink and then

slink out to find another bar maybe or head back to our suite to watch a movie.

'A few cocktails and Colin and Clive might start seeming more attractive,' Eli jokes – at least I hope he's joking. 'Bagsy Clive though. Colin talks too much.'

'Just one drink,' I insist. 'Then we'll make our escape.'

'Where do you think we're going to escape to?' he asks with a laugh. 'You're in the Atlantic Ocean. This ship doesn't dock anywhere until New York. And with this being the private dining room for our suites, unless you want to venture to one of the more casual ones and give up this incredible fancy food, you're going to have to make peace with your fellow diners.'

Oh joy. Still, at least it's just a week. Anyone can put up with anything for a week, right?

11

I wanted to go for a walk on the deck after dinner, but not only did Linda insist that it would be cold and dark and awful, I think Eli maybe thought I was going to try and boat-jack a lifeboat and head back towards Ireland. So instead of taking in the chilly sea air and staring out into the darkness, I am in the Backstay Bar, a sort of low-key (but still quite big) bar with speakeasy vibes. It's dimly lit and kind of cosy. There are little tea lights on each table and there is easy-listening jazz music filling the air. The piano is soothing against the almost harsh sounds of the wind instruments that accompany it. Both extremes are balanced out by the singer's gorgeous voice. I could almost forget I'm here with my ex, my parents and some random cruise people (and they really are cruise people through and through) – well, I could if I wasn't about to 'get wild' with them, whatever that means.

At the bar, the staff are wearing white shirts and black waistcoats with unfastened black bow ties – a clear stylistic choice, as opposed to scruffy barmen, one would assume. We order our drinks – a mai tai for me, even though that's usually my summer go-to drink – before gathering around two tables, my lot on one and Colin et al on the other. The tables are very close together though, so there's no escaping them.

'Breakfast early,' my dad says, a little more like his usual blunt self.

'I'm not great at eating breakfast early,' I say.

'And I like to do my workout first,' Eli adds.

'Listen to me,' my dad starts firmly. 'We haven't been on a family holiday in years. We are going to have a good time, so no more excuses, OK? Do it for your mum.'

My mum looks left and right as if to say 'leave me out of this'.

'Tim, what's this song?' Eli asks, changing the subject.

'"All Of Me",' he replies, keen to offer up a fact. 'Frank Sinatra did a few versions of it.'

My dad is a huge Frank Sinatra fan; this place is so up his street. I feel like we've somehow stumbled into my dad's dream holiday. I suppose it's nice that I can do this for him, even if it wasn't intentional. He and my mum deserve a nice break.

'This singer isn't half bad,' my dad says.

'He's a Michael Bublé impersonator,' Karen informs us. I forget that they're always listening, even when they're not a part of our conversation.

Now that I think about it, he's got the voice pretty spot on – even his speaking voice, as he introduces his next song, 'Feeling Good', proves that he has the exact same strong Canadian accent as the real Bublé, as well as a spot-on match with his vocals.

As the familiar, almost iconic intro to 'Feeling Good' plays, Eli bites his lip.

'God, he looks like him too,' Eli says, looking beyond me. 'He's like a younger, hotter Bublé.'

I've had my back to the stage since I walked in. I turn round to check him out, just as the song starts getting into it, and my jaw drops to the deck below.

I hop up from my chair and make my way closer to the stage.

'Rosie?' Eli calls after me. 'Rosie!'

I pause behind a pillar near the stage. Eli catches me up.

'OK, he's hot, but he's not "salivate at the front of the stage" hot, come and sit back down.'

This Michael Bublé impersonator is, without a doubt, a fantastic one. He's got his vocals spot on, with that same silky smooth voice. He's somehow managed to make himself look quite a lot like the real deal, in that uncanny way tribute acts often do, which baffles me. I always wonder what comes first, having the same voice as someone or looking like them – surely it must be so rare, to be blessed with both?

This guy has even got Michael Bublé's mannerisms down to a tee – the way he holds the mic, the way he moves his body... it's all so, so familiar. It's too familiar though – it's familiar to me.

'Eli, that's Josh,' I tell him.

'What, where?'

'On the stage, singing.'

'What, Fake Bublé? Fake Bublé is your ex?'

'Yes,' I reply in hushed tones, hoping Eli lowers his voice a little.

'Oh wow,' he blurts. 'Sexy Simon must really be something, if he took the title over this guy.'

Josh does look really good. So different to when we were together too. He had messy, longish brown hair the last time I saw him. He would be forever pushing it out of his gorgeous brown eyes – God, I loved his eyes. I always used to say the fact that they were almost always hidden behind his hair made them all the more powerful when I did get to look into them. It was a like a gift I didn't get all that often.

Similar to Eli's glow-up, Josh looks like a man now. A big, manly, Bublé-looking man in a sharp grey suit.

As the instrumental bit of the song plays, Josh pulls his tie a little loose with two of his fingers before dancing to the music, getting lost in it.

I glance around the room to see that almost all eyes are on him – especially the women.

'Get his attention,' Eli says.

'What, while he's on stage?' I squeak back. 'You're off your head.'

'You're just stalling because he's blatantly much hotter than when you were with him, that's why you're so awestruck... unless you grew up to be a massive Michael Bublé fan.'

'He's working,' I insist.

'So you're just going to hide behind this pillar and drool over him?'

'Yep, that's the plan,' I reply. 'I like this.'

'Fine,' Eli laughs.

'I can see a few familiar faces out there in the audience. Some of you regulars might know what happens next,' Josh says in his new-found Canadian accent. It's so creepy, seeing him look and sound so different, and yet he is so obviously my Josh. I can feel it. I could feel something from the second I heard his voice, I thought it was just the Bublé factor making him seem so familiar to me – not that I did grow up to be a massive Michael Bublé fan, but everyone loves a bit of Bublé, right?

Women in the audience coo and cheer. A decent handful get up from their seats and gather in a half-circle on the dance floor in front of the stage.

'This next song is called "Save The Last Dance For Me". For the instrumental I like to select a lovely lady from the audience for a twirl on the dance floor.'

Christ, no wonder they're queuing up. I'd be there myself, if I weren't hiding behind this pillar because he knows me.

As he starts singing, the volume of women gathered on the dance floor increases, with everyone hoping to be twirled by the next best thing to Michael Bublé.

God, he looks so good up there. I can't get over it. I can't believe that's Josh. My Josh.

I stare at him as he hops down off the stage, ready to select a lucky dance partner. I can't take my eyes off him, which is probably why I don't notice the almighty force that comes from behind me. A force that feels suspiciously like a shove from the hands of my new best friend. A force that sends me hurtling into Josh's arms.

Josh catches me, saving me from taking a tumble in the centre of the dance floor, in front of an embarrassingly large number of people – I honestly can't afford to have any more embarrassing incidents, my pride couldn't take it.

I don't know for sure if Josh recognises me because he doesn't falter. Assuming I am clearly just desperate to be the one who dances with him, he takes me by the hand and dances with me. It's worth pointing out that I can't dance to save my life. I don't know any steps or moves or dances – unless you count the Macarena or the entire work of the band Steps, but I haven't practiced those moves since I was a kid.

Josh does most of the hard work, dancing me round the floor, twirling me, leading me into the steps he wants me to take. I expect him to release me – just another one of the anonymous women who he dances with every night for show – but he keeps me there on the dance floor with him and serenades me for the rest of the song. It might not be as embarrassing as falling flat on my face in the middle of the dance floor, but it's pretty embarrassing standing here, being serenaded by a swoonsome man who probably doesn't remember me, while a gaggle of ladies much older than I am shoot me daggers.

I don't know what to do with my face or my arms. And then there's the fact I'm still wearing this super clingy dress – except now I've got three courses (that I ate in their entirety) in my stomach. I feel so awkward until I start getting lost in Josh's voice, and in his eyes... his eyes might have been a rare treat when they were hidden away from me, but now that I can see them all the time they're way too powerful, it's like I'm looking at the sun.

As the song comes to an end, the audience erupts with applause – for Josh, not for me. I've just been standing here awkwardly holding my tummy in for what feels like a lifetime but in reality is probably closer to under a minute.

'I'll come find you,' Josh whispers into my ear.

'OK,' I say without a hint of warmth or excitement or anything – it's barely audible. I feel sick with nerves. I'm not even sure if he knows it's me yet, perhaps he does this with all the ladies?

I exhale deeply as I make my way back to Eli.

'Cheers, friend,' I say sarcastically.

'I just got you to first base with Fake Bublé,' he says. 'Thank me later.'

I kind of do want to thank him. That was like something out of a movie.

I slink back to my table to finish my drink, where the adults are still chatting, seemingly unaware Eli and I even disappeared. I'm hoping this social vanishing act is something I'll be able to do a lot over the course of the week.

'Mum,' I say to get her attention, even though she's captivated by another tale of life at sea from Karen. This one is about the time she married a ship's captain – it doesn't sound like they're still together though. It sounds to me like she's cruising for another man, and by the look on Colin's face, it seems like he thinks he could be the guy for her. Maybe for her mum too.

'Mum,' I say again.

'What?' she asks me eventually. 'Karen is telling an interesting story.'

'I promise you, I have something better,' I say.

My mum leans in, ready for something juicy.

'You see that singer? The Michael Bublé impersonator. It's Josh.'

'What?' she squeaks – so that's where I get that reaction from. 'I knew he was a singer, but I didn't know he was Bublé.'

'You knew he was a singer?' It's my turn to squeak. 'Why didn't you tell me? I thought he worked in the coal room or something.'

'I knew watching *Titanic* while we were packing was a mistake,' Eli says under his breath.

'Oh, he's still a bit of all right, isn't he?' she says, checking him out on stage.

I wonder if my mum has always given my boyfriends a visual once-over or if this is something she has started doing recently. Perhaps my boyfriends just get more attractive when they cut me loose. I'm not ruling it out.

'Have you spoken to him?' she asks.

'She's danced with him,' Eli says.

'What? When?'

'He just did a bit where he dances with someone from the audience,' I explain. 'Eli... put me forward.'

He sniggers victoriously. Well, he literally put me forward – pushed me forward even.

'Well, that's one way to bump into him after all these years,' she says. 'What did he say?'

'He didn't say anything,' I reply. 'In fact, I'm not even sure he recognised me. He didn't say anything that suggested he knew who I was...'

We're interrupted by one of the barmen, who places a folded white piece of paper on a small silver plate down on the table in front of us.

'I thought it was supposed to be all-inclusive,' Eli moans before draining the last of his strawberry daiquiri. 'I was going to have a few more of these.'

'You're literally a millionaire,' I remind him. I don't know that he is, I'd assume that he is, but when you live from month to month on a small wage, it's hard to imagine large sums of money existing, never mind people living with it. 'I'll get it,' I insist. After all, it's my fault we're all here in the first place. But when I unfold the paper, I realise it isn't a bill at all, it's a note from Josh.

I look up at the stage only to realise he's not there. His band are currently playing an instrumental piece.

'It's from Josh,' I tell my mum and Eli. 'He says he only

has a short break tonight, but he's asked me to meet him for breakfast tomorrow.'

'You have to,' Eli insists. 'I know you're holding out for allegedly Sexy Simon, but this is your chance to have your weird little debrief.'

'I'm not having weird little debriefs,' I insist. 'But I'm definitely going to catch up with him, have a chat, see how he is...'

I probably will have a low-key debrief with him, just to see if there's anything he can tell me about what might be wrong with my girlfriend game, although with Josh, I think I might know... Still, it will be nice to have a chat with him. More than anything, there's just one question on my mind: how the hell did Josh wind up becoming a Michael Bublé impersonator?

12

Across a table of pastries, fruit, yoghurt, toast, eggs, sausages and bacon, Josh smiles at me.

'I remembered that you loved breakfast,' he starts. 'I just wasn't sure what you'd prefer.'

I smile back, finally secure in the knowledge he remembers me, because I do love breakfast, in fact, our first date was a breakfast date, and it was a bit of a disaster to begin with. After my bad break-up with Simon, it was a little while before I even wanted to go on another date – Chris Hemsworth could have got down on one knee and proposed to me in the heart of a flash mob and I still would have said no. Josh and I were friends for a while, before we started dating. He actually helped me through my break-up quite a bit, before he even knew about it. We really were just great friends who turned into something more. It was only once we started dating that I told him what a mess Simon had left me in, but he kept helping me. He's always helped me.

So, when we organised out first date and Josh said he would pick me up at 9.30 – double checking to make sure the

time was OK – I assumed it was because 9.30 in the evening
was a little on the late side. I planned my outfit the day before
and stayed up super late doing other miscellaneous date prep
before going to bed. The next thing I knew I was waking up
to Josh at my front door, at 9.30 a.m., because he was taking
me on a breakfast date, not a late dinner date, so not only was
I absolutely not ready, but the outfit I had planned was totally
inappropriate. I had to throw something together and rush
getting ready, without even washing my hair, but in the end
none of it mattered. It was an amazing first date. The best one
I've ever had.

'Any – or all – of this is great, thank you,' I assure him.

'Don't thank me too much,' he says. 'It's an all-inclusive
cruise, no one pays for food. I just assembled it.'

'Well, it's well assembled,' I point out as I make myself
comfortable in the seat opposite him, ready to unleash hell
on the food in front of me. On the walk here I was so nervous.
The thought of seeing Josh after all this time and having a
conversation with him terrified me, there was no way I could
even think about food... but now I'm here with him, I feel as
comfortable as ever – starving too.

The breakfast room – this particular one, anyway – has a
wall of large windows which the morning light pours
through. It's cool and bright and almost impossibly blue from
the sea and the sky. It's sunny, but I'll bet it's chilly out on the
deck.

I pour myself a cup of tea from the adorable little Silverline cruise branded teapot on the table.

'I can't believe it's you,' Josh blurts. 'Here, on a Silverline
Cruise. Was that your parents you were with? And...
boyfriend? Husband?'

'Yep, I am on a Silverline Cruise with my parents. In my

defence, I asked my dad to book me a trip on a cruise – I fancied a trip to New York while I'm off work – and he booked this one so... yeah. And Eli isn't my boyfriend, I'm single.'

I think it's probably for the best that I don't start banging on about my weird week or so. Josh clearly hasn't seen the video of me getting dumped on live TV and I don't exactly want to relive the embarrassment. I'm sure there will be a day, when I'm happily married with a couple of kids, where we'll all gather round the TV in the family room to laugh at the time Mummy was on TV. Yep, I'm sure one day I'll be able to see the funny side... but I am absolutely nowhere near that day today. And anyway, if he hasn't seen the video, and he's casually assuming Eli is my significant other, then he obviously isn't the person who sent me the flowers. It never really seemed like something he would do, but I hadn't ruled it out with all certainty until right now.

'Eli? As in your ex-boyfriend Eli?' Josh asks, raising his eyebrows.

'The one and only,' I say. 'We're just friends though.'

He nods thoughtfully.

'Never mind me,' I start. 'I can't believe you're a Michael Bublé tribute act.'

'Yeah.' Josh laughs awkwardly. 'I just sort of fell into it.'

'Do you enjoy it?'

'I love it,' he says. 'It might not sound very cool, but I have so much fun.'

Right on cue, a couple of old dears edge towards our table.

'Good morning, ladies,' he says, talking in a Canadian accent all of a sudden. I can't say I don't dig it, because I absolutely do. 'How are we doing today?'

'Oh, very good, Michael,' one of them says.

'Will I be seeing you for Luck be a Lady tomorrow?'

'Oh, yes, Michael,' the other one says.

'Well, all right, I'll see you then,' he says as he waves them goodbye.

'Do... do they actually think you're Michael Bublé?' I ask once they're out of earshot.

'Nah, I don't think so,' he says, snapping back to his gentle Mancunian twang. 'I think they just like the fantasy, to pretend it's real... For the regulars on these cruises, the ship is like a world away from the real world. They get way into it.'

'Sounds nice,' I say thoughtfully. That's exactly what I need.

'I never thought you'd be a cruise-goer,' he says as he sips his coffee.

'I never thought you'd be a Michael Bublé impersonator,' I say again. 'On a cruise ship!'

'I'll miss it when I give it up,' he says. I absolutely believe him. He might not be topping the UK Top 40 singles chart, but on this ship he's the man. Everyone treats him like he's a celebrity, he gets to sing fun, catchy songs every day – he's living the dream in a world away from the real world, just like everyone else on the ship. It's just nice to see him happy. 'Still writing?' he asks me.

'Yes,' I reply. 'Well, no... I suppose I'm between jobs at the moment.'

'Ahh, you'll find something,' he reassures me. 'You're a brilliant writer.'

'Thanks,' I say. 'I wasn't being properly utilised at my last job; it was soul-destroying. I just realised, all at once, that I'd had enough so I quit, booked a holiday and here I am.'

I don't need to mention the stuff about getting dumped

live on TV. In fact, if no one could ever mention it again, that would be great.

'Wow,' he blurts. 'That doesn't sound like you at all.'

'I'm going to keep coming back around to this,' I warn him. 'But you being Bublé is still the biggest shock of the day. You were this super cool indie kid with shaggy hair and scruffy clothes and now you're some clean-cut, super smart manly-man.'

Josh just laughs. 'I grew up,' he says. 'You...'

As Josh's voice trails off, I realise that he was going to return the compliment before stopping himself. Well, someone in her thirties who rage-quits her job before blowing a bunch of money on a carelessly booked holiday isn't exactly a girl who has blossomed into a grown woman, is she? I must look like such a hot mess, without too much emphasis on the hot part. I might still have youth on my side, but only just.

I pick at my croissant awkwardly as I wrack my brain for something to say, but Josh beats me to it.

'I'm sorry for the way things ended between us,' he says. 'Don't think I don't know this is the first time we've spoken since the last time... you know what I mean.'

'I do,' I reply. 'And don't worry about the break-up, we clearly weren't working and we knew it.'

'Hmm, nope, I'm not having that at all,' he says, starting out kind of polite before getting more insistent as his short statement goes on. 'We were great together. If I hadn't got that job...'

'We probably still would have broken up,' I point out.

'I don't think we would,' he replies.

'We obviously would because, as soon as I realised you

were willing to dump me for a job, that was it for me,' I say firmly. I've never told him that.

'It wasn't like that,' he insists.

'No, it really was,' I say, unable to hide the frustration in my voice now.

'If I hadn't taken the job, I wouldn't be where I am now, I had to take it,' he says. 'And I couldn't have asked you to just sit around and wait for me to come back.'

'You could've asked…' I start, but what's the point? 'You know what, I think I'm going to go. It was nice to catch up, but I think we both know we broke up for a good reason. You're here now. Well done.' Oh, God, I'm babbling. I really do need to go.

'Rosie, wait,' he says. 'Let's not leave things like this.'

'We had no trouble last time,' I reply. As I stand up from the table, I somehow clip my teacup with my elbow, knocking what's left of my cold tea all over the otherwise pristine white tablecloth. 'I need to get back to my family,' I insist, hurrying away, not even giving him chance to reply.

So much for not embarrassing myself again.

13

'Oh, God, Eli, seriously?' I ask, shielding my eyes.

I've just walked back into our suite where Eli is still fast asleep on the sofa, except he must have kicked his covers off while I was out. He's wearing an impossibly tiny pair of white underpants with an intimidatingly big bulge in them. He's leaving absolutely nothing to the imagination.

'What?' he asks as he wakes up. 'What's wrong?'

'We need to get you some pyjamas,' I insist, nodding towards his crotch.

He's still half asleep, but he laughs, looking at me through partially open eyes as he pulls the covers back over himself.

'It's nothing you haven't seen before,' he jokes.

'I definitely haven't seen that before,' I insist, finally lowering my hands. 'Either you're stuffing your pants or you've been lifting weights with it.'

Eli laughs. 'When did you turn into such a prude, huh?'

'Sorry,' I say, calming down. 'Just a bad morning.'

'A bad morning? It's not even 10 a.m. And weren't you having breakfast with Josh?'

'Yep, had it, spilled it on him, bickered with him about our break-up, felt myself getting upset, so I flounced off, probably shouldn't have – you know me.'

'Oh, Rosie,' Eli says sympathetically. 'Throw me that robe.'

I do as he says. Eli puts the robe on and comes over to give me a hug.

'We don't care about this one anyway, do we?' he reminds me.

'We don't,' I say. 'But it was still really embarrassing. At least we know he didn't send the flowers.'

'Good,' Eli says. 'He might be a babe, but I'm sure he's no Sexy Simon, and if he didn't send you the flowers, then fuck him – or not.'

I laugh.

'Ooh, grab me your laptop,' I say. 'I'll see if I can show you what Sexy Simon looks like.'

'Ooh, yes please,' Eli says excitedly. He grabs his MacBook from the coffee table, punches in his password and hands it to me.

When I looked Simon up before, as soon as I figured out where he worked, that was that. I had everything I needed. It didn't occur to me to look much further than that, but, for illustrative purposes, I'm sure I'll be able to find a picture of him online somewhere.

'That is a nice website,' Eli says enthusiastically as I scroll through Simon's site, looking for a picture of him amongst all the snaps of gorgeous models. It baffles me that someone could be around women like this all day and still send flowers to my chunky butt.

I notice an 'About Me' section and click the link before scrolling down to find a picture. There he is, Sexy Simon. It's a mid shot black and white photo of him posing with his camera. From his chiselled facial features to his slender but obviously toned body, right up to the tips of his blonde hair, it's safe to say that Sexy Simon is sexier than ever.

'Bloody hell,' Eli says. 'It's a good job I put this robe on.'

I laugh. 'Out of my league, right?'

'I'd be surprised if we could get him as a team,' he jokes. 'Why on earth did you let him go?'

'He dumped me,' I say plainly. 'And it was absolutely my fault. I was convinced that he was cheating on me. Absolutely sure of it. I was suspicious for a whole bunch of reasons, so I started checking up on him, going through his phone, following him around...'

'And how did that go down?'

'Not well,' I admit. 'Let's just say, it's a good job I didn't grow up to be a private detective like I had hoped, because I was not covert at all. It was frustrating because I could never quite get that smoking gun and a lack of any real evidence only made me more suspicious – like I'd hear his phone going off all night, but when I'd check it while he was in the shower he would have no messages. The lack of messages seemed just as damning as the messages themselves would've been, but I could never quite prove anything. Things escalated and by the time I realised he wasn't cheating on me, that it was all in my head, he'd had enough. He dumped me.'

'That's rough,' Eli says. 'Suspicion changes a person though. Once you've been hurt, you're just waiting for the next time. Do you still have trouble trusting?'

'Not really, not like that. Josh helped me through it. He'd spend hours listening to me talk, he'd always be ready with extra reassurance, he'd be so open about everything – I never got the chance to feel suspicious with him.'

'Wow, he sounds great,' Eli says, before quickly changing course. 'But not that great. Not Sexy Simon great. Perhaps now that you've got over your issues you won't fuck it up this time.'

'Thanks, buddy,' I reply as he gives me a meaningful squeeze. 'Great encouragement.'

'That's what I'm here for,' he says.

We're interrupted by a knock on our suite door.

'You'd better get it,' Eli says, nodding towards his robe.

'Oh, now you're modest,' I say with a chuckle as I head for the door.

I look through the spyhole to see what I'd imagine is my dad's enthusiastic doppelganger, but when I open the door I realise it is actually my dad... he's just in full cruise mode. He's wearing light, pastel colours which is unusual for him – chinos and a smart-casual shirt along with a pair of boat shoes that I suspect he bought for the occasion.

'Now then, you two,' he says giddily, clapping his hands together with such a force the noise makes my ears ring for a few second. 'Have you just woken up?'

I say no at the exact same time Eli says yes.

'You need to get up,' my dad says, ignoring me. 'I've got such a fun day planned for you two, and Evie, I left her getting ready while I explored the ship. It's big – it's huge. It's got everything.'

'I'm glad you like it, Dad,' I say. 'But... can't we just chill today?'

'I've already booked us in for a bunch of stuff. Come on, where's your holiday spirit?'

I frown.

'There you are,' my mum says, sticking her head inside

the open door behind my dad. 'You've been over an hour, Tim – where have you been?'

'I was just exploring the ship,' my dad says. 'It's massive. It has three spas; can you believe it?'

My mum laughs as she places a hand over her mouth.

'Oh, Tim,' she eventually says. 'It doesn't have three spas; it has one spa. You must have walked past it three times. Did you get lost?'

My dad scratches his head. 'I don't think I did... God, this ship is big.'

It feels like role reversal, me taking my parents on holiday instead of them taking me like they used to when I was a kid. I feel responsible for them, but it's also really, really nice to see them having such a great time. It might be strange, seeing my dad so enthusiastic, but it's wonderful too. He seems like a completely different person to the man who has, so far, spent the bulk of his retirement locked away in his shed.

'OK, Tim, what's first on the agenda?' Eli asks. 'I can be ready in forty minutes.'

'You can be ready in fifteen,' my dad corrects him. 'We're going to play shuffleboard.'

'I don't even know how to play,' I say.

'Don't worry, they show you,' my dad insists. 'Just wait until you find out what I've got planned for after.'

'Can't wait,' I say as enthusiastically as I can.

I dread to think what my dad has signed us up for, but, as long as it doesn't involve Fake Bublé, I don't suppose I mind...

14

Earlier this morning, if you'd told me that this afternoon I would be a shuffleboard expert, I'd tell you that you were crazy. And I'd be right. I still have no idea what I'm doing.

Eli and I played against my mum and dad, who claim they haven't played before, but I don't think I believe them. It was a disaster, they absolutely crushed us.

We all had a joint lesson with the same teacher – a guy called Saul – but somehow they ended up destroying us. I might be mostly to blame for this because there is a bit at the end of the court (the isosceles trapezoid was what Saul kept referring to it as, but I call it the 'bit at the end') where, if you land, you can actually end up losing points. So as fast as Eli was somehow scraping us points, I was losing them for us.

'I'm so sorry,' I told Eli after the game was over. He's never liked to lose.

'It's fine,' he said through gritted teeth. 'It's an old person game anyway, I'd kill them on a GTA game.'

Hopefully he didn't mean that too literally.

Now, in what I want to call a change of pace, but the pace

is still oh-so slow, we're doing water aerobics with my mum and dad – yep, Eli too. My dad nagged us both to take part, so, in the end, for a laugh, we agreed to do it if the other person did. It's so much fun having Eli around, he feels like the sibling I never had. On all those family holidays growing up, or even at Christmases and birthdays at home, when I could have done with an ally but didn't have a brother or sister to have my back... here, now, with Eli on my side, I know what it feels like and it's amazing. It turns out I don't mind doing lame, goofy crap when I have a buddy to do it with me and have a laugh with.

Thankfully the swimming pool is indoors, because I went outside for a stroll earlier and I was positively freezing. It's more than just 'indoors' though, it's like indoors but outdoors. The ship boasts an absolutely stunning atrium – a subtropical paradise – with a huge pool, lots of greenery, a bar with lots of tables and chairs. It feels a little bit like being at the beach, which is very odd and jarring given how freezing it is outside.

'Oh my days, it's like being at Center Parcs,' my mum exclaimed as we walked through the door.

It is definitely much nicer than Center Parcs – we're on a five-star cruise, for crying out loud.

It's so strange, being so warm, surrounded by so much greenery and water when you're in the middle of the Atlantic Ocean, in April. You walk into the pool like you would the sea, there aren't any steps and, bizarrely, people are seemingly sunbathing on sun loungers around the edges of the pool, lying back with their sunglasses on, or reading books, enjoying cocktails. So, so bizarre.

Not as bizarre as water aerobics though.

It seems strange that this is exercise. I mean, we're in a

swimming pool – swimming would probably be way better exercise.

'It's so the old dears don't put their hips out,' my mum tells me when I complain under my breath.

'I think it's exhilarating and relaxing,' my dad says as he navigates a foam noodle, although navigates is perhaps too optimistic a term.

'You look like you're making a low-budget remake of *Tremors*,' I tell him before turning to Eli. 'You almost look like you're having fun.'

'It is kind of fun,' he says as he lifts his knees up, one after the other, over his foam noodle. 'But maybe that's just because I'm good at it.'

'Implying I'm not?' I reply. 'Fine, and I know you think you're using reverse psychology on me, and you might be, but the fact that I recognise it cancels it out, so there.'

'And yet there you go, playing with your noddle in front of all these people,' he says.

God, it's actually quite tiring, now that I'm trying. The water makes it somehow easier and harder to move my limbs, especially my legs. On the one hand, my body wants to float, which is great on the way up, but on the way back down it's a battle. You've got to take your dorky mandatory swimming cap off to everyone in this pool giving it their all, I'm knackered.

'OK, now, I hope you're ready to make a splash,' our bright, bubbly instructor tells us via the headset sitting on her ear which pumps out through the sound system. 'We're going to take it up a notch.'

As she leads us into some kind of high-energy water dance, with lots of arm flapping and jumping up and down, I find myself having a blast, mucking around on the edges with Eli. Well, if a serious businessman like him can let his hair down, then so can I. I laugh, I sing along to the Abba medley we're working out to, I flail around in the water with all the grace of a sea lion (and potentially the figure to boot) even though I'm wearing a slightly too small two-piece that Eli talked me into on our shopping trip. If I'm honest, I bought the bikini completely sober because I didn't think I'd be using it except for maybe in the spa, where there wouldn't be too many eyes on me. Still, I'm styling it out here in the pool in front of all these people, I just keep having to give my boobs a courtesy grab to stop them popping out during the moves that involve the most movement.

As I bounce in the water with Eli to the tune of 'I Do, I Do, I Do, I Do, I Do', we serenade each other. With one boob grasped firmly in each of my hands, I look to the side of the pool. The music goes quiet for just me, as Josh and a pretty young woman with honey blonde hair walk past in what seems like slow motion. I notice them a split second before they notice me, but it doesn't give me enough time to take off my swimming cap, put down my boobs and stop Eli singing and dancing with me, even though I've stopped.

Josh gives me a wave and an amused smile. The woman must realise we know each other. She just laughs. It's only a few seconds, but it feels like an age. They don't stop to chat – thank God.

'Oh look, it's lover boy with a girl,' Eli says. 'You don't need him. You don't, you don't, you don't, you don't, you don't.'

He sings this in time with the music, which makes me laugh, but I can feel my face all flushed with neat embarrassment.

As the intro to 'Does Your Mother Know' plays, I make my way towards the 'shore' of the pool.

'That's it, my boobs can't take it,' I tell Eli. 'This one is too fast; it will be full indecent exposure.'

'Wait, I'll come with you,' he says.

We walk out of the pool and in the direction of our table, where our things are – including our towels. It feels like one of the longest walks of my life, hugging my body to hide how self-conscious I feel in my bikini.

'Cardio kills your muscles,' Eli explains to me as we walk. 'I really ought to get to the gym – I'll go in the morning, maybe.'

'Mmm, yes,' I say, not really listening as I pull off my awful pink swimming cap. 'Wait, what? Exercising is bad for your body?'

'Cardio kills your gains, everyone knows that,' he tells me. 'These are what I like to call vanity muscles. I don't want to exercise, I just want Tom Hardy to s—'

'Oh, for fuck's sake,' I blurt, interrupting him before he can tell me exactly what he wants Tom Hardy to do to him. 'They're sat at the table next to ours.'

'Oh,' he replies. 'Hmm, well, I'll just go and get your stuff if you like?'

'Would you?' I say. 'Thank you.'

'Yeah, no worries,' he says. 'Oh, wait, he's seen you.'

'Oh, great, now it will look weird if I walk away, won't it?'

'It will definitely look like you're avoiding him,' Eli replies. 'Balls to him. You don't need to hide from him. Go and get your shit with your head held high.'

'Yeah, except I feel self-conscious in my itsy-bitsy teenie-weenie red-would-make-a-porn-star-blush bikini,' I say.

'OK, you look incredible, for the record, but if you feel

that awkward, just walk behind me. I'll block their view of you while you grab your towel.'

'It's worth pointing out, you are the love of my fucking life,' I say, hoping it shows my gratitude.

As promised, Eli walks just enough steps ahead of me to block their view of me. As we reach the table, he casually tosses a towel back to me, which I quickly wrap around my body. After giving me a few seconds to get covered up, Eli steps out of the way.

'Hello, Rosie,' Josh says.

'Oh, Josh, hi,' I say as though I've just seen him. I'm not sure he's buying it.

'Enjoying the water aerobics?' he asks with a cheeky glint in his eye.

I feel the blood rushing to my cheeks again. I suppose it's good that he isn't being awkward with me after I bailed on breakfast. He's always been so chilled out.

'Oh, she just does that for me,' Eli says as he places a hand on my arse, pulling me close to him.

'Is this 'just friends' ex-boyfriend Eli?' Josh asks, sounding almost jealous.

'The one and only,' Eli tells him with a wink. 'We're... casual.'

Oh, God. Now I'm blushing for a different reason.

'Who's your friend?' Eli asks him.

'This is Amanda,' he says. 'She's one of the other singers.'

'Hello,' she says in a strong North London accent.

'Hey,' Eli says. 'Are you a tribute act too?'

'I am,' she says, all smiles. 'I'm the ship's answer to Adele. I used to be an Amy Winehouse tribute, once upon a time, but it didn't feel right after she passed away... so, I adapted, dyed my hair, and now I do Adele.'

'I suppose with your accent...' Eli points out.

'Oh, you don't have to be a cockney to be an Adele tribute, but it helps,' she jokes, ramping up the accent. 'I don't sing with it, obviously, but it helps with the on-stage persona.'

'Fab,' I say. 'Fab, fab, fab. Well, we're off for lunch, aren't we, Eli?'

'We're just meeting our band for a quick drink, chat through our set. We're the first ones here,' Josh points out. Old habits die hard, I guess, it's like he doesn't want me to think he's here alone with Amanda.

Right on cue, a twenty-something man with dirty blonde, blown-back hair approaches their table.

'Sorry I'm late,' he says.

'This is André, our cello player,' Josh explains.

With all the speed and ease that Eli pulled me close, now he sharply pushes me away before André looks over in our direction.

'This is my friend Rosie and Eli her—'

'Friend,' Eli interrupts Josh. 'Her friendly neighbourhood Eli.'

For the first time since we got reacquainted, super buff, super rich, super cool Eli doesn't seem all that cool at all. Take that dorky joke, for example. I can practically see his cringe ripple through his muscles.

'Nice to meet you both,' André says.

'Anyway, we were going for food, right, Eli?' I say, gesturing away from the bubble of awkwardness we've found ourselves in.

'Us? I don't think so,' Eli replies. 'That's later. Right now we said we'd sit at the table here and have a drink.'

'You're welcome to join us,' Josh suggests. I want to throw him in the pool. Him first, then Eli, I just might need someone to help me shift him. The only thing bigger than Eli's muscles is his ego, apparently.

'We'd love to,' Eli says, pulling up a chair. 'Wouldn't we, Rosie?'

'Oh, God, yes, love to,' I say. With each word, my faux enthusiasm grows, but my overcompensation just makes me come across as sarcastic.

As a few more members of the band arrive, I sink into my chair a little. This is made all the worse by the fact that everyone here looks lovely and then there's me, in my towel, with damp hair and I daren't even think about what my make-up must look like after being repeatedly splashed in the face during water aerobics.

I know what you're thinking, isn't Eli soaking wet and wearing a towel too? Well, no, Eli hasn't bothered with a towel, that would cover up his 'vanity muscles'. And he looks amazing soaking wet, like Daniel Craig fresh out of the ocean. I look like a wet mutt.

'We're sharing a set tonight, if you'd like to come along,' Josh tells me, trying to pull me into the conversation.

'We'd love to,' Eli says with the most enthusiasm of anyone I've ever witnessed.

'I can't tonight, I have plans with my mum and dad after dinner,' I say. 'But you should go, Eli.'

'Don't you need me for moral support?' he asks me quietly.

'Nah, I'll be fine, you go and have fun.'

'You're a star,' he tells me, patting me on the shoulder.

I frown at him.

'Well, I was going to kiss you on the cheek, but I don't want André thinking I'm straight.'

'Straight guys don't kiss me on the cheek,' I point out.

'They don't kiss you anywhere,' he jokes. 'Zing.'

I don't say much, trying to keep out of the conversations as best I can. Instead, I wait until my mum and dad show up at our table to get their towels.

'Oh, that's my mum and dad, I'd better go,' I say.

'Josh Pearson,' my mum says, before I get chance to make my escape. 'Look at you all grown up.'

Josh hurries to his feet to give my mum a kiss on the cheek.

'See,' Eli whispers to me under his breath.

'Oh, that doesn't count,' I say. 'You're allowed to kiss up a generation.'

'That's always been my experience,' he jokes.

'I was grown up the last time you saw me, Evie,' Josh tells her with a smile.

'Oh, I know, but you're all manly now,' she points out. 'Just like Eli. What is it with your exes, Rosie, getting all manly?'

I look at Eli, who looks at André to see if he's heard that. He has.

'I'm not just an ex... I'm like an *ex*-ex,' he babbles, whatever that means. 'I went out with Rosie before I realised I was gay.'

Oh, so that's what that means.

Everyone falls silent.

'Would you look at the time,' I say, with no plausible way of knowing what the time is. 'I'd better go and start getting ready for dinner.'

'Oh, I'll come with you,' Eli says. I think he knows he's said the wrong thing – well, not the wrong thing, but the wrong thing for me in this situation.

'No, no, catch me up later,' I insist as I hurry off.

I don't know if it's from cringing too hard or the water aerobics, but I get a cramp in my leg all of a sudden. It's so painful and the tightness makes it hard to put my foot down. Still, I carefully turn on my heels to walk away.

How on earth am I supposed to live that little display down, huh? So much for my 'Rosie Outlook'. It's really letting me down at the moment.

15

Something isn't right this evening; I can feel it...

I started feeling a little bit anxious when Eli announced that he was bailing on dinner to go and hang out with the band. Having already announced that I was busy this evening (and still not wanting to hang out with Josh and Amanda), he left me with no choice but to go for dinner alone. Well, I knew that I wouldn't technically be alone, I'd be with my parents and our fellow diners, but I – the only young/sane person – would be all alone for sure.

I slipped into one of my new dresses – a long, black number, because I'm mourning my dignity, apparently – and headed for the dining room, where my parents, mother-daughter duo Linda and Karen, and ship bachelors Colin and Clive were already seated, except this time everyone was positioned just a little differently. Rather than leave two spaces next to each other as you would expect, the two spare seats were separate, one between my dad and Linda, and one between my mum and Clive.

'Sit with me,' my mum insisted, so I did. We ordered our drinks and then our food, and it all seemed fine... until now.

'Clive is divorced,' my mum tells me.

'Sorry to hear that,' I tell him.

'Oh, don't be,' he says through a mouthful of whitebait. 'Better off rid. She was bleeding me dry – or trying to at least.'

'Got to protect the old bank balance,' Colin chimes in. 'I won't enter into anything without a signed agreement.'

God, I really hope he's talking about business, or marriage at least. Anything else doesn't bear thinking about.

'And, Clive is only fifty-two,' my mum says.

'Oh wow, only fifty-two,' I repeat back to her, but it goes over her head. She's being weird, but I can't quite work out why.

'Yep, retired early,' he says.

'We all do, in the oil biz, you know,' Colin adds. I don't know.

'I reckon that makes me the youngest bachelor on board,' Clive tells me smugly. 'Well, after your friend, of course. Your mum did tell me the two of you were just friends.'

'What a terrible shame, that a strapping young lad like that can't seem to get a girl,' Colin adds.

'Oh, for sure,' I say. 'I'm sure Eli would absolutely agree with you on that one.'

My mum gives me a semi-subtle nudge that is most likely designed to silently tell me to cut it out.

'So I'm single, you're single,' Clive says. 'Your mum thought it might be nice if we got a drink sometime, had a chat, got to know each other, just us.'

I choke on my drink.

'Oh, did she really?' I eventually reply.

'Yes,' he says hopefully. 'I'm game if you are, just putting that out there.'

'Speaking of my mum... Mum, I could do with popping to the loos, fancy coming with me?'

'OK, darling,' she says.

Oh, wow, she's oblivious. She has no idea I'm going to try and lock her in a cubicle and leave her there until we get to New York because she's trying to set me up with Clive. Oh my God!

'Don't be too long, ladies, I know what you lot are like with your gassing,' Colin says – I assume he's talking about chatting and not some other bathroom complaint. 'They don't give you long between the starter and the main.'

Well, when many of your guests are north of eighty years old, I don't suppose there's much time to waste.

'Mum, what the hell are you doing?' I ask her the second we are out of earshot. 'Are you trying to set me up with Clive?'

'I just thought it might be nice if you got to know each other,' she says. 'What's wrong with that?'

'He's literally old enough to be my dad,' I point out.

'He's a good man, he looks good, dresses nice and he could take care of you.'

'I don't need taking care of, Mum. I don't care if he's the most eligible bachelor on the RMS Over 55. Plus, I'm going to see Simon, remember? Simon who must have sent me the flowers because none of my other exes did.'

My mum stops dead outside the ladies' room.

'I just... I wouldn't hang all my hopes on that,' she says. 'Don't put all your eggs in one basket.'

'Why not?' I say. 'Mum, he obviously sent me flowers...'

I don't know how he found my address, but he's a man of

means, there are websites for this sort of thing, his mum is still in touch with my mum...

A cold wave worthy of the Atlantic Ocean washes over me.

'Mum...Mum, I'm only going to ask this once, OK?'

'What?'

'Did... Did you...' I pause for a second. I can't believe how stupid this is going to sound. 'Did you send me those flowers?'

'What? No! Of course not! Rosie Jones, how could you even ask me that?'

'Shit, I'm sorry, Mum, I don't know, I'm not thinking straight.'

Before the words had even left my lips I knew that they were stupid, but my mum's reaction is more than confirmation that she's telling the truth because my mum can't hide anything. She's ruined every surprise party she's ever tried to throw me and unless that was all in anticipation of needing to tell me one big lie (and have me believe it without question) one day, then I'm certain she's telling the truth.

'That's OK, but try not to swear,' she says. 'Are you going to the loo?'

'Oh, no,' I say. 'I just wanted to drag you away to tell you to stop trying to set me up with Clive.'

'OK, let's head back,' she says as she takes me by the arm. 'But, remember, you can do a lot worse than Clive.'

'I can also do a lot younger, Mum, I'm not going to start dipping into divorcées just yet.'

As we sit back down at the table, my mum's words about me doing a lot worse than Clive bounce around in my head. He might only be fifty-two years old, but I'd assumed he was older when I met him. It's his bottle-brown hair that I'm sure was intended to make him look younger, but somehow the extra effort just makes him look like he's trying to hide his age. I like to think that I'll grow old gracefully, but I'm thirty-one years old and slathering myself in anti-aging creams and lifting my breasts with super bras and I know that within seconds of spotting a grey hair I'll be running to the salon, but that's how we've all been programmed to think, isn't it? Societal standards make us feel like it isn't OK for a woman to age – for a man, it's practically a badge of honour, getting that hot dad, salt-and-pepper, distinguished look. If I were Clive, I'd cash in on that and make the most of it. Just one of many ways in which my life would be better if I were a man. Less worry about growing old, no need to be concerned about biological clocks (which, recently, if it's quiet enough at night, I hear ticking sometimes), no more pesky periods popping up when I don't want them to (or not popping up when I do want them to because it turns out a tendency to be late can affect all aspects of life sometimes), no need to cake make-up on every day, I might even have been promoted at work already, although you can't always just blame all of your problems on the patriarchy, can you?

'We were just saying how romantic these cruises are when you have someone to share them with,' Karen says, bringing me and my mum up to speed. Oh, great, we're still on this.

'Yes, no offence, Clive, but I'd much rather have a female companion,' Colin says with a wiggle of his eyebrows in the direction of either Linda, Karen, or probably both.

'You do have to be careful not to get carried away though,' Karen warns. 'I could tell you a story from when I worked on a cruise that you wouldn't believe.'

'Now this I'd love to hear,' Colin says. 'Go on.'

'Well, I'm sure we can all agree that cruise ships are great places for making love – but that the thrill of doing it outdoors is also an appealing concept,' she starts, looking around the table for nods of agreement. I abstain. 'Well, I'm sure you've all realised how thin the walls are on these ships...'

Karen is so sure of so much.

'Go on,' Colin prompts, getting impatient.

'We had this young couple – maybe in their mid-twenties – who decided to pop out onto their balcony for a bit of how's your father. Must have been so romantic, out there at night, looking at the stars... except she falls overboard during the throes of passion.'

'Oh my gosh, what happened to her?' my mum asks.

'He only goes and bloody jumps in after her, the daft git,' Karen continues. 'Sixty-foot drop from their balcony to the water. It was only once someone realised they were missing that we had to turn around, go back and look for them with the big searchlights on. We find him, naked as the day he was born, eventually, and we find her forty minutes later – he'd jumped in after her and not even bloody found her. Anyway, neither of them was seriously injured.'

Wow, Karen is right, I don't believe her.

'Oh, the things we do for the opposite sex, huh?' Colin muses.

I mean, let's just pretend that this ridiculous tale is true, and isn't just something someone made up to try and scare people off having sex on their cruise ship balcony, because I'm sure it isn't a practice that is as discreet as people hope it might be. Why on earth did he jump in after her? What did he think he was going to achieve? He would have been smarter throwing on a pair of pants and running out of his cabin to raise the alarm, that way they could have stopped and searched for her right away, save the two of them bobbing around in the sea for God knows how long. They're just lucky it wasn't this cruise because you wouldn't last long literally chilling in the sea out here, waiting for someone to realise you were missing – however, it's worth noting that this is also information that I have gathered from the movie *Titanic*, which, yes, I do regret watching before going on a transatlantic cruise, but I've never been on a cruise before so it's the only real point of reference I have. The only movie that would have been more stupid to watch would have been *The Poseidon Adventure*, which Colin made sound like an absolute nightmare.

'I'd risk it,' Clive tells me with a couple of awkward elbow nudges.

Actually, if the ship could just flip upside down right now, that would be amazing. Anything to get me out of this horrifically awkward situation.

16

You know, for an over-55s cruise, most of the guests have a lot of energy. More than I do, that's for sure. Me, on my best day, after a rare full night of sleep with no hangover, no worries or a post-pizza bloat, still wouldn't be able to keep up with the ship aerobics. I thought the water aerobics was full-on – it turns out they are for the people with reduced mobility; apparently it's much easier for people with problems to move around an exercise in water. And I couldn't even hack that.

Eli wanted to get up early and go to the gym – because it turns out that, when he meets someone he fancies, his motivation comes surging back – and he somehow managed to talk me into going with him. Not wanting to lift weights or bust my butt on a treadmill, I decided to join in with a little light aerobics, but honestly, I'm knackered now.

If there's one thing a Silverline cruise does, it is redefining what it means to be old. These people might be older, but they're certainly not like your stereotypical old person.

As I sat at one of the tables at the side of the gym, trying to get my breath and work out how to mainline my bottle of

Lucozade, a little old lady in a bright pink tracksuit sat down next to me. Her name was Doris and I was surprised to learn that she has fourteen grandchildren. I was even more surprised to learn that she had broken her hip last year and had it fully replaced because she was probably the person in the class with the most energy. She told me she had been through months of rehabilitation to get to where she is now, with the cruise at the end of it as her reward – it was the one thing that pushed her to get better, knowing she had a holiday to look forward to. I asked her how recently she had finished her rehab and she told me that right now was when she had finished. This was her first proper burst of exercise on her own, not for rehab or with a physiotherapist breathing down her neck. She did this for herself, and now she's knows that she's better. Isn't that amazing? This eighty-something woman who, even after going through so much, never gave up and can still run rings around me. What the hell am I doing with my life that's so impressive, huh? I'm on a cruise that I paid for with money that was handed to me for absolutely nothing I did right, heading to New York for a man I haven't seen in years, who may or may not have sent me flowers... I feel pathetic in comparison, and I absolutely should. I need to learn a thing or two from Doris, about motivation, life goals and personal growth. But not right now because I'm starving and, now that we're showered, we are meeting my mum and dad for breakfast, and thankfully, breakfast is a buffet, which means we can grab what we want and sit where we like, so our table buddies won't be there.

'You know my mum tried to set me up with Clive last night,' I tell Eli as I lean over to grab a chocolate chip muffin.

'You can do a lot worse than Clive,' he jokes as he loads his plate up with all the protein-heavy breakfast foods.

'Oh, stop it, that's what my mum said,' I tell him. 'What was she thinking?'

'She probably just saw – what looks to her at least –a young, successful man who could take care of her baby girl. The second-best one after me, of course.'

'Of course,' I echo. 'But she knows I'm only taking this trip to go and see Simon.'

'I just wouldn't put all your eggs in one basket,' Eli says as he grabs out teapots and cups.

'That's what my mum said too,' I say. 'Why does everyone keep saying that?'

'You just never know, do you? He looks good, it seems like he sent you the flowers, but don't pin your everything on one thing.'

'That's easy to say when you've got everything you want,' I point out. 'But point taken.'

'Speaking of things that I want,' Eli starts, lowering his tone slightly as we walk past a group of older ladies navigating the breakfast buffet. 'André... oh my God.'

'You two have a good evening together then?' I ask.

Eli got back to our suite last night long after I'd got back from dinner with my parents and fallen asleep watching *Sex and the City* on Eli's laptop. I didn't think he'd get back so late, I figured he'd join me and we could watch it together, just like we used to do when we first started going out. But the next thing I knew I'd woken up to go to the bathroom at 4 a.m. and there he was, fast asleep face down on the sofa, stinking of booze. At first I was a little bit annoyed that he'd stayed out so late getting drunk, but then I felt like the nagging wife getting her knickers in a twist over her seemingly carefree husband going out and doing his own thing while she's stuck at home watching TV and stuffing her face with the ship-branded chocolate coins she bought from the shop on the way back to her suite.

'I'm glad you had a nice time,' I say, and I do mean it. Eli is such an incredible man; he deserves to have everything he wants in life.

'It was great – I don't know if it's just because I've been around old people for too long, but those band kids can party. Most of them drank me under the table.'

'Was Josh there?' I ask curiously. I immediately kick myself for asking because it makes it sound like I care.

'He was,' Eli replies simply.

'What about Amanda?'

Oh, God, now it really sounds like I really care and I don't. I really don't. I swear, I don't. We all keep curious tabs on our exes, don't we? If not because we want good things for them, then just because it's a great way to measure our own success as adults, via theirs. With Eli, I have both. I care about him and want amazing things for him, but I can also look at how well he's doing and see that I have achieved absolutely nothing in my adult life. Seriously, nothing. I'm single, I don't own my own home, I haven't done a very good job at maintaining grown-up friendships and now, well and truly hammering that final nail into my coffin, I have bailed on my career. I do keep wondering about that last part, if it really was the best thing for me to do. They say that it's much easier to find a job when you already have one, don't they? And that gaps in CVs ought to have reasonable explanations. Telling potential employers that I rage-quit my job, because I hated it, after somehow landing myself on a quiz show, where I not only won a chunk of money but also went embarrassingly worldwide viral, doesn't sound like a reasonable explanation, does it?

'Yeah, she was there too,' he says. 'You think something is going on between them?'

'Do you?' I ask. 'You were out with them all night.'

'That's true, I was... but you only notice these things if you care.'

'Well, I don't care,' I say. 'So I haven't noticed.'

'Here they are,' my dad announces as Eli and I sit down at the table with him and my mum.

I cannot get used to this fun-loving, giddy, enthusiastic holiday version of my dad; it just doesn't feel right. If this were happening in reverse, they would probably be asking me if I were on drugs before organising some sort of intervention for me. I haven't seen someone's temperament shift so quickly since the last time I watched *The Shinning* (through the gaps in my fingers, admittedly – I really am a big baby).

'Raring to go?' he asks.

'You know it,' Eli replies enthusiastically. 'What's on today's agenda, Tim?'

'Luck be a Lady,' he says, as though we're supposed to know what that means.

I blink at him blankly for a few seconds until he realises.

'It's a special thing at the casino.'

'Yes!' Eli chirps.

'No,' I quickly add. 'What am I going to do in a casino?'

'Gamble,' my dad says.

'Cheers, Dad, I know that's what happens in casinos,' I tell him. 'But I'm not a gambler – I'm not a naturally lucky person. Never have been.'

'Didn't you just win £50k on a quiz show?' Eli asks.

'Yes, and it ruined my life,' I point out melodramatically. 'I finally get a blast of good luck and my entire life crumbles around it. I swear to God, that money is cursed.'

'OK, now you're just being ridiculous,' my mum chimes in. 'There's no such thing as curses.'

'OK, sure, but that money cost me my boyfriend, my job and my anonymity. I used some of it to book a cruise which I absolutely shouldn't be on, not for another three or four decades at least, and I bought a bunch of clothes I can't exhale in, thanks to one of the three ex-boyfriends I've bumped into so far – all of whom I've embarrassed myself in front of, big time.'

'Still, you might be good at blackjack,' my dad reasons.

I puff air from my cheeks.

'OK, fine, I'll come and watch,' I say, giving in. Sometimes it's just easier to give in, isn't it?

'And I'll come and play,' Eli says. 'I love casinos. Love cards, love roulette, love gambling – I'll happily ruin my life in there.'

God, I hope he's joking.

'But don't people say that the house always wins?' I ask. Everyone knows that.

'But you know what else people say, right? It's the taking part that counts.'

'They absolutely don't say that about gambling,' I point out. 'At least if I'm spectating, I can stop you betting away your flat or one of your kidneys or whatever.'

'That's the spirit,' he chirps giddily. 'Man, I thought this was going to be a dull old folks' cruise, but I'm actually starting to have the time of my life.'

'It's fantastic, isn't it?' my dad says. 'Thanks so much for bringing us, Rosie.'

Seeing that giddy little smile on his face does make the whole thing absolutely worth it, but I can't say I'm having a fantastic time. For me, the fun is going to start when I get to

New York. I've always wanted to visit but, perhaps this comes from being a writer and a huge *Sex and the City* fan, it just feels like somewhere someone like me should visit. I love the glitz and glamour that comes with life in big cities and New York is certainly a big city – way bigger than Manchester. I could definitely see myself living there, especially now I'm free of basically any and all responsibilities back at home. A new start would be right up my street, not that I'm getting ahead of myself or anything. I think Manhattan life would suit me, if I could bag myself a well-paid newspaper column, a Mr Big and a gang of very supportive, outrageous friends who all enjoy ridiculously active social lives. Gosh, that's the dream. So dreamy I'm not quite sure it exists.

This cruise might not be very me, but it's not exactly an unpleasant place to be, is it? Our suite is gorgeous, the food and drink are amazing. Sure, I've got Clive's advances to contend with now, and an ex-boyfriend I'd really rather not bump into, but that doesn't mean I'm having a horrible time. Keeping my head down and out of Josh's way for a few more days shouldn't be a problem, the ship is huge after all, and I'll just be civil, if I do see him. I just need to be smart about it and I'll be in New York before I know it.

17

I watched this TV show once – I can't remember what it was called, but it was a science fiction show about parallel universes. At one point, some of the same parts of the two worlds collide, matching up exactly, and what happens is that whatever is occupying both spots in the same place merge into one – I feel like that's what has happened here, in the ship's casino.

Imagine the glitz and glamour of a big, fancy Las Vegas casino if it collided with the retro day room of a nursing home in Bolton. It's a jarring combination of two extreme opposites that Eli doesn't quite know how to process.

'It's a casino,' I point out. 'You said you love casinos...'

'It is... and I do... it's just so...'

I let out an involuntary yawn, right on cue.

'Exactly,' he says.

'Go bet that Hermès belt on zero or green or whatever you call it,' I say, nodding towards the roulette table. 'That will cheer you up.'

'God, even the roulette wheel seems slower than usual,' Eli says. 'Still, we're here now, let's give it a go.'

We've separated from my mum and dad – my mum's suggestion, she said it was so that we 'young ones' could do what we wanted, but I think she was just worried that my dad would try to keep up with Eli and his gambling.

'So, how many chips are you going to get?' he asks me.

'None,' I tell him. 'Obviously. You?'

'Hmm, I don't know, I'll see how I feel when I get to the desk. I'll try not to go too crazy,' he says as he heads off to get his chips.

'Well, hey, miss,' I hear a strong, convincing Canadian accent say behind me.

'Well, hello there, Mr Bublé,' I reply. 'How's it going?'

'It's going good,' Josh says, keeping up the accent. 'I'm just about to do a set actually.'

'Ahh, is that why you're not letting the accent slip?' I ask.

'What accent?' he asks with a faux-blank stare.

'Nice,' I reply. 'So, what does a set in a casino go like?'

'They give me a microphone and I just walk around the table singing the classics – Frank Sinatra, Dean Martin – you know the stuff.'

'And does that, erm, liven things up at all?' I ask. 'Because right now...'

I pretend to fall asleep and make snoring noises.

'These lot can get pretty wild, don't let them fool you,' he insists. 'They'll perk up when the music starts.'

'Hey, Josh,' Eli says as he butts between us.

'Hey, Eli,' he replies. 'It's Michael right now.'

'That's pretty weird,' Eli says. 'Where's André?'

'No band with me today,' he replies. 'Last night was a lot of fun – Rosie, you should have been there.'

'Hmm, maybe next time,' I say.

The three of us fall into a slightly awkward silence.

'OK, well, I'd better go make a start,' Josh says. 'Can't keep the fans waiting.'

'It's so bizarre,' Eli starts once Josh has gone. 'Hearing him flit between sounding like someone off *Hollyoaks* to actual Michael Bublé.'

'Yeah, it's completely weird. I can't get my head around it.' I say. Then I notice the tray of casino chips in his hands. 'Go on, how much did you get?'

'Not much, I promise,' he insists. 'I got you some too.'

'Oh, no, Eli, honestly, you shouldn't have, I'll only lose them,' I say.

'Rosie, don't worry so much, they're not proper chips, they're cheaper ones, they don't really win you anything, they're just for playing with, for fun.'

I glance down at my chips. Little blue plastic disks with a sliver cruise ship etched on them. Around the edges, they say 'ship token' on them. They look pretty real to me. I suppose it's kind of cute of him, pretending they're not real so that I don't worry about using them. I guess I could play with a few, see what happens.

The ambient music switches from gentle background music to the blaring trumpet of the intro to 'Have You Met Miss Jones', before Josh starts circulating the room, singing along, doing a bit of that light Bublé dancing that's not really dancing, mixed with a little serenading of whichever old dear he's passing at the time. It's amazing how the women on this ship look at him, it's like everyone thinks he's an absolute rock star. A god, walking amongst us mere mortals. Poseidon himself could rise up out of the water, climb aboard the ship and stroll the decks in all his buff, beardy glory, brandishing his trident, just generally being the god of the sea, and I honestly don't think that anyone on board would notice, not if Josh was here in his suit crooning along to 'I Get a Kick Out Of You'.

It must be so surreal for him, being treated like a celebrity on board but then stepping off the ship and going back to complete anonymity. I suppose that's the best way to do it, isn't it? To get the best of both worlds. I think he has the ratio right too, having a small group of people thinking you're a big celebrity but then going back into the real world and no one caring who you are and just letting you live your life.

On the flip side, there's me, with things completely the wrong way round. It's on this ship where I'm anonymous, where no one knows or cares who I am, and it's in the real world where I've gone viral, where everyone and their social network of friends are laughing at me on YouTube. I wonder if things have died down yet? I mean, how funny can it be, watching someone get their heart broken on live TV? Like, I don't know, maybe it's funny once (it's hard to say because it's impossible for me to see the funny side yet), but it can't have much re-watch value, can it? It's more cringey that it is funny, right? Cringey must have a shelf life. Perhaps I'll get off the ship and everyone will have forgotten about the girl who got dumped by the dinosaur nerd on a quiz show. Hopefully someone else will have done something funnier or dafter or stupider and they'll be the new star of the show. Failing that, I don't suppose it will take much more than ditching my blonde locks for a slightly darker hairdo for people to stop recognising me. I'm just hoping that the internet is so satu-rated with memes and people who have gone viral that these days, anyone who does fall victim won't have to endure the embarrassment for too long. I hope, anyway.

'So, roulette?' Eli says.

'Sure, why not?' I reply.

We make our way over to the roulette table. There are a couple of men playing, but otherwise, it isn't exactly alive with excitement. Hopefully Eli will change that.

'So, can I teach you how to play?' he asks me.

'I really don't need you to teach me,' I insist. 'I'll just keep an eye on you, maybe be the person who blows on your dice like you see in the movies...'

'If you think roulette involves dice, then you absolutely need me to teach you how to play,' Eli replies.

'You know what I mean,' I say. 'I know how to play, I think... you just put your chips down on whatever, the wheel spins, if the ball lands on where you put your chips, you win.'

'I mean, that's an oversimplification of a very beautiful game,' he insists. 'But, yes, I suppose you can get by on that knowledge.'

I watch as Eli places chips down on the green felt. Putting little stacks of them in different places – some on number 22, which I remember to this day is his lucky number, some on the edges around it, some on the corners...

Eli's chips are all red and gold which makes me think that they must be worth much more than mine are. I'm not really sure how much mine are worth, this is the first time I've held a casino chip – then again, it's the first time I've ever been in a casino.

'It helps to spread it out a little,' Eli says. 'Don't put everything on one thing.'

'Don't you mean: don't put all my eggs in one basket?' I tease, repeating exactly what he said earlier.

'Well, yes,' he says. 'That's solid advice in every situation.'

Hmm. I hate that he's making this a teachable moment –

and I hate even more that it's a teachable moment that proves that he's right. What's so wrong with getting your hopes up? Why do I need to manage my expectations to the point where nothing is worth getting excited about? What people don't seem to grasp about being an optimist is that you look on the bright side and hope for the best. You don't worry about what you'll do if things don't work out. Sure you can plan for the worst and hope for the best, but the stakes are important too – surely a hardcore gambler like Eli should know that. If you have nothing to lose, then you might as well see what you can gain; whether it's gambling with baby chips that won't lose me any money if I don't do well or travelling halfway around the world to reconnect with an ex who might still have feelings for me – it's worth a shot because there's nothing to lose. In situations like this, I'd be crazy to not try?

Keen to prove a point, and feeling just a little bit rebellious, I take four of my chips and place them on red.

'There isn't much point doing that,' Eli says.

'Why not?' I ask.

'Well, it's kind of boring,' he says. 'The odds of winning are pretty equal, you'll either lose or just win what you put down, it's not a very good strategy.'

'Well, I have faith,' I tell him. 'So we'll see.'

'Nineteen, black,' the croupier announces.

Son of a...!

'See,' Eli says.

I can't help but pull a face at him.

'Same again,' Eli says about his chips.

'Yeah, same for me,' I say, placing another four chips down.

'You're not learning any lessons,' Eli points out. 'You're

setting yourself up for a fall if you don't learn from your mistakes.'

'OK, thanks,' I say. 'But I'm sticking with red.'

'Twenty-three, black,' the croupier says.

Eli knows better than to say 'I told you so'.

As he collects his winnings, I look down at my chips. I have just eight left now.

As Eli shifts his around the board a little, Josh slinks up alongside us. He's just finished a song, so he chats to us, but it's all part of the act. He keeps his accent at all times and talks to us with the microphone, so that everyone can hear what we're saying.

'Any big wins over here, guys?' he asks us.

'I'm doing great, thanks,' Eli tells him. 'I can't say the same for my friend.'

'I'm doing just fine,' I insist. 'In fact...'

I take my last eight chips and place them on red.

'Rosie... doubling down, seriously?' Eli asks.

'What? It's been black twice, surely it has to be red this time?'

'That's not how roulette works,' he insists.

'Whoa, look at you two, bickering like an old married couple,' Josh says.

Gosh, he doesn't know the half of it. From me making him sleep on the sofa to being annoyed when he gets in late drunk, we're every inch an old married couple, just without the sex. Then again, if everything you see on TV is accurate, that's very much the defining characteristics of an old married couple.

'Well then, ladies and gents, let's see how Rosie does, shall we... she's bet everything she's got on red and...'

I shoot Josh a look. I really don't need an audience for this

– in fact, I can now safely say that I don't need an audience for anything. Been there, done that.

'Thirty-three, black,' the croupier announces softly. I think even he is starting to feel bad for me now and he probably sees people lose at this all day, every day.

'Oh, unlucky. Better luck next time,' Josh says, ever the professional. He swiftly moves on though, which I appreciate. I think he can tell that I'm not enjoying the attention. Eli absolutely is though.

'See, I told you so,' he points out unhelpfully.

'OK, OK. I'm going to leave you to it, go and see what my mum and dad are up to,' I tell him. 'Try not to ruin yourself.'

'I'm not making any promises,' he says, focusing on his chip placement.

As I take a step back from the table, I notice that I've dropped one of my chips. It's my last one, I'm tempted to keep it as a souvenir, and also as a reminder that a) gambling is stupid and b) I didn't quite lose all of my chips... I quit while I was ahead, and I am technically ahead, because Eli paid for these.

As I walk around the room, I search for my parents. I can hear Josh singing 'Luck be a Lady'. She might be a lady but she's a different kind of lady to the one I am. I just don't seem to get much good luck and while I might be offsetting that fact with my optimistic nature, it's actually starting to get to me now, just a little.

I spot my mum and dad in the distance, feeding chips into a slot machine. I'm about to head in their direction when I notice a slot machine on its own, away from all the others. A massive version of the blue chip in my hand sits on top of it – identical in every way, apart from its size. I look at my chip. My one, sad, sorry little chip. Do I keep it forever, cash it in or throw caution to the wind and put it into the slot machine and see what happens?

A wise man once said that we make our own luck – Billy Zane, *Titanic*. I mean, it sounds right, right? But then again he is the movie's main antagonist if you don't count the iceberg (and why on earth would you count the iceberg?!). I really, really need to stop living my cruise life in accordance with things I saw and learned whilst watching *Titanic* in a cocktail-induced blur as I packed my bags.

If a real man – or woman, in my case – makes his or her own luck, then I can just decide to be lucky, right? I can stop worrying about it, feed my last chip to this bloody machine and be over it already. There's no good luck or bad luck, these things run on algorithms, don't they? It's predetermined if I'm going to win or lose.

I sigh. I have no idea what I'm talking about. Even I've stopped listening to myself babble in my head. I'm just going to do it and see what happens.

I pop the chip in and pull the lever. I don't really under-stand what's going on, but the three dials behind the glass spin, stopping one at a time to reveal a picture that also means nothing to me.

The first one is a cruise ship, just like the one on the chip I just said goodbye to. So is the second. So is the third. I only have a second or two to ponder what this means before the machine comes to life. Alarms start ringing, lights start flashing. I'm beginning to wonder if I've broken it before I see a light flashing on the large, plastic chip that sits on top of it. It's flashing £1,000 in lots of little, bright white lights.

'Oh my goodness, we have a winner,' I hear fake Bublé announce to everyone.

I spin round, only to see him walking up to me. That's the

problem, with him being amped up, it's hard to avoid someone when you can hear them from every speaker in the room, it makes it impossible to work out what direction they're coming from.

'Congratulations, Rosie Jones, you've won the big prize of £1,000,' he announces.

As everyone in the room cheers excitedly, I feel my cheeks blushing at their support. It's nice to be embarrassed by attention, rather than because I did something stupid, but it makes me blush nonetheless.

I can't believe I've won even more money. Can't I just make a career doing this? It sounds better than ever working again. Then again, I definitely spent much more than £1,000 to get here. At least it will offset the cost of that a little.

As Josh gets back to his song, my parents and Eli rush towards me from different directions.

'Oh my gosh, Rosie, you won,' my mum says excitedly.

'Ah, don't get too excited,' Eli says. 'It's just ship credit.'

'What?' I ask him.

'You've won £1,000 of ship credit.'

'What does that mean?' I ask him.

'It means you can only spend it on the ship,' he points out.

Wow, he really did buy me chips that weren't worth much. If I'd known that, I wouldn't have agonised so much over what to do with my last one.

'Yeah, but we're all-inclusive,' I remind him.

'Oh, yeah... Erm...'

'You can spend it in the gift shop,' a casino employee tells me, handing me a voucher for £1,000. 'You take this to the front desk and they'll credit your account with it. Congratulations.'

'The gift shop? That's lame.' Eli says with a snort. 'Anyway, I need to get back to my table.'

'Well, I think it's wonderful,' my mum says.

'Me too,' my dad adds. 'There's some right fancy stuff in that gift shop.'

'Well how about I take the two of you there and you can pick out whatever you want?' I suggest.

Well, they're clearly buzzing about it, and I doubt there's going to be anything in there that I want.

'Oh, Rosie, that would be amazing,' my mum practically sings.

'Yes,' my dad says as he clears his throat. He sounds like he's getting a bit emotional. 'This really is a wonderful, wonderful holiday.'

'And, see, you're not always unlucky,' my mum reminds me.

Oh, yeah, I'm not always unlucky... Sometimes I win things – there's just always seems to be a downside. Other than using it to make my mum and dad happy in the gift shop, what the hell am I going to do with £1,000 credit on a cruise that I've paid to be all-inclusive on? I suppose I'll have to wait and see what they have in the gift shop, they might sell things like perfume or maybe even duty-free booze.

I hear frantic cheering coming from the roulette table, where I see Eli kissing the elderly lady next to him on the cheek victoriously. That, right there, is good luck. Not the elderly lady who got the kiss on the cheek (although she does look absolutely delighted with it). Eli could fall into a pile of manure and come out smelling like Creed Aventus – although that might be because he uses it so liberally.

Lord knows how much money he's just won and then there's me, rolling in it, but only if it is in the gift shop.

18

Eli, super smug from winning big in the casino, has taken me for lunch.

Except he hasn't taken me for lunch, because it's all-inclusive. And he hasn't taken just me for lunch, he's invited André along too.

He's absolutely right about him, André does seem like a really lovely man, but it's so strange for me, seeing my ex cracking on with a man right in front of my face. I'm so happy for him, don't get me wrong, it's just not something you ever expect to see, is it?

Still, at least I can't measure myself against him. If this were the Olympics, we wouldn't be judged in the same categories, would we? That's what I'm telling myself anyway because, if women and men can be judged against each other equally, then André is better than me in pretty much all ways. He's younger, better looking, doing what appears to be his dream job, and now he's on a date (that I feel so much like I'm crashing) with a dreamboat like Eli.

It's so cute, watching them together. I'm not an expert in

love – I'm barely a novice – but they seem so into each other. It's making me feel so, so single though, and very much like the third wheel.

'Are we still on for dinner tonight?' Eli asks him.

'Of course,' André replies. 'We could meet at my cabin first, have a drink? I have my own cabin.'

Damn, I'm not sure if that's a flex on me (who is sharing with her ex) or a come-on to Eli. Either way, I think it's time I make my excuses.

'Oh, look, it's Josh,' I say, pointing him out at the other side of the bar. 'I'm going to go and say hello.'

Eli gives me a grateful smile. He invited me along in the first place, but I think he feels like I'm a third wheel now too.

I head towards Josh meaningfully, fully intending to make a swift exit from the bar when Eli and André stop watching me but before Josh spots me. It doesn't quite work out that way though.

'Hey, Rosie,' he says, back to his Mancunian accent. 'Spent any of your winnings yet?'

'Not even touched them,' I say. 'But I did only win ship credit.'

'Yeah, I saw that,' he says. 'Are you all-inclusive?'

'Yep,' I reply.

He laughs. 'That's rough. We do have a wonderful gift shop on board though.'

'Is it wonderful?' I ask.

'Not really,' he admits. 'It's full of tat.'

'Marvellous,' I reply. 'I've made plans to take my mum and dad later, I just couldn't face it right now.'

'You having a nice time with André and Eli?'

'I kind of feel like a spare part, thought I'd leave them to it, go for a walk.'

'Do you mind if I join you?' he asks. 'I was actually just about to go for a walk out on the deck, get some air.'

He picks up his coat from the barstool next to him.

'Erm, yeah, sure,' I say.

Well, I was just going to walk alone anyway – probably inside though. I may as well keep Josh company. Plus, if I'm chatting with him, I won't be agonising over my life choices.

'I really am starting to feel quite claustrophobic,' he says. 'I think it's because we're at sea for a week without stopping, and even though it's spring, it's just so cold outside and when it gets dark, it gets really dark. It's disorientating.'

'Nothing like working in Australia then?' I say, kicking myself for bringing up the job he left me for. It's going to sound like a dig when, in fact, it's just one of the few bits of information I actually have about him. I somehow feel like I know him so well but also like I don't know who he is at all now.

'No, nothing like that,' he says. 'Fewer murderous spiders.'

'I'd take the freezing cold ocean over hot weather and big spiders any day,' I tell him, not that he needs me to, he had to remove many a bug from the bathroom back when we were together.

We walk up a big, wooden staircase to the top deck of the ship where there's a door that leads out on to the deck. The ship must be so well heated because stepping outside from the cosy warm ship to the icy Atlantic weather feels like walking through a wall.

It's so strange, life at sea. You lose all sense of what's what. For starters, all of the little things you do over the course of the day that anchor you in time don't exist, whether it's having lunch, getting home from work or watching a particular TV show. Also, it gets dark kind of early – I think – it certainly feels like it does. It's dark outside now and I'm not sure if I love it or hate it. I don't suppose it matters much because whether you are out on the deck during the day or night, you can only see one colour wherever you look: blue or black. Although I suppose you can't really see the black, the black is more of a lack of sight which makes you feel like – even though you are outside the ship – you are still inside something. You're inside the icy blackness of the Atlantic Ocean. The jury is still out on whether I feel free or trapped.

'I feel like I'm getting a tour of the ship from an insider,' I joke.

'Would you like that?' he asks.

'Probably,' I reply. 'I find the ship so fascinating.'

'Well, miss, you are currently on board the longest, largest, tallest, widest ocean liner ever built. It is the equivalent of 24 storeys, measuring around 1,200 ft long – just 50 ft shorter than the Empire State Building is tall.'

'Oh, wow, you really are giving me a tour – *the* tour,' I say.

'Well, I've heard it many, many times,' he replies. 'It's also the fastest ship, hitting speeds of just under 40 mph. Have you done much exploring?'

'I haven't,' I admit. 'My dad has roped me into a few things – the casino, where I won my worthless money. Water aerobics, shuffleboard. I went to the gym with Eli this morning and I've eaten and had drinks in a few different places. I'm a little scared to venture too far out of my comfort zone, if I'm being honest.'

'It is pretty intimidating, when it's your first time on board,' Josh says. 'But, seriously, there is so much to do. For example, here's something you might like. There's a library – the biggest at sea – with 10,000 books.'

I gasp. 'There's a library on board?!'

'There is,' he says. 'I can show you where it is, if you like?'

'Please,' I say. 'What else is there?'

'There's a cinema, there's loads of unusual activities like fencing. There is even a planetarium – seriously, it's incredible, if you still like nerding out over things...'

'Oh, God, you know it,' I say. 'Did you ever think, on all those nights we would spend watching weird documentaries, that the world would catch up with us?'

'True crime is really having a moment, isn't it?' he says. 'It's quite odd really, when you think about it, how interested people are in serial killers and mysterious murders.'

'Oh, yes, super weird,' I say as we stroll. 'Do you still watch them though?'

'Oh, God, yes,' he says with a laugh. 'Out here at sea for days at a time, with a lot of downtime, my Netflix subscription is my best friend. I plough through them.'

'Have you seen *The Staircase*?' I ask.

'Yep.'

'*Evil Genius*?'

'Of course.'

'All of the Ted Bundy stuff?'

'Rosie, please, I watched Ted Bundy documentaries before it was cool,' he jokes. 'Have you watched '*Til Death Do Us Part*?'

'I have...' I say. 'What do you think?'

'*Til Death Do Us Part* is a five-part documentary that I actually only watched a couple of weeks ago. The show follows Terry Mackie as he prepares to marry his fiancée Joanna. Joanna is actually Terry's fourth wife because the previous three all met grizzly ends shortly after tying the knot with him. In each case, the deaths were a little more than suspicious, but despite it seeming like Terry might be involved in the demise of each wife (or like he is some kind of jinx at the least), no one has ever been able to charge him with anything. He's a self-made multimillionaire with a huge house, he always seems to be on holiday, he has lots of cars and properties – he could give any woman the life of her dreams... until they wind up dead. So, with Joanna seemingly ignoring the fate of her predecessors in (supposedly) the name of true love, the series follows them during the wedding planning process, right up to their big day. Ever since I watched it I've kept one eye on the news, expecting to hear any day that something awful has happened to Joanna.

'Come on,' Josh starts. 'He definitely did it. There is no way that man hasn't killed at least one of them.'

'I know, right? He's so... so... nice, but in such a weird way. He's like nice enough and softly-spoken enough to make him seem so far from being a murderer, that he actually definitely seems like a murderer, do you know what I mean?'

'I absolutely do,' he says. 'You're spot on. Something just isn't right about him.'

Wow, I've missed having someone to talk about weird TV shows with. I tried to get David into true crime, but he said it was too depressing. He'd watch documentaries about dinosaurs – of course – and the occasional history documentary, so long as the findings were in accordance with his own studies (he had no time for any documentary that tried to put forward a different version of events to the ones he had learned), but he said that true crime was just too grizzly and too depressing. He would describe his students as a bunch of depressed gen Z-ers, all miserable from too much exposure to things like these documentaries and the news. He said we'd all be much happier if we stuck to the interesting facts and stopped obsessing over the gruesome ones. It's just human nature though, isn't it? To be interested in the unspeakable.

The main thing this reminds me is just how much I have in common with Josh. I suppose because we started out as just friends, he always felt like a best friend and a boyfriend rolled into one.

An overwhelming wave of longing for the past washes over me and it stings way more than the cold. I feel like Josh and I had a great thing, we were just moving in completely different directions, getting further and further apart. Here on this ship, with nowhere to go (I mean, we can't get more than the Empire State Building apart, can we?), no matter how far apart our lives may have gone, we can't get away from each other and, this close together, looking into those eyes, it's hard to stop the old feelings rushing back. When we were happy together, we were *really* happy together.

I hug my body.

'Here, have this,' Josh says, shrugging off his black coat before holding it out me.

'Oh, no, don't be crazy,' I insist.

'No, come on, what kind of Bublé would I be if I weren't chivalrous?'

I laugh.

'Thank you,' I say as I slip my arms into it. It's warm from his body heat and it smells like his aftershave. It's so comforting.

'Why are you smiling?' he asks me. I didn't realise I was.

'I was just thinking about *Titanic*,' I say, improvising.

'Does that usually make you smile?' he asks.

'No, of course not,' I say quickly. 'It's just that, when we were packing our cases for the trip, Eli and I thought it might be a good idea to watch the movie, and it's amazing, how many similarities there are... like you giving me your coat. There isn't a diamond in the pocket is there?'

'Sadly not,' he says. 'I think Eli is more likely to have an expensive diamond in his pocket than a Michael Bublé tribute act, don't you?'

'Yes, but he'd sooner die in his coat than give it to me. On the off chance he survived, it would pain him to see me mishandle his couture.'

'He isn't at all like you described him when we were together and we spoke about our exes,' Josh points out.

'He isn't at all like the Eli I knew,' I say. 'But then sometimes he is... He's an amazing man though.'

'He seems it,' Josh says. 'André seems to like him a lot.'

'It's nice to see him happy,' I say, but my face falls as I realise that I probably wouldn't feel quite so happy seeing Josh move on. Perhaps, deep down, I did know (without knowing) that Eli and I were never right for each other. It's impossible for me to feel jealous of him moving on (well, only in a different way, because I wish I had someone, but that's envying what he has, not someone else having him), but with Josh... I don't know, it just doesn't sit well with me.

'Well, speaking of *Titanic* comparisons, we have a cigar room on board,' he says, changing the mood.

'Really?' I ask.

'Yeah, I always find it really interesting... I've never been, obviously, because I don't smoke.'

'Yeah, I imagine it's awful, but it's cool that it exists. Feels so old-fashioned.'

'This is the door we need to go through,' Josh says.

As he leads me back inside, the warmth of the ship starts to soothe my chilled bones. We don't have to walk far before he ushers me through another door.

'Oh... my... God!' I whisper – well, we are in a library after all.

I imagined the ship library being big but nothing quite as grand as this. It's massive, the shelves are stacked to capacity with books, it has a real art deco vibe to it – I love it.

I hurry my eyes across the shelves, taking it all in. There is fiction, non-fiction, old books, new books. I run my hand along a shelf until I locate my favourite novel – *The Bell Jar* by Sylvia Plath. I find the nearest armchair and sink into it, cuddled up in Josh's coat, before carefully opening the book – quite an old copy, or at least a well-read one.

I look up at Josh, who is just smiling at me.

'Listen, I need to go,' he says. 'I've got a set tonight to get ready for. You'll be OK here right?'

'I'll be more than OK here,' I insist. 'Thank you for showing it to me. Here, let me give you your coat back.'

'It's OK, hang on to it for now,' he insists. 'You look so cosy. And, come on, what am I going to need it for? There's nowhere to go and I'm working all night.'

I smile at him. 'Well, thanks again, for bringing me here, and for chatting to me, it's nice to talk to an adult who isn't related to me, sharing a room with me, or over the age of fifty-five.'

'Welcome to my world,' he says. 'See you soon.'

'Yeah, see you soon,' I call after him.

Before I get stuck back into a book that I must have read a hundred times, I watch Josh walk away. Man, he's so cool now. So cool, but still such a dork on the inside. I can't believe we're both still watching the same kind of TV shows – shows that no one else in my life seems to understand the appeal of.

It's such a shame Josh and I were never able to work things out, but he was always destined for bigger things, always drifting away from me. We might be on the same ship now, but once I get to New York, that will be it. He'll set off back for Liverpool and, by the time I fly home, he'll probably be on his way back to New York again. I suppose we'll always just miss each other, like ships in the night, which is such a shame. I'm not sure anyone will get me like Josh does.

19

I have known, since the day we boarded this ship, that we could order room service, twenty-four hours a day, completely free of charge (well, covered by our all-inclusive tickets). Breakfast, lunch, dinner, snacks, desserts – anything at all. That's quite an appealing concept, isn't it? You would be crazy not to take full advantage of that... and yet I have resisted. It's not really a willpower thing, it was more of a social call. With my mum, dad and Eli all on board, I made a decision to enjoy all of my meals with them, instead of hiding in my suite, working my way through the menu, all alone.

Tonight was no exception. I got dressed for dinner, I met up with my parents (alone, because Eli had plans with André again), I didn't complain when they wanted to eat in the same restaurant. Apparently they love the food there and they are really enjoying the company of Linda, Karen, Colin and Clive, who are also creatures of habit, dining in the same restaurant every night. Personally I'm a little bored of the super fine dining, I'd happily 'rough it' in one of the other restaurants – preferably one that has pizza on the menu, but still, I accompanied my parents as I said I would.

That was until we got there and I realised my mum was edging me into the seat next to Clive again. Bloody boring, weird, oil-anecdote-telling Clive. Clive who could (and probably would) be my dad. Ew.

My mum is about as subtle as a steam train, so I could see her ushering me in Clive's direction long before it was obvious to Clive, who, in his defence, I suppose, jumped up to pull my chair out for me.

Standing there in yet another clingy dress, holding in my tummy for pretty much everyone's benefit but my own... I don't know, I just decided I'd had enough. That I deserved a night off.

So I made an excuse about feeling seasick, headed back to my suite, hopped out of my dress, into my cosy pyjamas and I called for some room service. I say some... it was loads. I called for more room service than one girl needs. A Hawaiian pizza (because pineapple absolutely does belong on a pizza), courgette fries, a salad (probably just for appearances though, if I'm being honest – a healthy but completely empty gesture) and a salted caramel brownie with ice cream. All for me.

At first I felt a little bit bad for bailing on my parents, but now that I'm watching a movie and pigging out, I feel much better. I needed this time for myself.

It's kind of nice to be alone for a bit. I've lived on my own for a while and as much as I have always craved my independence and my own space, I'm a people person. Night after night alone in front of the TV before climbing into an empty bed is not my favourite. That's why I've always been way happier with a boyfriend, because it gave me someone to share moments with, share my bed with. Here, on this ship, it's kind of hard to feel lonely, even though I am alone. I know there are so many people on board, who aren't going anywhere, so even though I'm in this suite on my own, I don't feel it. In fact, I am really enjoying my own company right now. I suppose the grass is always greener, isn't it? Too much time on my own and I'm sure I'll go back to missing Eli hogging the bathroom, my mum trying to set me up with old geezers and my dad emotionally blackmailing me into playing shuffleboard.

Now that I'm suitably full (no, of course I didn't eat it all and, yes, I left more than just the salad I didn't really want), it has occurred to me to change into something I can venture out of my cabin in, maybe and go and find Josh, watch him perform, but then I wonder why? Why would I do that? It's not like I'm a big Michael Bublé fan, is it? Although I know that's not why I would be going. I'd go because I liked spending time with him earlier. I liked it a lot. But not only is it probably not a good idea to get reattached to someone who, in a few days, I'll go back to never seeing again, but if he's on stage performing, I'll just be sitting on my own anyway, technically just staring at him, and that's way worse.

Instead I'll probably just keep watching movies, maybe move on to TV shows if I can't sleep (Eli told me not to wait up for him in a way that implied he wouldn't be coming back at all tonight) and I can always pick at my leftover pizza. I need to be up early tomorrow anyway, I promised my mum and dad I'd go for breakfast with them before taking them to the gift shop to spend my prize money – my second lot of prize money, that is. My ship money that isn't actually real money. I'm just going to let my mum and dad go to town on it and then maybe pick myself up a few bits if there is any money left and anything I fancy.

As for my real prize money, I'm scared to look at how much is left. No doubt this cruise (plus the tickets I bought for my parents) and all my pre-cruise shopping have made quite the dent in it. I'm sure I still have plenty left but, if I'm not careful, I'm going to need to spend my gift shop money on stuff that I can flip once I get back home.

I suppose the elephant in the room is that I need a job, and fast. I just can't worry about that right now. I'll worry about it when this is all over. I just hope things work out the way I want them to.

20

Gift shops are always full of tat, aren't they? Random objects branded with the name of wherever you are on them. Stationery, clothing, ornaments, lighters...

The Silverline gift shop is no exception. I'd be tempted to say it's even worse. Five-star gift shops are just the same as one-star gift shops, only gaudier. Luckily, my mum and dad are completely captivated by it.

'Oh, exquisite,' my mum says as she admires the Silverline-branded scarf she's wearing in the mirror. 'Just... wow, so beautiful.'

'Yeah, it looks great,' I say. I mean, it doesn't look bad or anything, but it's not exactly a really nice scarf. It's just navy blue with the ship name and logo embroidered on in silver thread.

'Can I... can I really have it?' she asks me.

'Of course you can,' I say.

'What about this pen?' my dad asks me. 'Would you look at this stunning pen.'

The supposedly stunning pen is silver with the ship's

name and logo on it in navy blue. There's a real theme here. No one was all that inventive when it came to branding the items and yet my parents love it all. They are like kids in a toyshop. This is like complete role reversal because it used to be them who would take me to the shop and ask me what I wanted them to buy me. It's kind of nice, to be able to return the favour, even if it isn't exactly my own hard-earned cash I'm spending.

I stroll around, looking at the tat, trying to see if there's anything I might like, even just to serve as a reminder of the trip. There's a snow globe with the ship inside and a real surge of bad weather when you shake it up, but I can't imagine breaking that out at Christmas every year. There are tea towels, bath towels, face cloths. There is actually a Silver-line bathrobe, which does feel lovely and soft, just like the ones that we have in our rooms. I think that might be it for me though. I can't imagine anything else taking my fancy. I *definitely* couldn't spend £1,000 here.

'Stationery!' my dad enthuses. 'Look at this gorgeous Silverline stationery!'

It's off-white paper and envelopes with, surprise surprise, the ship's logo on them.

'Who are you going to send letters to?' my mum asks him. 'You don't even say hello to people if you pass them in the supermarket.'

'I'd send letters if I had this gorgeous stationery,' he insists 'I can send letters to everyone back home, when we get to New York, tell them what a lovely time we're having.'

'Yeah, sure, chuck them on the pile,' I say casually.

We do actually have a little pile of tat on the counter, where a small brunette lady is ringing them up as we go along.

'Can I have this mug?' my mum asks me. 'I know I have a lot of mugs, but—'

'Mum,' I say with an amused laugh. 'You guys should just grab anything you want. Anything. Anything at all, OK?'

My dad stops in his tracks in front of a glass cabinet. He gaps with delight as he stares up at a navy blue blazer with red edges and a big, gold Silverline cruise logo on the sleeve and little gold badges on the collar. It is bizarrely futuristic in the way that it is cut, with the buttons off to one side. It's also completely ugly.

'What is this?' my dad asks.

'That's the captain's jacket,' the cashier says. 'Well, a replica captain's jacket.'

'I must have it,' he says, the wonderment apparent in his voice.

'Dad, there is no way the captain wears a jacket like that,' I insist. 'You'll look fresh off the Battlestar Galactica.'

And I know this because *Battlestar Galactica* is one on my dad's favourite TV shows. I've seen someone on there with something almost identical, in fact, I think he was the captain. The Battlestar Galactica captain might wear this jacket, but I guarantee you the captain of this ship does not.

'Does the captain of this ship wear this jacket?' my dad asks the cashier.

'You bet,' she replies in a strong East Coast American accent.

'Doesn't he wear like a white shirt, bits on the shoulders, maybe badges on the chest...?'

'He wears this jacket to relax,' she explains.

Absolutely no one is relaxing in this jacket.

'Can I have it?' my dad asks. 'I know it's £290, but—'

'£290!' I squeak. Still, it's only ship credit. 'Sure, go for it.'

When my mum and dad are happy that they've got everything they want and the cashier has rung it all up, it comes to a grand total of £512.

'Is that it?' I ask.

'I know,' the cashier beams. 'You've got yourself some amazing bargains.'

'That's just over half what I have to spend,' I say. 'Let's see...'

I grab another robe, this time for Eli, along with a few bags of chocolate ship coins because they are amazing, but I'm still not even over £600.

'What's the most expensive thing you sell?' I ask curiously.

'It's like... a piece of glass, like a glass disk, with the ship and the date we sail etched into it... it's kind of cool, they only make so many per trip, so they are rare too. We keep them locked away. Would you like to see one?'

'No, it's fine, I'll just take it,' I say.

'Yeah?'

'Yeah,' I say. It can be the thing that reminds me of the trip and blah blah blah.

'Well, OK then,' she says. 'It will be delivered to your suite, Miss Jones.'

'Marvellous,' I reply. 'Thank you.'

'Oh, Rosie, thank you so much,' my mum says, giving me a big squeeze before quickly releasing me to pick up her bags of ship merchandise.

'Yes, thanks, love,' my dad says. 'I can't wait to wear my jacket.'

'Probably don't wear it while we're on the ship,' I say.

'What? Why not?' my dad asks, like I'm his mum and won't let him go to school in a Darth Vader costume.

'Well, people might mistake you for the captain,' I say. But they won't. There is no way the captain wears this weird, space-age, movie-prop jacket.

'Actually, anyone who buys one gets to meet the captain,' the cashier says. 'It gains you access to the Captain's Bar – a private drinking joint for the captain and a few, very lucky select individuals.'

'I... I get to meet the captain?' my dad asks. He can't believe his ears. You'd think he'd been told he was getting to meet the Queen or something – he'd probably be less excited to meet the Queen.

'Yes, of course,' she tells him. 'You can take your family with you. Just pop to reception and they'll help you schedule something.'

I massage my temples. Why oh why did she have to tell us that?

'Do many people buy these?' I ask.

'They don't,' she replies. 'Very exclusive.'

More like very crap.

'Perhaps he can fit us in this evening?' my dad says.

'Perhaps,' the cashier replies.

'OK, well, we should go and get ready,' my dad insists.

'I thought we were going to play shuffleboard?' I say – and now I can't believe my ears. But I really, really don't want to meet the captain. I have nothing against the man, he's doing a fine job, but my dad is going to treat him like he's Clint Eastwood. He's going to fanboy the captain, I just know it. My mum has this overwhelming respect for anyone who she thinks has an important job, so she'll probably be throwing herself at his feet too. It's nice that they're excited, but it's going to be so, so embarrassing for me.

'I might pop for a drink,' I say.

'We can get a drink with the captain later,' my dad says.

'Yeah, I mean I'll go for a pre-drink,' I say. 'You know what us millennials are like with our prinkies.'

'I have no idea what that means.' He looks at me, confused. 'But OK, sure. We'll see you back at our suite to go and meet the captain.'

My mum does a little, excitable jig.

Wow, this ship really is like Disneyland for retired people. We went to Disneyland, when I was younger, with my auntie, my uncle and my cousin Tom, who was about four at the time. Tom was a huge fan of Aladdin, which hadn't been out long, so it was a pretty big deal at the park. Characters from the movie were strolling around and, when Tom got to meet Genie, he got so excited and nervous that he wet his pants. Tom, as an adult, thinks that this is hilarious, but his mum still says it was the most embarrassing moment of her life.

I'll grab a drink, loosen up a little, and then we'll see about going to meet the captain. Let's just hope I don't embarrass myself, or my excited parents don't do it for me. No one wants a repeat of Disneyland.

21

'Well, hey there,' I hear fake Bublé's voice say as he sits down next to me at the bar.

For a big ship, I sure do bump into him a lot. I am in the ship's stunning champagne bar – definitely the fanciest prinkies I've ever had, in this beautiful golden room with free-flowing booze and gentle ambient music.

'I cannot get over that accent coming out of your mouth,' I say. 'I can't get over how different you are generally. You were such an indie kid the last time I saw you.'

'Well, looking like an unkempt Oasis fanboy was never going to be a look that would get me far, was it? When I landed in Australia, the first thing they made me do was get a proper haircut.'

'I can't say I'm surprised,' I admit. 'I don't think the wild, messy hairstyle was cool until Harry Styles made it so.'

'Yeah, I was ahead of my time,' he says with a laugh. 'I got to be a Josh Groban tribute precisely once – couldn't quite match his tone – and I got to grow my hair out for that gig, but that was it. Anyway, Bublé is a much better fit, you know me, I love the sound of my own voice. I get to chat, be charming, sing, I can do my weird dad dancing...'

'Oh, I'm sure the cheeky chap in you loves it.'

'I really do,' he says. 'I get to be kind of a wild card, which I like.'

'What does being a wild card entail?' I ask curiously. 'Is it like diplomatic immunity?'

'Sort of,' he chuckles before bursting into a rendition of 'When I Fall in Love'. Propping up the bar, nursing the drink he already had when he sat down next to me, he somehow blends right in and captures everyone's attention. His voice, unaccompanied, without a microphone stands on its own. He has such a smooth voice which simultaneously sounds so romantic and yet so heart-breaking – then again, it's a fine line between the two.

I rest my chin on my hand and just stare at him. It's almost impossible to believe that my Josh is inside this smooth, sexy man. It's like he went on one of those TV makeover shows where they completely rebuilt him. He was always an amazing boyfriend but now he's made of 100% boyfriend material. I'm not sure what you'd want to change about him (not that I ever wanted to change him before) except maybe to get him a job on dry land.

'See, Josh Groban doesn't get to do that,' he tells me when he's finished singing.

I feel so relaxed and yet so nervous. I don't even know what to say.

'Gosh, don't tell my mum you were Josh Groban,' I eventually blurt. 'She's obsessed with him. Anyway, for what it's worth, I like your hair like this. The sleek, suave Bublé look suits you. It's nice to be able to see your eyes.'

'Yeah, I should have known you'd be into it – don't think I

don't remember how you used to hold my hair out of my eyes when we kissed.' Josh laughs.

'Why is that funny?' I ask.

'Because you would move my hair from my eyes, lean in for a kiss and then immediately close your eyes again,' he says. 'I never understood it.'

'Well, I always felt like you were hiding something behind that fringe. Those few seconds getting to look into your eyes... it felt like the one moment I got to glimpse inside your head.'

Josh scoots up a little closer to me, placing his face just inches away from mine.

'Can you tell what I'm thinking right now?' he asks.

Truthfully, I have no idea. I just hope he can't tell what I'm thinking. I'm thinking about what it used to be like to kiss him and how I'd love to give it another try, just to refresh my memory...

'Maybe,' I lie.

He only lingers a second longer before getting out of my personal space.

'Hmm,' he says with a laugh before finishing his drink. 'So, what are you and Eli up to this evening?'

'I have no idea what Eli is up to, he's still with André – I haven't seen him in twenty-four hours, they must be having fun.'

'We did a set earlier, André was there, but Eli wasn't with him... Are you sure that's where he is?'

'Erm, yeah, well, he said he was probably staying with him last night but—'

'Don't worry, I'm sure he's fine,' Josh says, squeezing my shoulder.

'Yeah,' I say, except my brain is considering a different

version of events. A version where he's drunk, staggering around on the deck before taking a tumble overboard... and then there's that balcony story that Karen told us. Eli just found it funny, he won't have heeded it as a warning, he would've seen it as a challenge if anything. Some kind of extreme sport sexual activity to add to his resume.

'Your brain is running away with you, isn't it?' Josh says.

'Yep,' I admit.

'Some things never change, do they?' he laughs. 'Well, how about I take you to André's cabin and we see if he's there – I'm sure he is.'

'I'd really appreciate it, thank you.'

Josh offers me his hand to help me down off my stool.

'Here's one for your *Titanic* tick list,' Josh says. 'I'm taking you down to the cabins where the staff live. No suites down there.'

'So long as it isn't underwater, I don't mind,' I say.

'Are you not a high-society girl now?' he asks. 'With you guys all staying in suites, I figured... I don't know...'

'Oh, no, I'm still a lowly pauper,' I say. 'I won the money to buy the tickets.'

'Well, that's almost Titanic-y, isn't it?' he says as he ushers me into the lift.

'I guess it is,' I say thoughtfully. 'I'm definitely more Jack Dawson than Rose DeWitt-Bukater though.'

'Me too,' he says. 'It's nice to pretend to be something better – something more successful – isn't it?'

'It is,' I reply. 'I think I keep forgetting that this isn't my life, and once I get back home, it will be back to reality.'

'Are you not enjoying reality?' he asks.

'Is anyone?' I say with a laugh.

God, I'm really bringing the tone down, I need to change the subject.

'Are we nearly there?' I ask.

'Yeah, just down this corridor,' he says. 'Rosie, honestly, I'm sure Eli's fine.'

'God, I hope so.'

Eli has been back in my life for about five minutes and I'm not sure I could live without him now. I didn't realise he was missing from my life but now that he's here I can see the hole that was there before. You might think you can get through life without a proper best friend, but you need someone you can count on, someone you can tell anything to, someone who is always going to have your back and never ever judge you.

'Here we are,' Josh says. 'This is André's cabin.'

I take a deep breath and knock on the door.

Eli answers, eventually, wearing nothing but a Silverline cruise robe.

'Oh, thank God you're OK,' I say, grabbing him for a hug.

'I'm fine,' he says cautiously. 'What's wrong with you?'

'Nothing, nothing,' I insist. 'I was just worried because I hadn't heard from you in a while.'

Eli hugs me back. 'Oh, you're your mother's daughter,' he says with a chuckle. 'Yep, I'm fine. Hey, Josh.'

'Hey,' he says.

'Sorry I missed your set earlier, I was going to come, but André talked me into just relaxing, ordering some room service... He was going to the gym before coming back to hang out more.'

'Do you fancy going for a drink?' I ask.

'I've had a bunch.'

'Yeah, well, it's a drink with the captain,' I explain. 'My

dad bought this jacket that gets you into the captain's lounge and apparently we're all invited to have a drink with him.'

'You know, I've always wondered who buys those,' Josh says.

'People like my dad,' I say. 'So, come on, Eli, will you come with me?'

'You know I'd love to, but when André gets back he's going to play me like a cello, if you know what I mean...'

'I'm not even sure you know what you mean,' I point out.

'I can come with you if you like,' Josh chimes in. 'I've got the night off, I'd love to. We can catch up, keep an eye on your folks, have a few drinks.'

'Oh, there we go, all's well that ends well,' Eli says. He pulls me for a hug before pushing me away just enough to close the door. 'See you, sis.'

'I feel like I've just been dumped,' I tell Josh. 'You know you don't have to come, right? I'll be fine on my own.'

'I'm sure you would be, but I'd like to come... if you want me to?'

'Yeah,' I say. 'I'd love you to.'

I actually would. Now that we've spent more time together, I'm starting to really enjoy Josh's company.

'Great,' he says. 'Well, let's go and see if we can get jackets.'

'Don't even joke,' I say. 'You know my dad is going to be wearing his.'

'He'll make it work,' Josh says.

'I'm so nervous,' I admit. 'What's the captain like?'

'Have you been paying attention to his announcements?' Josh asks me.

'Yes... they sound kind of kooky, I think I'd assumed it was just an actor.'

'Nope, that's the captain, and kooky is exactly what he is.'

Oh, wonderful, that's just what I need. Drinks with the kooky captain. If anything was going to make me think that we won't make it to New York, it's finding out that the Joker is steering this ship.

Still, at least I'll have Josh there with me. I'm actually really pleased he's coming along. The more I'm around him, the more I want to be around him. I'm really starting to enjoy hanging out with him again. It would be nice if we could be friends, but while he's doing this job, there's no way I can maintain any sort of friendship with him, unless I reactivate my social media profiles, but, honestly, I'm kind of enjoying life without them, and exchanging the occasional Facebook message would hardly count as maintaining a friendship, would it? Never mind anything else that I may or may not be thinking about...

22

Guess what... the captain could fit us in tonight. Because of course he could. Because no one else is buying these jackets.

I really don't know what I was thinking, when I imagined a captain's private bar. At first I thought it would be big, lavish, super exclusive with fancy décor and stylish furniture. Then, I'd think a little more logically and it would shrink into something small, intimate, maybe with a globe in the middle, ocean charts on the wall, leather-bound books and big armchairs.

Now that I'm here it's, well... it's sort of both. It's not huge, but it's not tiny either. It's not too fancy, but it's not too serious. The only thing that it does have, that I didn't float in either scenario in my head, are taxidermy animals on all available walls and flat surfaces. So, while it might be just the one bartender behind the bar, along with me, Josh, my mum and my dad, we are still under the watchful gaze of birds, fish, a stag's head, foxes, rabbits and a few reptiles I can't accurately identify. Their beady eyes are so lifelike, yet so cold and dead. The only real animal in the room is a golden retriever, fast asleep by a fireplace that I can't quite figure out. I'm not sure if it is real or decorative. I imagine, if it is real, it might be one of those bioethanol fireplaces, as opposed to a real one that needs a chimney. That just feels like asking for trouble.

The captain himself is yet to join us, although you could be forgiven for thinking otherwise because my dad is proudly wearing his captain's jacket – not that I think the captain would wear a jacket like this.

My mum looks lovely, in a pale blue skirt and jacket combo. She always looks so effortlessly classy in a way that I know I never could.

I am wearing a silver cocktail dress that looks just right next to Josh, in his black suit and white shirt. He popped to his cabin to get changed before we came here. I hovered outside his door while he dashed in. In less than ten minutes he was back out in the corridor with me, and while his suit is still very much like something Michael Bublé might wear, there is an unidentifiable difference between his stage clothes and his real clothes. Even after his sexy new glow-up, in his own clothes he somehow looks a little more like himself, although still admittedly more handsome than when I used to know him. With his own accent, without a microphone or an audience in sight, he's just Josh, and it feels even easier to be around him.

'You know, I was talking to one of the old dears by the pool about you earlier today,' my mum tells Josh. 'She was telling me all about your wife and kids.'

My heart jumps into my mouth – well, it's my heart or it's all the chocolate I ate before I left my suite. I feel my body stiffen as an anger I didn't expect surges through my veins, pooling into my arms and legs, making me feel so tense. I wrack my brains for snippets of our conversations up to now – didn't he say he was single? I remember telling him that I was single, back when he thought Eli was my boyfriend, but did he actually say that he was? If he did, I'm so so angry at him for lying to me, but, if he didn't, well, I suppose if it was to mislead me then that's just as bad as lying. Then again, why would he mention it? It's not like I'm a potential love interest, is it? He doesn't owe me any kind of explanation; his private life is his private life... so why am I getting so upset?

I need to excuse myself, to get out of this room and clear my head. I don't want anyone to think this topic of conversation is having any effect on me.

'I'll be back in a sec,' I say as I pull myself to my feet, careful not to burst any seams on my dress in the process. It's a full-time job at the best of times, but when I'm in a hurry, a wardrobe malfunction feels more likely, if not imminent.

'Whoa there, wait a second,' Josh insists, jumping to his feet too. 'This is how misunderstandings happen, when people leave mid-conversation. I absolutely don't have a wife and kids.'

He's either doubling down on his spectacular lie or he's telling the truth. How can I know which one it is? And, worst of all, he knows that I have had problems trusting in the past, he knows this will play on my mind. I suppose that's why he's quick to insist it's not true, but what am I going to do? Make him prove it? Why would I bother? Why do I care?

'Oh, I know that,' my mum says. 'This is the thing. She kept talking about your wife and kids, the time she saw you on *The Graham Norton Show* – and then I realised she was calling you Michael. Most of the ladies on this ship think you're the actual Michael Bublé.'

Josh laughs. 'I know, I know, I do tell them I'm just a

tribute but... I don't know, they seem happy believing what they believe. So a few of them get a bit mixed up sometimes.'

'You want to be careful,' my mum starts. 'If I had been an eligible bachelorette, it might have made me think you were off the market... Are you off the market?'

'Mum,' I snap. 'Don't interrogate him.'

I'd actually quite like to know the answer, now that I think about it. I wasn't expecting to feel so strongly about the thought of him having a family already. I'm weirdly glad that he doesn't.

'It's OK,' Josh says with a laugh as he sits back in his seat. 'I am very much on the market, sadly. At sea, you don't meet too many women looking to settle down.'

'So, you do want a family?' my mum persists.

'Mum!' I say again.

Josh just laughs. 'Honestly, it's OK,' he insists. 'By the way, Rosie, now you know I don't have a secret double life, you can go to the bathroom or wherever you were heading.'

'Oh, I wasn't going to the bathroom,' I say, although that would be the most logical explanation. I suppose I could have just pretended and gone anyway, but I kind of want to see where this conversation is going. I'm curious about what Josh does want in his future. 'I was just, erm...' I glance around the room. 'I was just going to pet the dog. I love dogs, I miss them, being on this ship, I used to see a bunch, every day, just going about my business...' Awkward, horrible, embarrassing babbling.

'OK,' he says.

I walk over to the golden retriever and squat down next to him. His eyes are closed. He looks fast asleep, so comfortable and so peaceful. Still, if I know dogs like I think I do, I'm sure he won't mind a few pats and some ear scratches.

I gently extend my hand and place the back of it on his head, but right away I can tell something isn't right. He doesn't feel soft and warm he's hard and... Oh God.

I scream as I recoil in horror.

'Oh my God, the dog is dead, the dog is dead,' I say.

'I should hope so,' a deep voice bellows across the room. 'Or getting him stuffed was a grave mistake.'

A broad man with a deep voice walks towards us. He reminds me a little of Lou Ferrigno, the bodybuilder who played the Hulk in *The Incredible Hulk* TV series back in the 70s. My dad used to watch it on VHS when I was growing up. But even more distinctive than his voice or his frame is his jacket. His ugly, sci-fi-looking jacket that is exactly like my dad's, only it looks like it's made out of more expensive materials, with more care. Wow, I guess the captain really does wear a jacket like that. It appears, as the cashier had suggested, to be his relaxing jacket, who'd have thought?

My dad gives me a side-eye that absolutely oozes with sass. He looks so smug to be right about the captain wearing the jacket and pleased as punch to be wearing one (not quite) just like it too.

Sadly, the captain's arrival and his jacket can't fully detract from the fact I've just petted a dead dog. I feel sick to my stomach. I would say that taxidermy is an arguably grim practice anyway, but touching it, expecting it to be a warm, breathing, alive lovable golden retriever has made it all the more repulsive. I just want to wash my hands.

'Have you been trying to feed the birds too?' the captain asks with an amused chuckle. I'm so glad he finds it so funny.

'I just wasn't expecting it to be stuffed – I didn't realise people stuffed dogs,' I point out. 'Everything else in here is a wild animal.'

Don't get me wrong, it is all absolutely repulsive. But dogs are household pets – practically family members to most people. I wouldn't stuff a dead pet any more than I would stuff my granddad, I can't think of anything more horrible or upsetting.

'Yes, well, when you're at sea all the time, you really miss your pets. You can't bring them on board with you, not alive at least, so I had them pull old Stanford's plug out and make him a little more ship-friendly,' he explains.

I place a hand over my mouth.

'Look at your face,' the captain laughs. 'I'm joking, I'm joking. You can bring pets on board, there's a special part of the ship where you can walk them. No, poor old Standford croaked naturally. But I did have him stuffed so that I could keep him forever. He was such a good boy, such a great friend. I'm Captain Martin, by the way.'

'So great to meet you, captain,' my dad says, offering him a hand to shake.

My mum shuffles on the spot, as though she's fixing to curtsy, but thankfully she doesn't. She just reaches out to shake his hand, but Captain Martin has other ideas. He snatches up her hand and plants a kiss on the back of it. My mother blushes and giggles.

'I'm Timothy,' my dad tells him. 'This is my wife Evelyn, our daughter Rosie and that's her ex-boyfriend Josh.'

My eyebrows shoot up to the deck above. Why on earth did he have to introduce him as my ex-boyfriend? I know he is, but still, just say friend, surely?

'Oh, hey, it's our very own Michael Bublé,' the captain says. 'How's it going?'

'Very well, thank you,' he replies politely. 'And you?'

'Yes, can't complain, can't complain. Drunk as a skunk,

but pretty sure we're going in the right direction... I'm joking, I'm joking.'

I cannot believe this man is in charge of the ship. It's terrifying to think that the running of the ship, the staff, the passengers, their pets... this man is the person taking care of all of it. This man, who can't stop joking for two minutes, whose idea of a joke is arguably completely unfunny.

'That's a fine jacket you have there, Timothy,' Captain Martin says. 'A fine choice of purchase.'

'Thank you,' my dad replies. 'It's just so stylish. I had no idea it came with the opportunity to meet you, I have so many questions to ask you.'

'Well, it's my night off,' he says. 'Let's order some drinks, get some food brought in here – I would love to chat with you, Timothy, and with your gorgeous lady wife.'

Given this man is in charge of the ship, I'd expected the meet and greet to be a quick in and out jog, maybe a swift drink, before we would be shown the door, and that was fine by me. I mean, it wasn't really fine by me because I didn't even want to do that much, but knowing that it would be quick and painless meant that it might not be the weirdest night of my life – except now it's turning in to being exactly that.

'Please, call me Tim,' my dad says. 'All my friends call me Tim.'

'Right you are, Tim,' the captain replies.

Oh my God, it is like I'm trapped in a nightmare. From the embarrassing encounters to the dead animals decorating the place, this is exactly how I would describe my worst nightmare. The only thing it's missing is a TV camera, for full, mortifying, oh ground please swallow me up, embarrassment.

I yawn theatrically. 'Oh, would you look at the time,' I say, glancing at my bare wrist. I actually have no idea what time it is, nor am I tired at all. I just want to get out of here.

'I'd love to pick your brains about the plumbing on this bad boy,' my dad continues, not even listening to me, and he heads to the bar with the captain, my mum following close behind.

I take a few slow steps towards Josh.

'I don't even think they would notice if we left,' I tell him. 'I definitely don't think they would care.'

'I think you might be right,' Josh says. 'Shall we do a bunk?'

I nod decisively before we slowly but surely make our way towards the door. Josh opens it quietly for me. I slink out, with him hot on my heels. As the door slams closed behind, thanks to a little unexpected whatever ship turbulence is called, we both instinctively run down the corridor. Of course no one is chasing us. A tidal wave could've burst in through a window and taken us off out to sea, but my parents would have been way too engrossed in their conversation to notice.

We finally stop when we get to the lift.

'I know you said he was kooky, but oh my God, what an odd man,' I say as I try to catch my breath. Is there anything more embarrassing than being so unfit that, as soon as you exert yourself a little in front of an audience, you have to try and hide the fact that you're dying because your body isn't used to exercise in any way, shape or form? I've done more exercise on this ship than I have this year.

'Yeah, he's eccentric, all right,' Josh agrees. 'He is a good captain though, everyone loves him.'

'Oh, yeah, I'm sure he's lovely until you die and then he stuffs you and hangs you from the wall,' I say.

Josh laughs. 'I'll walk you to your suite, if you're tired,' he says.

'Oh, thanks,' I say. 'I'm not really tired though, I just wanted to leave.'

'Oh, don't let me force you into bed then,' he says. He bites his lip as he regrets his choice of words. 'You know, I've never actually seen inside a suite. The cabins they give us are the small, standard ones, low down in the ship, usually without windows. One time they had miscalculated how many rooms they needed for staff so I got an upgrade. I was so excited to have a window with some natural light coming in, but instead it had a digital balcony.'

'What the hell is a digital balcony?' I ask curiously.

'Imagine a real balcony,' he says as we walk. 'Looking out during the day, your curtain blowing in the wind, then the night sky at night... except you're actually in a windowless room and your wall is covered with a large screen that makes it look like you have a balcony.'

'Oh my God, that's... is that genius? It's either genius or depressing.'

'In a way, it did make a nice change,' he starts. 'But you could tell it wasn't real.'

'Well, you can come in if you'd like,' I say. 'We could maybe have a drink, watch a documentary about a serial killer like old times?'

'I would absolutely love that,' he says. 'Let's do it.'

'Great,' I reply, trying to contain my smile. 'But don't get too excited, I don't think we have the best suites you can get. I heard some have multiple floors and Jacuzzis... We do have a balcony though, and a nice big sofa that we will be able to actually sit on because it sounds like Eli has well and truly bailed on me now. Still, it could be worse, I—'

Another jolt to the ship sends me hurtling into Josh's arms. He catches me and helps me back to my feet, keeping his hands on my sides to steady me.

'You OK?' he asks me.

'Oh, yeah, that could've been much worse,' I say. 'I usually hardcore embarrass myself at every opportunity.'

'I don't remember that about you, you know,' Josh points out.

'Hmm, maybe I didn't used to be so bad... maybe it all went wrong at some point. I've definitely always had bad luck, maybe it comes from that.'

'You do not have bad luck,' he insists with a laugh.

'I could tell you some stories that would prove otherwise,' I say.

'Such as?'

'Just trust me,' I say.

Josh reaches up to push a piece of hair from in front of my eyes. It must have messed itself up a little when I stumbled. His hand brushes my cheek for a few seconds as he places my hair behind my ear. It's like there is an electricity that transfers from his fingers to my cheek, down my neck before working its way down my back.

Josh moves his face closer to mine. I lean forward to meet him in the middle. Our lips touch. It's like a kiss that isn't quite a kiss. A peck that could be something so much more except Josh pulls away.

'Shit, sorry,' he says. 'I... I shouldn't have done that, I'm...'

Oh God.

'No, I, erm...' I don't know what to say either.

'I'm going to go,' he says. 'Sorry.'

Josh doesn't even wait for me to reply, he just turns on his heels and practically runs away from me. He regrets kissing me so much he can't even look me in the eye.

Now do you see what I mean? If there is a way for moments to turn so completely and utterly embarrassing for me, they absolutely will. It's just my luck.

23

It's nice to wake up in bed with someone next to you, isn't it? Someone to cuddle up to when it's cold. Someone to make you feel better when you've had a nightmare. Someone to spoon with on lazy Sundays, kissing, listening to the rain, watching TV while you drink tea and make plans for the day, for the week, for the rest of your lives. One of the things I miss the most when I am single is having someone to share a bed with. It's a kind of company you just can't get from anyone but a partner, isn't it? Well, how often do you share a bed with someone you're not romantically involved with?

Yes, I absolutely love sharing a bed with someone... if I remember going to bed with them in the first place. I can safely say there is nothing nice about waking up in a bed with someone you don't remember going to bed with because that's what I'm dealing with right now. I woke up on my side, facing out of the bed, and thought I could feel the warmth of a body behind me, but I assumed it was just single-girl early-morning delusions... but then, when I extended my leg behind me I collided with someone else's leg. Now I'm too scared to move. I'm petrified to roll over and see who it is.

I wouldn't say that I was a huge drinker – in fact, I get drunk quite quickly. Usually I hit the point where I feel emboldened to do things that I wouldn't usually – like spend a bunch of money on a bunch of dresses that make me look like an overstuffed sausage – but I never get so drunk that I have a *Hangover*-style night where I wake up the following morning with no recollection of what happened the night before, but I absolutely don't remember getting in bed with a man last night, so what the hell happened?

I remember my awkward kiss with Josh that sent him running for the hills... I went to my suite, I had a few drinks on my own... did he come back? Did he see the error of his ways or just double down on his mistake? Would I really not remember?

I ponder alternatives, but the best I can come up with is that perhaps someone somehow walked into the wrong suite. Or did some random drunk wander in? Perhaps I didn't close the door properly... Such a terrifying thought gives me the surge of energy I need to jump to action, sitting up quickly, spinning round to see who my bed buddy is, all while carefully pulling the covers up high over my upper body, even though I'm wearing the vest top I've been sleeping in.

'Oh my God, what? What?' the man says, jumping up too.

It turns out that a drunk has wandered in and got into bed with me. It isn't a random drunk though, it's my drunk. It's Eli.

'You gave me a bloody heart attack,' I say as I lie back down, now I know that I'm safe.

'Who the hell else did you think was going to be in bed

with you? A different ex?' Eli is joking, but as he says this, he remembers that I do actually have another ex on board, and he reads me like a book. 'Were you with Josh last night?' he asks. 'In here? You saucy minx!'

'No, I wasn't,' I quickly insist. 'We were on the way back here, just to hang out, I hasten to add, when... I don't know what happened, something happened, and we kissed... sort of... our lips barely touched for three seconds before he pulled away, like he was making the biggest mistake of his life, and then he ran away. Literally ran away. Like, the speed with which his legs removed him from the situation only dented my ego further.'

'Aww, baby,' Eli says as he lies back next to me. He lifts an arm and pats his chest, silently telling me to rest my head there.

I shuffle into place.

'He obviously wanted to kiss you,' Eli says as he strokes my hair.

'No one wants to kiss me,' I point out.

'I'll kiss you, if you like,' he says, and I'm 99% certain he is joking, but you never quite know with Eli.

'So the only person who is willing to kiss me is a gay guy, and it's only out of pity, he doesn't actually want to kiss me,' I say. 'Great.'

'No, I do want to,' he says. 'It's like... you know how when you always eat a pepperoni pizza and every now and then you decide to have a Hawaiian for a change, but it only reminds you that pepperoni pizzas are the one for you...'

At least now I know he's winding me up.

'So in this scenario I am not only a pizza you don't want, but the most divisive pizza on the planet? Marvellous.'

'There she is,' Eli says. 'I can feel your little cheeks smiling down there, don't pretend you're all depressed.'

'I know, I'm fine,' I insist. 'It was just embarrassing.'

'That's just life,' he says. 'Why don't we go for breakfast and put it all behind us? Eat a bunch of pastries, that will make you feel better.'

'How did you end up here? In bed with me?' I ask. 'Where is lover boy?'

'He was up early for a rehearsal for something or other... I figured I'd just come back here. My plan was to wake you up, but you looked so peaceful, snoring your little head off.'

'I do not snore,' I insist.

'You will never know, will you? Anyway, I plonked myself down next to you, saw you sleeping, thought I'd let you get another hour or so and I guess I dropped off... Next thing I know, you're waking up in a flap.'

'I promise you, it was scarier for me,' I tell him. 'Breakfast would be good though.'

'OK, well, why don't you go and have a quick shower, freshen up, sort that hair out – lord knows, it needs a brush – I just have a little bit of work to do.'

'I thought you weren't working on holiday,' I remind him.

'It's just a couple of quick emails, it's no big deal. Now go and have a shower so we can eat. And wash your hair, I can't handle any more dry shampoo. Honestly, it's like being in a sandstorm.'

I know that Eli's teasing is a form of affection and it comforts me more than he will ever know.

'OK, fine, fine, I'll go and wash my hair. Just know that I only do this on special occasions.'

'I already know this,' he assures me. 'Hurry up.'

I already feel a little more relaxed, just for having Eli

around. He really does help to put things in to perspective, or, at the very least, distract me from the things that are on my mind. Perhaps if I keep him with me all day I'll be able to face bumping into Josh, because I know I'm going to wind up face to face with him sooner or later. That is, if he doesn't run away again.

24

There are three different sizes of plates next to the breakfast buffet. The first is a tea plate, not very big, perfect if you just want to grab a quick croissant to go with your morning cup of coffee. Then we have your average dinner plate, a decent size, perfect for a full English, no matter where you stand on what actually belongs in a full English, because my dad got quite upset about hash browns the other day, despite actually eating four of them. And then there are the large plates, and they are *large*. Today is absolutely a large-plate day. I load it up with all the usual fodder – the beige junk that makes my taste buds happy but my metabolism sad. I don't want to look like a complete piece of trash, so I take a yoghurt and some fruit too, giving my plate a much-needed dash of colour that will most likely remain there after I OD on pastry.

'Oh, look, there's André,' Eli says innocently, although he's not fooling anyone.

André is sitting at one of the large round tables with Josh, Amanda and a couple of other members of the band. Rather suspiciously, there are two empty seats available at the table.

'Let's sit with them,' Eli suggests.

He doesn't give me chance to reply before marching over with his plate, taking a seat next to his new squeeze. The only seat for me is between Eli and Amanda, the Atlantic's answer to Adele.

'Good morning, campers,' Eli says.

'Morning,' I say sheepishly.

I can hardly look at Josh, not that it matters. It turns out he can't look at me at all, he just stares as his scrambled eggs.

'How is everyone doing today?' Eli asks.

'I'm doing great,' André says, all smiles. You can tell he's so into Eli, and who can blame him? Despite being completely different types on paper, they are perfect for each other, and they make a really gorgeous couple. 'We're having a bit of a party, after our set this evening – it's our last evening set before we arrive in New York, we usually make a big thing of it. It's going to be an incredible show, then we're all going to meet in the aft lounge.'

'They let us commandeer it for one night per crossing,' Josh says, still not really looking up. 'It's a public event, but most of the passengers would rather be relaxing in the posh bars, rather than listening to music, drinking and dancing with us.'

'Sometimes a few people show up,' Amanda adds. 'It's rare they stay long though, with so many other places to go.'

'Sounds awesome,' Eli enthuses.

'You should come,' André insists. There's a real optimism in his eyes, coupled with a case of the nerves. I think it's cute that he's still so nervous around Eli, even though Eli is completely smitten. Perhaps that is the key to a long and healthy relationship, to never get too comfortable or feel too safe. I'm not saying we should be on edge all the time, just that perhaps if we all considered our relationships to be a little more delicate, despite how solid they may seem, we might just take care of them a little better.

'Can I bring a friend?' Eli asks.

'Of course, bring a friend, have your friend bring a friend,' he replies excitedly.

I pick up a pastry from my huge plate. An almond croissant, which I pull the end off aimlessly. I can't quite bring myself to eat it, not sitting at this table with the awkward energy there is between me and Josh. You could cut the tension with a knife, even the blunt butter knife Eli is using to slather butter on his toast. I can't believe, after I told him what happened last night, he has actually brought me to this table to sit with these people. I shouldn't be annoyed with him though, perhaps he isn't thinking about me at all, perhaps all he's thinking about is André and how much he wants to spend time with him. He probably doesn't even think I care about what Josh thinks of me, given that this is mostly a trip for me to go and see Simon. Sexy, successful Simon, who took one look at me making an arse of myself on YouTube and still sent me flowers telling me that he missed me.

I wonder if he'll be surprised when I turn up on his doorstep – well, his work doorstep anyway. It will be nice to surprise him, and hopefully it will show him that I'm open to a reconciliation, if it feels right. Our relationship didn't just leave me with trust issues, it left me with a lot of guilt. Guilt because I know that it was my fault that we broke up. I spent months suspecting that Simon was cheating on me. There was always just enough almost evidence to make me suspicious, but never the smoking gun that I needed to prove it. Keep in mind that this went on for so long that checking up on him practically became second nature to me. It might have been a bad learned behaviour, but it became a part of me, it grew roots that tangled my rational thoughts until I couldn't find them in all of the mess. Things just went too far. I should have confronted him, but I was worried that would have just made him more careful. I just needed to catch him, to prove to myself that I wasn't imagining it.

One day, while Simon was in the shower, I noticed his phone on charge next to his bed – unlocked. I'd spotted his passcode over his shoulder a few times, but he was forever changing it (which only added to my suspicions), and at that particular moment in time it felt like it had been a long time since he changed it – and he hadn't let me within a mile of his phone since. Unable to help myself, I snatched it up and began riffling through his messages, looking for girls' names, or boys' names, that I had never heard him mention before, but what caught my eye before any of that was a message sent by Simon, to his best friend, which said: I've got the ring, we're going out for dinner tonight, I think I'm going to do it.

Suddenly it all made sense. Simon wasn't being suspicious because he was cheating on me, he was being sneaky because he was planning on proposing. This shook me up in a different way. For starters, we had only been together for a year. Surely that was too soon to be getting married? It's not that I didn't love him, I was so sure that I did, but marriage...

I didn't know what to do, but I prepared for every eventuality, and by that I mean I quickly returned Simon's phone to his bedside table before spending an extra long amount of time getting ready. I made sure that my hair was perfect, my make-up was perfect, I even removed my red nail polish and replaced it with a gorgeous nearly nude pink shade, ready, just in case I might be snapping a photo of my ring-clad hand later in the evening. I still had no idea if I wanted to get married, but I trusted my instincts and felt confident that, whenever Simon did pop the question, I would just know the answer, like it would only come to me in that moment. Until then, even I didn't know what my answer would be and that made me as nervous as it did excited.

Simon was always a snappy dresser, but I didn't think much of it when he got ready and appeared to be dressed on the casual side. I'll admit, I did think it was a bit weird when he took me to a crappy diner on the outskirts of town, rather than a nice restaurant which was more our usual scene – I just thought he was planning something elaborate; I didn't think anything strange was going on. But we ate our food without much conversation (which I put down to him being nervous) and I carefully ate my dessert in tiny little bites, just in case there was a ring lurking somewhere in my ice cream, but by the time the bill was placed on our table, nothing had happened, until Simon placed a hand in his pocket and started rummaging around.

'Rosie,' he said. 'I have something to ask you.'

I felt my heart jump into my mouth – I think I might have been on the verge of panicking, but then Simon pulled his wallet out.

'Will you go halves on the bill?' he asked.

Obviously I was expecting a much different question – I didn't know what to say.

Simon, judging by my reaction, finally confessed to something, that *he* had been suspicious of *me*. It turns out that my sneaky searching through Simon's phone was not actually all that sneaky. He had suspected for a while that I was checking up on him and, like me, he had never quite been able to prove it. So he'd set me up, laid a trap for me, pretended he was going to propose to me and then just watched me squirm all night, waiting for him to pop a question that was never going to come.

Naturally I was furious – well, what a dirty trick. I was so angry that I threw a cup of tea at him (just the contents, and they were already cold). We argued all night before Simon eventually called time on our relationship, saying that I needed to be able to trust him and he needed to be able to trust me.

I was so upset and angry, but, after I thought about it – long after our break-up – I realised that I drove him away with my insecurities. I suppose I always knew, at the back of my mind, that Simon could get any girl that he wanted and I guess, as far as I was concerned, that meant that he was getting any girl he wanted while he was with me. I imagined the whole thing and in the end it cost me my relationship. I just want to show him that I've changed, I've matured, I have put my issues behind me and I am open.

'I watched a very interesting video last night, would anyone like to see it?' Amanda asks, bringing me back to the present.

No one seems all that interested. Still, she whips her phone from the pocket of her jeans, loads something up with a few taps of her screen and then turns it around for us all to watch.

I'm probably the least interested of everyone, so I don't even look. Instead I finally try to eat some of my breakfast. I'm no sooner chewing on a piece of croissant when I hear a familiar voice – *my* voice.

I snap my head in the direction of her screen to confirm my worst fear. It's the video of me on *One Big Question*, getting dumped by Dinosaur Dave.

'Oh, God, can you turn that off,' I say.

'Come on, Rosie, it's just a bit of fun,' she says before shushing me.

I'd made myself so comfortable on this cruise, knowing full well that none of the passengers would have seen my hit viral video, that I had almost managed to put it out of my mind. It had stopped being the movie playing behind my eyelids when I got in bed at night, it was no longer the conversation I was constantly replaying in my head in the shower, wondering what I could have said differently to make things not turn out like they did.

Yep, I knew that I would be safe from the passengers... I didn't stop to think about the crew.

Josh isn't having trouble looking at me now. His gaze keeps shifting from the real me to the me dying of shame on Amanda's phone. I want to slap her phone from her hands, hoping it will land in her fruit salad and never work again, but it turns out that cruise ships have their own prisons (they have their own morgues too, which is a horrible thought) so I'd best keep out of trouble. The whole place seems like such a dream, but you forget that it has to be ready to tackle all the horrors of real life too. As much as it feels like life is put on hold for the week you are at sea, it isn't at all.

'OK, look, let's not watch it,' Eli says, speaking up for me. 'You've seen it, we get it, she got dumped, who cares? If it hadn't happened, she and I probably wouldn't have reconnected, so, Rosie, as shit as it sounds, I'm glad it happened.'

I smile at him. My boy Eli always has my back. Always.

'Wait, you got back in touch after this?' Amanda asks. 'This was less than a month ago and now you're on holiday together. Didn't you say you were exes? And aren't you and Josh exes? Oh my God, is that why you're here, for Josh?'

'No,' I insist a little too quickly. 'Of course not.'

'My girl has had fellas way hotter than this one – no offence, buddy,' Eli tells Josh. 'We are on our way to New York to see Sexy Simon. He took one look at that hot mess on your phone and he just knew he needed her back, so he sent her a gorgeous bunch of flowers begging her to give him another chance.'

'Simon cheated on you,' Josh blurts. 'He cheated on you and then he dumped you in the most cruel, spiteful way I could even imagine – if I could even imagine something so horrible, I can't believe he came up with it.'

'Did he?' Eli asks me quietly.

'Everything that happened there, I deserved, OK?' I say before turning to Eli and whispering: 'I'll tell you later.'

'Wait, so... you get a bunch of flowers and now you're just going to New York to get back with your ex, with one of your exes in tow, on a ship where your other ex works, after another one dumped you on live TV?'

God, it sounds awful when she puts it like that. The thing is, it's not that bad. I am not going to New York to get back with Simon, no questions asked, like how would that even work, with him living across the Atlantic Ocean from me? I am just taking some time to enjoy a break from work, reconnecting with my exes and then just going to find Simon and see what happens. I really do feel like we need to have a chat and clear the air – at the least – because I've done a lot of soul-searching since what went on. I'll bet he has too.

Then again, what if it is fate bringing us back together? If I have the time and the resources, and the sense of spontaneity and courage to just go for it and see what happens, then why they hell not, right? As you get older, and deeper and deeper into adult life, it gets harder to do wild things like this. Amanda is probably just jealous because she spends her life at sea, singing Adele songs night after night, unable to forge a real life for herself because she lives in a cabin on a ship full of pensioners. She can't pop to Primark to spend £40 on twenty-five random items, or nip to The Alchemist for a few cheeky midday cocktails. If she's bloated or has cramps and doesn't feel like slipping into a tight sparkly dress and would much rather spend the evening cuddled up on the sofa with a hot-water bottle, she can't because, guess what, she's Adele. The show must go on. All of that or just the fact that she's a bitch, and a bit of a bully, given how much she's enjoying everything that is happening right now.

'I can't believe you would go back to him,' Josh says. 'After everything you went through – after everything we went through.'

'Christ, you all need to calm down,' I insist. 'You're all so serious, I think you've been at sea too long. You need a little time on dry land to get your heads straight. Of course I'm not just going to New York to try and get my ex back. Spoiler alert, for anyone who hasn't seen the video, I won a shit-ton of money. I'm on the holiday of a lifetime with it. A nice cruise, a week in New York – I have my new best friend with me. I'm doing OK. And anyway, I have a date tonight, so I can't come to your little party, sorry.'

'You have a date?' Josh asks.

'A date with someone on this ship?' Amanda continues. 'What's his name?'

'His name is Clive,' I tell them.

They both laugh.

'Clive doesn't sound real,' Amanda insists.

'Believe me, I thought the same when I met him,' Eli

chimes in. 'But he's real all right. Real and... dating my friend.'

'Clive is pretty much the most eligible bachelor on this ship,' I say. 'And the youngest. And he's a lot of fun. And I'm going for a drink with him tonight because I am casual and I have fun and I'm not on a mission to stalk all my exes, OK?'

'OK, sure, well, if he's so real, you can bring him to our party, can't you?' Amanda says with a smirk. She thinks I'm bluffing.

I mean, I am bluffing, but how dare she not just believe me, right?

'OK, sure, I'll ask him,' I say. 'But I'm certain he doesn't want to hang out with a bunch of kids.'

'We're mostly your age,' Josh reminds me.

'Fine, I'll bring him,' I say.

'Fine,' Josh replies. 'Can't wait to meet him.

'Fine,' I say again.

God, this is going great, isn't it?

'Well, I think I'm going to take my breakfast back to my room,' I say. 'I'll see you all later.'

I'm only at the other side of the room when Eli catches up with me.

'I'm so sorry,' he says. 'I had no idea she was going to do that. I just thought it would be good for you to have breakfast with Josh, to nip the weirdness from last night in the bud.'

'How did that work out?' I ask sarcastically, but I'm smiling soon enough. I can't stay mad at Eli; his intentions are always good.

'OK, point taken,' he says. 'You know she has a huge crush on Josh, right? Unrequited though, that's what André tells me.'

I just shrug my shoulders.

'Are you really going back to eat in your room alone? Shall I come with you?'

'That's OK, go and sit with André, have fun. I'm not going to my room, I'm going to find Clive, see if he'll have a drink with me later.'

'Are you actually going to bring him to the party?' Eli asks in disbelief. 'Do you really think that's going to make you look good? Like, he's an OK bloke, but he's quite weird, and he's really old... it's going to make you look like a gold-digger or something.'

'No it's not,' I insist. 'It's just two friends having a drink, and that will be clear from our body language. You think I'm going to drape myself across his lap, laughing at his jokes and pouring champagne into his mouth?'

'That was quite a vivid description, so yes,' he replies. 'One hundred per cent.'

I send Eli back to his man before heading off to find mine. Well, I can't turn up alone now, can I? That would be so embarrassing. Plus, my mum really wants me to grab a drink with the guy, so why not? I'm sure he has no expectations and obviously neither do I.

I just need to do my best to get through the next couple of days and then I'll be in New York where I can have fun with Eli and my parents, go sightseeing, visit all the places I've seen in my favourite TV shows and movies, and, of course, catch up with Simon. Now, more than ever, I am looking forward to seeing him, making peace with him and seeing if this whole ordeal has been worth it.

25

'My word, that is a tight dress,' Clive points out as I lean over our table to pour him another glass of champagne.

'Thanks,' I say. I don't think it was a compliment. Little does Clive know that this dress was not actually that tight when I tried it on in the shop fitting room when Eli and I went shopping for holiday clothes, but I have eaten so much over the last few days that my tummy has bloated right up. Sadly this was the only dress I haven't worn yet and I figured it was better to just hold my tummy in all night, or at least until I drink enough to care less about my body hang-ups, than to wear a dress for the second time. I don't think I've seen anyone wear the same outfit twice yet.

I was fortunate enough (if that's what you'd call it) to find Clive playing shuffleboard earlier, which is where my mum and dad were too. I invited him to the party and he bit my hand off, but when I went to tell my mum what I had done, she seemed almost annoyed at me.

'But... you were trying to set up us,' I said.

'No, I was trying to give you perspective,' she replied. 'To show you what would happen if you didn't get a move on and sort your love life out. This would be your future. Sitting at a cruise table full of old, divorced singles, the leftovers that no one wants any more. I just wanted you to see that sometimes you need to jump on a ship and travel around the world to find love, if you want it enough, but sometimes it is right underneath your nose, wherever your nose may be at that particular time...'

I stopped her there. Well, I still didn't want to turn up to the party alone, and I couldn't exactly bail on poor Clive now, so soon after inviting him, could I? Tomorrow is our last full day at sea and we arrive in New York the following morning, so there is hardly time to reschedule, and even though I am absolutely not on an actual date with Clive, and I did make it subtly clear that this was just a friendly drink, I know what it feels like to have someone raise your hopes and then bail on you. I invited him to a party, so I have brought him to a party.

It did inspire me to do something else though. I might have deactivated all of my social media accounts, but I still have my email account, so I looked up Simon's photography page and sent him an email saying I would be in New York in a couple of days and would he like to catch up. I was surprised when I got an almost instant response from his personal email address, saying that he would absolutely love to make dinner for me. We made a plan to meet up on my first night there – he seemed so keen. I think the reason I changed my mind about surprising him was because I was scared, but now that I've seen this eager reply from him, I feel much more relaxed, and so so excited.

I top up my glass. I'm starting to feel as close to drunk as I will usually allow myself to be, but I'm going to carry on drinking anyway. Well, I'm on holiday and I'm in a bad mood, if I don't drink now, then when, huh?

Clive has actually scrubbed up really well. You can tell he takes his cruising seriously, so all of his outfits are completely appropriate. The only downside to inviting Clive was the fact that he turned up with Colin, Linda and Karen. Thankfully he never got chance to invite my parents.

Karen keeps shooting me daggers. I'm not sure if perhaps Clive was the one she had her eye on and she sees me as competition. I keep trying to think of a way to subtly let her know, without announcing that I have no romantic intentions with Clive because that might hurt his feelings or embarrass him, but I'm far too distracted.

The daggers that Karen is shooting me are ricocheting off me, in the direction of Amanda. She is dancing with Josh – in a very familiar way, if you ask me, and the only thing annoying me more than the fact that she is dancing with my ex-boyfriend in front of me is the embarrassing and confusing fact that it is making me jealous.

'It's a bit loud, isn't it?' I hear Linda say, her voice raised a little more than is necessary for the volume of the music. It is a bit loud, but not massively so. I am mostly talking in my regular voice and no one is having any trouble hearing me – that or I'm so drunk that I am doing that thing drunk people do where they raise their voice without realising.

'What?' Colin shouts back, pretending to be deaf. 'I'm joking, I'm joking. It is too loud though.'

'Why don't we all go to Neptune's?' Linda suggests.

'Aww, but my friends are here,' I say.

'Well, we're going,' Karen says. 'You coming, Colin?'

'Yes, this isn't my scene,' he says.

'OK, fine, be like that,' I say. I can feel my words starting to catch in my teeth a little. 'I am going to go and dance. You coming, Clive?'

I stand up from my chair and begin dancing on the spot. I'm not usually one for dancing and, lord knows, I'm not very good at it, but all of the booze has made me feel brave.

Clive stands up, walks over to me and kisses me on the cheek.

'Sorry,' he tells me quietly. 'You're just a little too wild for me.'

And with that he leaves with the rest of his friends, leaving me alone.

'Fine,' I say to myself. 'Who needs you?'

I glance around the room for Eli. He's over by the bar, semi-dancing with André. I knock back the remains of my champagne and head over to them.

'Hey, fellas,' I sing. 'How's it going?'

'Rosie,' Eli booms. 'Are we pleased to see you?!'

Eli leans over the bar and orders some shots.

'Let's get drunk and weird and see what happens,' he says.

André laughs. I'm sure he knows what Eli's strange sense of humour is like by now, otherwise he'd be long gone.

'Aww, no, has your date gone?' Amanda asks me.

Christ, where did she come from? Josh is standing next to her. The pair of them appear to be thick as thieves and it's really boiling my alcohol-laced blood.

'Worn him out,' I say. 'Now it's time to get weird with my bestie.'

I snatch up a shot from the bar and knock it back.

'I got cocktails too,' Eli says.

'Sweet,' I say, picking up the large cocktail glass and sipping from it. As I do so, I notice the barman hand Eli three straws.

'It's a sharing cocktail,' Eli tells me with a laugh.

'Maybe for you, bitch,' I tease. 'This is a Rosie-sized cocktail, as far as I'm concerned.'

'You might want to take it easy, Rosie,' Josh chimes in. 'You know...'

'What, you don't think I can handle my drink?' I ask accusingly. 'Oh, I can handle my drink. You don't know me any more, bud.'

It's so weird, the words are coming out of me, but it's like my mouth is just firing them out, without any assistance from my brain. I feel like, if I could just take a second, to think about what I wanted to say, it would come out much better. But everything is racing – my mouth, my thoughts, my heart.

I take another big slurp of a cocktail that is intended for three people.

'Those things are usually for four people,' Josh points out.

OK, four people, but it's no one's business but my own.

'I know my limits, but thank you both for your concern,' I say. 'Now, if you don't mind...'

'We'll see, won't we?' Amanda says as she takes Josh by the arm and leads him away. 'You're so much better off without that one in your life,' I can just about hear her tell him as they walk off.

Oh, what a bitch.

'Meh, forget them,' I tell Eli and André.

'Yeah, screw them,' Eli says. 'Let's dance.'

I carefully but still clumsily place my glass down on the bar before heading out on to the dance floor with them. I feel a little bit queasy as I dance between them, but I just need to power through it. I can and will hold my drink – of course I will. Even if it is only to prove a point...

26

When Josh told me all about the virtual balconies on board the ship I did ponder, only briefly, whether he might be pulling my leg. Well, while it sounds completely possible, it just sounds a bit... gosh, almost dystopian. It's a screen to hide the fact that you are in a windowless room. It isn't hard to imagine a future where we live in homes like that. Anyway, I looked them up and they're definitely a thing, 80-inch tall, wall-mounted TVs, hung vertically to give the appearance of a balcony door. At first I assumed they just had a day loop and a night loop which shifted from one to the other as the sun came up and went down, but the screens are actually linked to a webcam outside the ship which allows your virtual balcony to display the actual view you would have if you were higher up with a real balcony. That means you see real sights, real weather and the actual level of daylight outside. This is arguably far cooler than what I imagined it would be like, but I think they have missed a trick not giving it a manual override so that, at the push of a button, if you want to be in daylight instead of the dark of night (or vice versa) you can. I mean, it's hard enough to tell what time it is on the ship anyway, so being able to manipulate the light in your cabin would make it even easier to trick yourself.

The reason I'm thinking about this is because, right now, the sun is pouring through our suite's balcony window like water, and my eyeballs feel like they're shrivelling away. I wish I could plunge my suite into night mode. Without the option, I want to get up and close the thick, heavy curtains. Well, I don't want to, I do need to though. I just can't bring myself to move. There's a loud banging in my head, it's loud and unbearable – it's almost rhythmic too. I've seen a handful of old movies with ships that are being rowed manually by an army of men on a lower deck, all rowing to the beat of a man playing the drum, which instructs them when to go faster. The beat of the drum in my head is fast and frantic, telling the ship to go faster and faster, like it's in battle mode.

I'll admit that the pounding in my head is most likely from the worst hangover I have ever had in my life, after I drank, without question, the most alcohol I have ever had in my life. It wasn't my intention to get absolutely, completely, life-ruiningly wankered, but I missed my sweet spot, or rather, I pushed my luck and carried on drinking past my point of no return. I don't know what it was last night, I just felt like surrendering control. Well, I rarely have much control over my life anyway, do I? Last night I just wanted a break from swimming against the tide, to just let it wash me out to sea and see where I ended up. Well, it dragged me out into the empty, pitch-black night, where I had no idea what was going on, and then sent me hurtling back towards dry land where I most likely hit my head on a rock, ensuring that I wouldn't remember a thing. That might have been fine by drunk Rosie last night, but, this morning, sober

Rosie is wracking her brains, searching high and low, for just a hint as to what went on. This is only making my headache worse though, and it's not even turning up any results.

I'm lying in bed on my stomach with my head facing away from the window and my eyes tightly closed. My body feels weird, like I can't move it properly, so I'm doing my best to shield my eyes from the sunshine with the tools I have.

Why is it that free booze leaves you with the worst hangovers?

I hear the suite door opening. Has it always been that loud? I can practically map out every millimetre of the locking system, based on each sound and the order I heard them in (probably not though, I'm just being dramatic).

'Good morning,' Eli sings.

'Leave,' I insist. 'Close the curtains and then leave.'

'You don't mean that, lover,' he jokes.

'Why aren't you as hungover as I am?' I ask accusingly.

'Because I'm twice your size and used to drinking way more than you,' he replies. 'I am hungover, just not dying-in-my-bed, wearing-clothes-from-the-night-before hungover.'

Oh, I still have my dress on, that explains why I can't move.

'I brought you a coffee,' Eli says. 'Sit up and have a little, it will help.'

'Nothing will help,' I insist. 'Alcohol is evil. I'm never drinking again.'

'OK, let's not say things we'll regret,' Eli jokes. 'You made enough bold claims last night, let's not make more big promises today, shall we?'

'What was I saying last night?' I dare to ask.

'Come on, let me help you sit up,' Eli says as he takes me

by the arm. 'You were almost violently insistent that you could hold your drink.'

'Oh, God, I can't hold my drink at all,' I whine, finally opening my eyes just enough to see Eli, without letting too much light in. Eli looks fresh as a daisy, it's almost annoying.

'I know, drink this,' he says, handing me my coffee. 'When you started showing your arse, I brought you back here.'

'Oh, God, did I split my dress?' I say, trying to roll onto one side so that I can see my bum.

'Not literally showing your arse,' Eli laughs. 'Embarrassing yourself, being too much, too drunk, too wild. I started worrying about what you were going to do next, so I brought you back here and put you to bed. I was going to undress you and put you in something more comfortable for sleeping in, but that felt so weird, and anyway, you flopped straight onto the bed and started snoring your head off, so I thought I'd just leave you in peace.'

'Thank you,' I say.

'You're welcome,' he replies. 'If we pretend you are just a wild drunk, then I don't suppose anyone has any reason to think you can't hold your drink, and I won't tell them otherwise.'

'Thank you,' I say again. 'And thank you for the coffee.'

I feel so sick, but I take a tentative sip.

'Is that OK?' he asks.

I nod my head as gently as possible.

'Are you going to be sick?'

'I don't think so...'

'OK, well, now is your chance to prove you can handle your drink and everything you said and did last night was intentional. We're going to get you a very small something to eat, just enough to line your stomach so that you can take a couple of painkillers, and then... your mum has been nagging us to go to water aerobics with her and your dad, she says she loved it last time. I know that André and the gang are meeting in the atrium for lunch before their last show of the voyage in the afternoon, so get up, get your bikini on and let's show them all how great you are feeling, yeah?'

'Yeah, OK,' I say, mustering up a little of that Rosie Outlook that used to get me through the day.

I feel like absolute crap, but if pretending to feel fine will make me look better than I imagine the events of last night did, then I'm all for it.

'Have a quick shower, because you smell like a pirate,' Eli says. 'I'll pop to your mum and dad's suite and tell them we're game. OK?'

'OK,' I say, although I feel far from OK.

I take a few more sips of my coffee before very bravely pulling myself up and carefully heading for the bathroom. The room is spinning slightly, which makes me think I might still be just a little bit drunk. I'm hoping the hangover doesn't get worse, although I'm not sure how it could.

I carefully step under the shower and try to blast away all evidence of the night before. It's just a shower though, not a fairy godmother, so it can't work miracles.

I just need to show my face, appear to be fine and then I can come back to bed for a bit, until this hangover clears off. Then I'll be able to enjoy the rest of my final day on board.

Absolutely no drinking today though, under any circumstance. There is no way I am turning up to see Simon, smelling like a pirate, doing... whatever I was doing last night.

One thing I know for sure though is that, whatever I was saying and doing last night, I hope I never find out.

27

You know, I never thought I would struggle to eat a croissant. A third or fourth croissant, perhaps, but never a first one, and absolutely never on an empty stomach.

When people talk about the evils of alcohol, this must be what they are referring to, because coming between a girl and her favourite breakfast food is almost unforgivable.

I don't suppose I would have tried to eat anything at all, if I hadn't needed to take painkillers so badly, and taking them on an empty stomach only replaced my headache with stomach ache, so I had to try and force something down.

I had a few nibbles on a croissant with an ibuprofen chaser and, I don't know, what must have been a gallon of water. I've had so much water, I can practically feel it sloshing around inside me.

Speaking of water sloshing around, water aerobics is not a good idea, not when you have a stinking hangover. The last time I did it, to ABBA music, must have been the beginners' class. Now, much further along in the week, things have been kicked up a notch. Today we are grooving to songs by the Bee

Gees, and I didn't feel any rougher than I did outside the water while we warmed up to 'More Than a Woman'... but now, picking up the pace with 'Stayin' Alive', the title of the song feels very much like a goal.

'Is this blowing the cobwebs off?' Eli asks me. 'Or, washing them off, I suppose...'

'I'm not going to make it,' I insist. 'Are you enjoying this?'

'It's a lot of fun,' he admits. 'Not very cool, and not at all masculine, that's for sure – and I can't imagine taking this up back home, I'll definitely be getting straight back to wearing tight vests and throwing weights around in front of a mirror... but here, on holiday, it's kind of fun... with no witnesses.'

'Oh, there are witnesses,' I tell him, subtly nodding towards the table where the band are sitting. They're not just sitting by us, they're watching us. 'When did water aerobics become a spectator sport, huh?' I ask.

'When did it become a sport?' Eli asks. 'André wanted to watch me – can you blame him? And anyway, I thought you wanted to prove to Amanda that you can hold your drink and handle your hangovers?'

'What hangover?' I ask, putting on a brave face, trying to hide the fact I'm struggling to keep my breakfast down.

'That's my girl,' he replies.

Halfway through the session, my dad gets cramp, so my mum helps him out of the pool. If you ask me, they just want to go and get something to eat, because they disappear pretty sharpish. Eli doesn't make a move, which makes me think he is actually enjoying this. I suppose I'll stick it out, lest people think I'm making excuses to give up too.

As the Bee Gees medley softens, I feel my body floating into 'How Deep Is Your Love'. This is more my kind of pace, gentle hip exercises, minimal upper-body movement. All morning I've felt this... like... knot in my stomach. Like a big, heavy lump, rolling around in there every time I move. For the first time, I can't quite feel it as strongly, so perhaps the hangover is starting to pass. Maybe I'm not the hopeless drinker I thought I was – not that I plan on taking it up professionally. I'm not sure I'll ever drink heavily again, but I suppose this is a lesson that everyone needs to learn once, right? Was anything I drank last night worth feeling like this? Well, I think the fact that I pretty much did it out of spite, or to prove a point, means that it wasn't. Last night felt like me finally coming undone, after weeks of crap. The bubble needed to burst so that I could start building myself up again.

I glance over at Amanda, who is still watching me like a hawk. I look at Josh, who gives me a smile and a half-wave. I feel great doing this exercise knowing that, even if I feel like death warmed up, to them it must look like I really have my shit together. Being seemingly right gives me an extra spring in my step. By the time the music shifts into 'You Should Be Dancing', the pace well and truly picks up, and I am raring to go.

Eli, a water aerobics convert, gets way into it and his enthusiasm is infectious. Having a laugh with my friend, messing around in the pool, dancing to awesome music – this is what holidays are all about.

I am in my element until something funny comes over me. I'm not sure what it is... the gentle lapping of the water against my body, the almost frantic guitar playing in the song, the bright sunlight pouring in through the glass roof of the atrium... I feel like my own Saturday Night Fever might be catching up with me. And then there's that lump in my tummy again, that big hard lump... it feels like a cannonball. I thought it had disappeared, but, before I really know what is going on, I feel it hurtling its way from my stomach to my chest to my neck to my... Oh God.

An old woman screams, as though she's just witnessed a body emerge from the depths of the pool and float towards her. More infectious than enthusiasm is hysteria, and as more and more people realise I have thrown up into the pool, they all freak out and scramble towards the other side.

Eli, my darling friend, is on hand to help me. He pulls me away from the murky water and lifts me out of the pool like I'm weightless. He plonks me down at our table, which is, annoyingly, the one next to where André, Josh and Amanda are sitting. They all stare at me (in horror), and this certainly isn't a spectator sport. Josh looks concerned, but Amanda looks a combination of smug and repulsed. As horrible as I felt before, I feel even worse now, because she thinks she's winning this one. Well, I'm not going to let her. I need to try and save face.

The aerobics instructor comes running over to me.

'Are you OK?' she asks. 'What happened?'

'She got drunk last night and just threw her hangover up into the pool,' Amanda suggests with a chuckle.

'No, that's not what happened,' I say as I wipe the sweat from my brow with the back of my hand. 'I have a stomach bug.'

'Are you sure?' the instructor asks me. 'Are you certain it isn't just from drinking?'

'Nope, it's definitely a stomach bug,' I insist, very aware that lots of passengers are all staring at me. The last think I want is for everyone to think that this is what a young person is like, crashing their holiday, getting hammered, throwing up in their pool while they are trying to exercise.

'Rosie, are you *sure* you have a stomach bug?' Josh steps forward to ask me.

There's a weird tone to his voice, like he's trying to get me to own up to just being hungover – well, I'm not going to do it. 'Of course I'm sure. I might have had a couple of drinks last night, but this started yesterday lunchtime. It's just some kind of bug, probably one of those twenty-four-hour things...'

'OK, if you can just wait here,' the aerobics instructor says as she backs away from me. 'I need to go get someone.'

I look back over at Josh and Amanda – why does Amanda still look so smug?

'Christ, that was a display,' Eli whispers into my ear. 'Nicely covered up though, that was a quick-thinking save.'

'Do you think she bought it?' I ask.

'For sure,' he whispers back. 'I think she's gone to get a medic or something.'

'Oh, Rosie... you should just admit you're hungover,' Amanda says. 'Honesty is the best policy.'

'I'm not hungover, honestly,' I insist. I'm rather proud of myself, for my acting skills. I mustered up a ton of faux sincerity there – so much so I almost believed myself.

'It's a shame you're not just hungover,' Josh says.

'Why?' I ask curiously.

'Because you're probably going to be stuck in your cabin until we get to New York now.'

28

So, enthusiasm is contagious, hysteria is more contagious still, but you do know what tops the list on a cruise ship? A stomach bug. The most contiguous thing on a cruise ship is a stomach bug, and if they think you have one, they will treat you like an alien.

I'm in quarantine... or is it isolation? What's the difference? I think I'm technically in isolation, given I am supposedly ill, kept from the well people, to save them from getting ill too. I think quarantine is when you might be ill, or to stop you from getting ill or... I don't know, the point is, I'm neither ill, nor potentially ill. I'm just hungover and I should have just admitted it, but I was too proud, too scared to be shown up in front of Amanda, unwilling to look bad in front of the other guests.

So now I'm here, in my suite, all alone. Eli knows that I am absolutely fine, of course, but he didn't want to risk being confined to the suite for the rest of the trip too, so he's staying with André tonight. I suspect he would have stayed with him anyway, with this being the last night. I think they are in desperate need of a conversation about their holiday romance, and what happens next. Well, you can't exactly have a traditional relationship with someone who lives at sea for most of the time, can you?

My mum and dad dropped by to check on me too, but I told them to go off and have fun. Well, I don't want them to suffer being locked away for the rest of the trip either.

As nice as my suite is, the thought of being in here alone until we get to New York is driving me crazy. It might only be another twelve hours or so, but I tell you what, the five-star service soon vanishes when people think you are contagious. My cabin feels more like a prison now – just a really nice one with room service and wi-fi. I've spent many a night alone on my sofa with a takeaway and only Netflix for company, so tonight isn't exactly going to be unusual for me, but perhaps that is the problem. I've had a couple of crazy weeks, but, as embarrassing and life-altering as they have been, I can't say they haven't been exciting, and I certainly can't say they have been lonely. I've had my mum, dad, Eli and even Josh around me for almost all of it. I guess being alone in here tonight is a glimpse into what my life is probably going to be like, when I finally get back home, if this little trek across the globe doesn't actually alter anything for me.

There is a knock on my suite door. I carefully climb out of bed – not because I'm ill, but because my painkillers must have worn off and my headache is still very much present.

Standing behind the door is a man with a large box.

'Hello,' I say. I look down at the box and then back up at him.

'Rosie Jones?' he asks me.

'That's me,' I confirm.

'Here is your delivery, from the gift shop,' he says.

He hands me the box, which is actually rather heavy, before hurrying off, which makes me wonder if there is a ship-wide black mark against my name, telling people to keep well clear of me.

I take the box inside and place it down on my bed. Inside is the 'most expensive thing' they had in the gift shop. The girl described it as a 'piece of glass with the ship and the dates we sailed etched into it' and that is what it is... it's just that the piece of glass is the size of a large dinner plate, and almost as thick as the length of my thumb. It's gorgeous, if not a little tacky, but it's probably way too big for my tiny flat, and it's definitely going to tip me over my baggage allowance on the way home. I'm not sure what the hell I'm going to do with it... perhaps I could just leave it in here. Well, there's no point returning it, is there, for what? More gift shop credit. Perhaps my dad would like a few more jackets...

I place it on the sideboard and climb back into my bed. I suppose a night in my bed, in my cosy pyjamas, will do me some good, especially in my delicate state, it's just so annoying that it's the last night of the cruise and I'm stuck in here.

Still, my main holiday starts when I arrive in New York, and there are so many places I want to visit. I've been looking into it, while I've been killing time in here alone for the past three hours, and there are loads of places for TV and movie buffs to visit. For starters, there is the beautiful white brownstone apartment where Holly Golightly lived in *Breakfast at Tiffany's*, as well as Carrie's brownstone from *Sex and the City* – in fact, *Sex and the City* opens up a whole world of locations to visit that will be familiar to fans of the show, especially big fans like me who have watched it time and time again and know it like the back of their hand. There is so much that I want to do, perhaps I can take the time this evening to plan it all out, to try and squeeze as much into my trip as possible.

I grab Eli's laptop, which he has considerately left for me to use while he's off having fun with André, and get back to planning my trip. Giving myself something to look forward to will make my evening go much quicker. I'll be too excited to care that I'm locked away... hopefully.

There is another knock at my door. It's amazing, how popular I am, given that I'm supposed to be locked away to contain my pretend germs.

Standing outside the door, in his full Michael Bublé get up, is Josh.

'Well, hey there,' he says in his faux-Canadian accent. 'I heard there's a sick young lady in here who might appreciate a visit from her favourite cruise ship celebrity impersonator.'

Well, he's not wrong about the title. Then again, when there is only him and Amanda in competition with one another, he's an easy favourite by default.

'Hello,' I say brightly. 'Are you allowed in here?'

'Are you actually sick?' he says with a laugh.

'Fair point,' I reply.

'Can I come in?' he asks.

I nod and step back so that Josh can follow me in. We don't mention the kiss and that suits me just fine right now.

'Oh, wow,' he says, back to his own accent. 'The suites really are gorgeous.'

'Yeah, less so when you're trapped in them,' I reply. 'But up until today, yes, it's been like a dream.'

'I tried to warn you,' Josh says, shifting his attention from the furnishings to me.

'I know, I didn't know this would happen,' I start. 'I was just so embarrassed.'

'Well, it was pretty embarrassing,' he says.

'Anyway, what can I do for you?' I ask him.

'Have you heard of Annabelle Bateman?' he asks.

'I haven't...'

'She's an American woman who, after being diagnosed with terminal cancer, went on to raise loads of money for her experimental treatment and extra care that might buy her more time or even cure her. She held these big fundraisers where she would perform songs – she was a talented singer – and she gathered loads of media attention.'

'OK...' I say, confused as to why he's telling me this. 'You do know I'm just hungover, right? I'm fine...'

He laughs at me. 'Well, what happened next is,' he continues, making himself comfortable on the sofa as he builds suspense, 'a journalist started doing some digging into Annabelle because, she couldn't quite put her finger on it, but for someone who was supposedly dying, Annabelle seemed so full of life, so healthy... So she started this big investigation to try and prove if Annabelle was even ill at all. It was an interesting case, so someone has made a documentary about it, and it's available on Netflix. Do you want to order some food and watch it?'

'What, watch it together?'

'Yes, if you'll have me,' Josh says with a laugh. 'It's my night off, I have nothing better to do and I'll bet you could do with the company... it will be just like old times.'

'I'd love that,' I admit. 'Thank you.'

'You're welcome,' he says. 'Are you feeling up to eating now?'

'I am so hungry,' I confess.

'OK, well let's order a bunch of stuff and get this documentary on,' he says.

'OK,' I say excitedly.

As we both look over the room service menu together and wind up choosing the exact same things to eat – bacon cheeseburgers with pineapple, sweet potato fries, and choco-late torte for dessert – it really does feel just like old times, and, do you know what? It feels really, really good.

29

Josh and I have been eating, drinking (soft drinks only, I feel it is important to point out), hanging out, watching true crime documentaries, and just generally being merry for nearly four hours now – four hours, and believe me, they have flown by.

Time is a strange, strange thing. It can really drag itself out, for so long, when you don't want it to. Other times, it can pass you by in the blink of an eye. Before Josh arrived, the time I spent in my own company today was time I felt every minute of. I felt each hour, each minute, each second as it slowly passed. Now that Josh is here, hours have rolled into a blur – whenever I look at the time, we've clocked another hour together. Similarly, even though it's been nearly five years since the last time I saw Josh, it doesn't feel like we've been apart for more than a few days, but while I was living those years, with each day it felt like time was taking me further and further away from him. It's incredible really, how Josh, who was a distant memory last week, is here with me now, sitting on my bed, eating chocolate coins with me while we watch *The Good Place* – a welcome break from the heavy documentaries, We're both fully up to date on the show, it is mostly just on for something in the background while we chat. Josh and I are getting on like a house on fire – I feel like we're getting on even better than we used to, and that's quite the achievement, because, despite the eventual difference that broke us up, we always got along so well, something which I credit to being friends for so long before we finally got together.

We have chatted about the various jobs we have had and where we have lived since the last time we saw each other – admittedly, Josh's stories are far more interesting than mine; he's been all over the world, I've only moved around the Greater Manchester area. We have updated each other on our families – I always really liked Josh's mum. His dad died when he was seven, so he was pretty much raised single-handedly by her. She is such a kind, caring woman, it has always been so easy to see where Josh gets all of his good qualities from. He used to tell me how his mum would always instil good, feminist values in him, help him to understand his emotions and teach him that it is OK to cry sometimes – yes, even for men.

Josh never did tell me what happened to his dad, but it doesn't sound like he was in the best headspace near the end. I think that is what has always given Josh his drive, whilst still keeping him so closely tethered to his mum. He told me tonight that, although he might work away from home a lot, his mum is forever flying out to where he is, or cruising on the ships he has worked on. He's always been so close to her and it is nice to see that he still is, no matter where he is in the world.

With everything laid out on the table, we have fully caught ourselves up on each other's lives. Well, almost.

'I can't believe you're going to see Simon,' he says softly. 'After everything he did to you...'

'We don't know what he did to me,' I remind him. 'I was stupid and upset and kind of a crazy girlfriend by the end of it... I was thinking all sorts of things and... Look, it doesn't matter. I'm just going to see him, hang out, it's no big deal, you don't need to worry about me, OK?'

'I do worry about you though,' he says. 'I worry about you a lot – I always have. When we broke up... I don't know, it just never sat right with me. I got the job offer, we tried to talk about it...'

'You wanted that job more than anything,' I remind him.

'Not more than you,' he replies, his eyes fixed firmly on the screen in front of him.

I could just let it go, get back to watching TV – I mean, its ancient history, right? Except...

'Why did you go then?' I can't stop myself from asking.

'Because you told me to,' he replies. 'You didn't just tell me to, you insisted. You were so insistent, in fact, that I thought this was your way of dumping me, like you'd been looking for a reason and suddenly you had one... you laid it on so thick.'

'Yes, to see if you would go,' I admit. 'You told me that it was your dream job, probably your only opportunity, your foot in the door... if I loved you, how could I possibly try and stand in the way of that?'

'Because I loved you too,' he says, looking at me now. 'I don't know if it was just easy to believe that you wanted me to go because I was young and stupid, or if I really did believe that you didn't want to be with me any more, but I have thought about it so often since, wondering if it was the right thing to do, and don't get me wrong, I love singing for a living, but can I honestly say I wouldn't have had a happy – if not happier – life with you, if I'd fought for us? We could be married with kids by now.'

'Josh, honestly, don't worry about it, please,' I say. Someone needs to shut this down. We can replay this conversation in our heads all day, but we can't rewrite history.

'I thought you were all about retreading old ground at the moment,' Josh says. 'Since you got that bunch of flowers – what's that all about?'

I'm not sure if Josh sounds curious or just a little bit jealous.

'After I was on TV and the clip went viral, my social networks blew up, loads of people were sending me messages – even people I didn't know. But then this bunch of flowers turned up on my doorstep, from someone I obviously did know, because it said something like "I love you... I should have never let you go... I want you back".'

'That certainly sounds like it was from an ex,' Josh replies.

'Well, my first thought was David, the guy who dumped me on TV, but it turns out he only sent me a text afterwards asking to see me because he wanted a share of the prize money. He didn't send any flowers.'

'What a bastard,' Josh says. 'Seriously? After what he did to you? And that is absolutely not how quiz shows work. Imagine if everyone who phoned a friend on *Who Wants to be a Millionaire* was obliged to hand over their prize money? If you want to win money as a duo, go on *Pointless*.'

It's kind of nice, to see Josh so outranged on my behalf. He must still care about me. I still care about him too. More than I realised, in fact.

'I know, right?' I reply. 'So, at the newspaper I worked for, one of the other girls wanted to write an article about the local girl who went viral and I just didn't want to be around that, and I didn't like my job anyway, so, knowing that I had my prize money to keep me going for a little while, I quit. That's when I decided to go and stay with my mum and dad for a while. It was in their garden, while I helped them clear out the spider-infested shed, that I bumped into Kevin, my first boyfriend. We chatted and it turns out he's married, he has a couple of kids, so I know he didn't send the flowers. I just happened to be walking by Eli's work afterwards and, I suppose I kind of sought him out, but I'm so glad that I did because he's the best friend I never managed to make in my twenties. I'm so glad he's back in my life because I can't imagine it without him now, he's been my rock through all of this.'

'And then there's me,' Josh says.

'Then there's you,' I reply. 'I'm sorry if you feel like I've just kind of invaded your work. My mum and dad mentioned the cruise and I had some time off, Eli encouraged me to take the trip, maybe have a little catch-up with you and Simon but... I don't know...'

'You don't have to apologise,' Josh insists. 'I'm really, really glad you turned up. it was a lovely surprise.'

'So you didn't send the flowers then?' I say.

I'm aware that was a really nice thing he just said to me, and I'm just focused on those bloody flowers, but until I can definitely rule him out...

'No, I didn't send them,' he says. 'If I were trying to win you back, it wouldn't be a bunch of flowers left on your doorstep.'

'Oh, what would you use to win me back?' I ask.

'Cheese burgers, true crime documentaries, the risk of a stomach bug – although that does seem minimal, when I remember how much you drank last night.'

'Was I awful last night?' I ask, bracing myself for the answer.

'You were just drunk,' he tells me with a smile.

'Did I say anything?' I ask curiously.

'You told Amanda that you didn't like her shoes,' he says. 'And then you took me to one side and told me that Eli was your favourite ex.'

I laugh.

'I suppose he is,' I admit. 'He's definitely the one that has worked out best for me.'

'You told me that Eli was your favourite ex, and that I was the love of your life... and then you drank my drink, and you asked the DJ if he had the "Time Warp".'

'Oh, God, no, I don't want to hear any more, sorry that's... I was just drunk, I didn't know what I was saying,' I babble quickly.

'None of it was true then?' he asks.

'Well, Eli probably is my favourite ex, and I've loved dancing to the "Time Warp", even at school discos, before I had even seen *The Rocky Horror Picture Show*, which I suppose is kind of weird but...'

Was Josh the love of my life? I'd never given it much thought until right now, but, sitting on this bed with him, staring into those eyes I never could quite resist, it doesn't just sound right, it feels right.

This time it is me who leans in to kiss Josh, and this time he doesn't panic and push me away. Completely different to our previous kiss, and any kiss I've had over the past five years for that matter, this one is kind of frantic and wild. It's like five years of something has built up and this is the only way to ease the tension.

I break from kissing him only to close the lid on Eli's laptop. I love Ted Danson as much as the next girl, but he doesn't need to see this. As soon as the lid smacks shut, our lips are drawn together again. As we start tugging at each other's clothes, a voice in my head tells me to stop and think about what we're doing.

'Wait, wait, wait, wait,' I say, my voice muffled by Josh's lips. 'This is too fast, right?'

'You're right,' Josh agrees as he tries to pull himself together. 'Yes, too fast, that's exactly what I was thinking.'

We pause for a few seconds, but as our eyes meet again, all I can think about is kissing him.

'Maybe... just slow, gentle kissing?' I suggest.

'Yeah, great idea,' Josh says eagerly.

The slow and sensual kissing lasts for around thirty seconds before the pace picks up again. There's no time to stop and think, this just feels right. Being away from my 'usual life' makes me feel like I can take a step back from 'usual me' too. I would never usually do anything like this, but I'm here, and this is Josh, my Josh, and, maybe I have cabin fever, and we're in international waters, right? Admittedly I don't even know what that means, I just know that, right now, all I want is Josh. We can deal with the fallout in the morning.

30

I will never take waking up without a hangover for granted again, I promise you. Every day that I wake up, not feeling like I felt yesterday morning, will be the greatest day of my life, because I won't feel that rough, have that headache, be that repulsed by food; I won't throw up in a pool full of poor pensioners who just want to enjoy their retirement in clean, five-star water.

Today I'm waking up with a different problem entirely... Josh, in my bed, fast asleep.

Well, is it a problem? I had an amazing night with him last night. Just like old times, but way, way better. I feel like we're both older and wiser and able to act on feelings without it being some big drama.

By some strange miracle, I have woken up an hour before my alarm is set to go off, when it will be time to get ready to pack up and get off the ship in New York. This means that I am awake and Josh isn't. He's peacefully snoozing without a care in the world. I am awake and overthinking everything. I am a weird combination of elated, because it really was such a good night together, and terrified of what happens when he wakes up, and then what happens after that? These are uncharted waters for me, in more ways that the obvious one.

I'm sure Eli will be here to pack his bag soon and I do not want him to catch us like this. I'm not even sure how I would explain it.

'Josh,' I whisper as I lightly shake his shoulder to try and wake him up. 'Josh...'

I raise my voice a little, shaking him with a little more force.

'Josh,' I persist.

For some reason the thought of waking him up – him opening his eyes to find me peering down over him, trying to get him to leave before Eli gets here (it really is only to save us both a lot of embarrassing questions), makes me feel so uncomfortable. I need a plan B.

My first, albeit completely unnecessary step, is to slink out of bed and into the bathroom, where I brush my teeth, my hair, and apply enough make-up to not seem like I'm wearing any, but enough to make me look less like I just got out of bed.

I sneak back to the bedroom, carefully climb into bed and, like the absolute coward that I am, I set myself a phone alarm to go off in one minute's time – the soonest it will allow. Then I lie down and close my eyes, just waiting for my alarm to go off and 'wake' us both at the same time, in a completely normal, natural, not at all awkward way.

This one single minute drags longer than any of the hours I spent in here alone yesterday. I worry it must have passed already, and feel tempted to check and make sure that I actually did it right, but I resist for what feels like another thirty seconds before the alarm finally goes off.

I hear and feel Josh stirring next to me.

'Good morning,' he says sleepily.

'Morning,' I reply, rolling over to face him.

'This sounds clichéd but... you look beautiful,' he says. 'How do you wake up looking like that?'

'Moisturiser,' I say casually. 'How are you?'

'I'm good,' he says. 'Great, in fact. You?'

'I'm great too,' I tell him.

Ergh, why am I being so weird? It's like the harder I try to sound normal and casual, the less it actually happens.

Josh leans forwards and kisses me. It's not at all like the kissing from last night, it's soft and sweet. I did wonder if last night was just old feelings with an old flame firing us both up, but whatever it was, it's still here, only much softer now. It's like a more manageable passion, if such a thing exists.

'So, we'll be in New York soon,' I tell him.

'We probably already are,' he replies.

'I need to pack up my things, and Eli will be here to pack his, if you want to put some pants on – not that you wouldn't make his day.'

Josh laughs. 'It's OK, I'll leave you to it,' he says. 'So, what's the plan?'

I sit up in bed.

'Well... pack my bags, assemble my travel companions, try and navigate New York with them, which should be fun. My dad took me to London once when I was a teenager, he put us on the wrong tube and took us so far in the wrong direction we had to pay £40 for a taxi to take us back, so I'll be taking a proactive role in the navigating, that's for sure. I have plans tonight, but, after that, it's going to be non-stop tourist locations, there are so many places I want to go.'

'Plans tonight,' Josh repeats back to me. 'Plans with Simon?'

'Yeah, well... I told you that. We're going to catch up.'

'I suppose I didn't think you would go now,' he replies.

'Because we slept together?' I ask.

'Well... yes,' he replies. 'Did you feel it last night?'

I raise my eyebrows.

'Not like that,' he says, allowing himself a smile for a second. 'Didn't you feel anything between us?'

'Of course I did,' I tell him. 'But you work here, I'm just on holiday and then I'm going back home, we have the same problem we had before...'

I really don't want to go through all this again.

'Except we don't,' Josh says as he sits up next to me, taking my hands in his. 'The next voyage, the one back to Liverpool that leaves tomorrow afternoon, is my final one.'

'What?'

'It's my last one. I don't want to live my life on a ship any more, I want to get back on dry land, I want to start my life properly.'

This piece of information has floored me. That's the last thing I expected to hear him say. Singing professionally has always been his dream, and now he's doing it. Like he said, he gets to enjoy all the pros of being a famous singer without all the cons that come with it. He's living his dream.

'You would really give this up just to be with me?' I ask him.

'Well, yes, of course I would, but I'd be lying if I said that you were the reason I was quitting. I gave my notice sometime ago. I meant what I said, I don't want to live and work at sea, I want to start my life properly... and now that I've found you again, I want to start it with you. What we had between us is clearly still there, Rosie, I know you feel it...'

'Wait, wait, so you're not doing this for me? You were doing this anyway?'

'I was,' he admits. 'My plan was to quit, move in with my mum in the short term, start a new job in Manchester...'

'So, you're not doing this for me,' I say, only this time it isn't a question, it's a statement.

'Rosie, I was already doing this,' he says.

'But... this isn't some big gesture for me, this is you deciding you've had enough of jetsetting around the globe and now you want to go back to life before, moving back in with your mum, start things up with me again – make it like you never left?'

Josh laughs in disbelief, but it's not an amused laugh, it's closer to an angry one. 'I didn't know you were going to be here, Rosie,' he reminds me. 'Yes, the wheels were already in motion for me to quit singing on the ship, but – as much as a person might be able to make a case for this being some kind of course correction, I mean, what are the chances? – I don't think that we're just going to get back together and pick up where we left of, I just want the chance to be in your life again, if we're both living in Manchester... I thought you'd be happy.'

I take my hands back from him. I'm annoyed at him, but do I have any right to be? I suppose I just wanted to feel like he had finally chosen me, rather than a case of good timing opening the door for him to pick up where he left off. If he hadn't been quitting the Michael Bublé gig, and this had still happened between us, would he still want me, or would he be helping me pack my suitcase and hiding my big chunk of Silverline branded glass in the wardrobe so I don't have to take it with me before waving me off? I can never, ever know what the truth is, and that worries me.

'Look, I have plans with Simon tonight– and I can't stress enough that we're only catching up,' I remind him. 'I'm not going to bail on him just because you're, what, ready for me now?'

'I can't believe you're willing to spend a second with him,' Josh says. 'After everything he did, I can't believe a bunch of crap flowers has turned your head.'

'Whoa, OK, first of all, they weren't crap flowers, they were quite nice. Second of all, it takes two to tango, and it was me who tanked that relationship. You know how insecure I was.'

'Because he was cheating on you,' Josh says.

'I don't know for sure that he was though, do I? I was clearly imagining it, and he proved that to me when he set me up, to catch me snooping.'

Josh puffs air from his cheeks. 'Rosie, I was the one who was there for you after Simon set you up – in the most unforgivable way. I don't care if he thought you were snooping. If you have a problem with someone, you talk to them, you don't trick them into thinking you're going to propose to them, get their hopes up, only to embarrass them and then dump them. I was the person who comforted you, held you while you cried, helped you overcome your issues.'

'And I'm so, so grateful to you for that,' I tell him honestly. 'You saved me – if it weren't for you, I never would have trusted another man again.'

'As someone who got to know everything about your relationship, take it from me, he was cheating on you. He absolutely was. I know that you think he proved you wrong, but you were right. It never seemed worth arguing that point with you before, but now it feels important. He cheated on you, he set you up, and then he dumped you, because he was at the end of his rope with the situation. There was nowhere to go from there.'

'I know you think badly of him, because he tricked me, but that doesn't make him a cheater...'

'Lying to you, setting you up, manipulating what you could and couldn't see on his phone – that doesn't sound like the behaviour of a dishonest person to you?'

'Josh, we could argue about this forever,' I say, trying to nip it in the bud. 'But there's no point. I'm going to get off the ship, I'm going to enjoy my holiday, I'm going to go and see Simon for just a catch-up – which I am sick of saying – and then, when and if I end up back in Manchester, if you're serious, maybe we can talk, OK?'

Josh gets out of bed and hurries his clothes on.

'Go and see Simon,' he tells me. 'Have a great time together, see that he's changed, stay in New York with him, if that's what you want – it sounds like that's what you were implying.'

I suppose I was, not that it seems like something that would be on the cards. I'm just so angry that Josh thinks that we can just pick up where we left off, now that he has space in his life for me. It's not fair. You don't get to just pick me up and put me down as and when you get a better offer. I deserve better than that. I might be happier when I have a boyfriend, but I would rather be single and secure for the rest of my life, than waiting for the phone to ring with Josh's next big break that's going to take him away from me.

'We can talk when things are back to normal,' I tell him. 'When we've both had time to think. This is just so fast...'

'In other words, you want to go and see if Simon sent you

the flowers first, see how things are with him, and then come back to me if they're not what you want…'

'That's not it at all,' I insist.

'Well, I'll save you the trouble,' he says. 'Have a lovely holiday, sorry things didn't work out.'

With that, Josh storms out.

I quickly wipe away the tear that has escaped from one of my eyes, just in time before Eli walks in through the door.

'What?' he bellows theatrically. 'You haven't packed my suitcase for me? It's no wonder I'm off women, I feel like they have been completely missold to me.'

I laugh. It's so nice to see him.

'You OK, kid?' he asks me, sitting down at the foot of my bed. 'I thought you'd still be asleep, I was coming to wake you, to see if you fancied grabbing a quick breakfast before we pack.'

'Yeah, I'm…' I cough, trying to clear the emotion from my throat. 'I'm OK, just ready to get to New York and see the city.'

Eli stands up, takes me by the hand and gently pulls me out of bed before leading me to the balcony. Without saying a word, he opens the curtains and points outside.

'Oh my God,' I blurt. 'We're here.'

'We're here,' he says. 'Did you not notice we'd stopped moving?'

'I didn't,' I admit. 'I think I'd finally got used to the feeling of being at sea.'

I expected to be in some ferry port, like the kind we have back home, but, here at the Brooklyn cruise terminal, I already feel like I'm in New York. I can see the city, I can even see some of its most famous skyscrapers, right here in front of me, in real life, just far enough away to still seem like something out of a movie. I can see the One World Trade Center, standing the tallest of them all, I can see the Empire State Building, I can see what I believe is the green roof of the Trump Building... it is so surreal.

I can't quite get Josh out of my head but I'm here now and I need to make the most of it. I've been looking forward to visiting New York for so long, I need to make sure I enjoy myself.

'It's incredible,' I say. 'It kind of all seems worth it, now that we're actually here...'

'While that might be true for you, the only thing I have done to get to this point is go on a cruise, so it has literally been plain sailing for me,' he says with a chuckle.

'How is André?' I ask.

Eli's face falls as I bring him back to earth a little. That wasn't my intention, I was just curious about what happens next for them.

'He'll be fine,' Eli says. 'So will I. It was just a holiday romance, as much as I liked him, this is his home, most of the time, right? Nothing was ever going to come of it... it's a shame but... we're going to stay in touch. You never know.'

Oh, but I do know. I know all too well.

'Speaking of which,' he starts. 'I just saw Josh in the corridor, face like thunder, no time to talk...'

'Oh really?'

'Yes, really,' he replies, mocking my voice. 'So unless he copped off with an old lady last night, I'd hazard a guess he was coming from this suite.'

I shrug my shoulders.

'We need to pack our bags,' I tell him.

'We do,' he replies. 'OK, well how about we pack our bags now, while you unpack your baggage?'

'I see what you did there,' I say with a smile.

I tell Eli all about what just happened with Josh. He bites his lip thoughtfully.

'Ergh, that's messy,' he says. 'That is very messy. I completely see where you're coming from, and where he is... but you're right, now isn't the time for you to just drop everything and go running back to him. You came here to see Sexy bloody Simon; you will see Sexy bloody Simon. OK?'

'OK,' I say, although I'm starting to have second thoughts for some reason.

'For now, let's forget about Josh – good things are coming, I promise you that. With or without a man, I promise you will end this holiday much happier, OK?'

'OK,' I say. 'You really are my favourite ex, do you know that?'

'I do,' he says. 'You would not stop telling me when you were drunk.'

I really am never ever drinking again.

31

I have only been in New York for a few hours and I am already head over heels in love with the place.

Eli and I were so excited when we arrived, and I was so desperate for a distraction, that we thought we might send my mum and dad (plus all of our luggage) straight over to the hotel in a taxi, because we fancied doing part of the journey on foot. Well, when in Brooklyn and heading for Manhattan, why not walk over the Brooklyn Bridge?

It took us just over an hour, all in, to get from the cruise terminal to the other side of the Brooklyn Bridge. Honestly, I couldn't think of a cooler way to enter the heart of the city, it was like the city was revealing itself to us a bit at a time. It was just incredible, checking off landmarks that I've only ever seen on screen or read about in books. We could see the Empire State Building, amidst a forest of skyscrapers – we could even see the Statue of Liberty, across the water, standing tall (although not looking all that tall from where we were squinting) on Liberty Island.

I think, perhaps because New York is so well represented

on TV and in movies, that, even standing here with these iconic landmarks in my sight, I still feel a little detached from them. Staring at the Statue of Liberty in the distance still feels like looking at it through a screen, you almost have to meet the feeling in the middle, accept that it doesn't feel real and pretend that you're in a movie or something. My life certainly feels that way at the moment.

By the time we crossed the bridge, we were ready for a taxi to take us the rest of the way. There is just so much I want to do and I know that time is limited. The last thing I want is to give myself blisters on the first day, only to spend the rest of the time limping around.

As soon as you arrive in Manhattan, there is something to see almost everywhere you look. Our hotel is pretty much on Times Square – my dad booked it, and I've been so scared to ask him where we were staying, just in case it sounded like a nightmare (à la cruise for people double my age), but he really has picked a good one. It's a chain hotel, so nice enough, and being in the heart of the touristy bit is what I wanted, so no complaints from me. Well, I could potentially complain about the fact that he only booked two rooms for the four of us, but to be honest, I love sharing with Eli. Now more than ever, I really don't want to go back to living on my own.

When we arrived at the hotel Eli and I laid all of my new dresses out on the bed and I ranked them in terms of comfort while Eli ordered them in terms of sexiness. In the end, we worked out that the long, slinky red number with the plunging neckline (well, I call it plunging, but Eli says it's practically a turtle neck – I'd imagine it is somewhere in the middle) would be the perfect dress for this evening, although now that I'm out in the world in it, on my own, I feel a little…

I don't know, dressy. I should probably go shopping while I'm here. I mean, I should absolutely go shopping while I am here, I'm in New York! But I should probably shop specifically for some clothes to fill the gap I seem to have between casual and super formal. I feel like Jessica Rabbit's bloated sister in this dress, as gorgeous as it is. I guess it's too late to do anything about it now.

It turns out that where Simon lives now is actually not that far from where we are staying. A twenty-two-minute walk or a seven-minute taxi – guess which I selected to do, in this dress? Well, I might as well use my money to make my life easier while I can, right? And, anyway, catching a cab in New York is all part of the experience.

It did occur to me, when I was only a couple of minutes away, to check that Simon was still expecting me, and that he was actually going to be there. Well, when someone from thousands of miles away tells you they might drop in, how much do you actually expect them to show up?

Thankfully Simon replied, saying that he was preparing dinner for us, so that is both a huge relief and also really nice of him.

So here I am, standing outside an apartment building on 5th Avenue, the leafy green of Central Park behind me, as I wait to see Simon for the first time since the last time, when I threw a cup of cold tea over him.

Here we go...

32

I honestly don't know which way to look. To my right is Simon's living room window. He lives in a decent-sized apartment that overlooks Central Park, and he's above the tree canopy, so he has views of the city too. It's incredible, seeing all that green and all those skyscrapers, side by side, the most unlikely neighbours, but I quite like the way the park is this neat square of green in an otherwise concrete jungle. To my left is Simon himself, buzzing around the kitchen in his open-plan living space, preparing dinner, which smells amazing, but it's Simon himself I can't stop staring at. He looks so good – so different to the last time I saw him, but still Sexy Simon, all right. Perhaps Sexier Simon should be his new nickname...

Simon has grown his blonde hair a little longer, pulling it into a manbun on the back of his head. He's got a bit of the Chris Hemsworths about him, with his hair, his stubble and his muscular frame. Simon is wearing a tight grey T-shirt and jeans, which makes me feel like my outfit is way over the top, but he keeps telling me how great I look, which is putting me at ease a little.

He walks over with two glasses of champagne in his hands and, I know I said I would never drink again, but one glass to be polite won't hurt anyone, will it? Plus, imagine trying to explain not wanting one...

'Dinner is nearly ready,' he tells me. 'Sorry, I let you in and then immediately ignored you, I am a terrible host.'

As he jokes around, I notice how his accent has changed. I don't know how long he has lived here, but it must be long enough for a New York twang to have infiltrated his vocal cords. It suits him though; he seems like an uber cool New York creative type. I guess life here just suits him. God, I wish life here suited me. I know that I've only been here a few hours, but all I want to do is abandon my old life and start a new one here. I think I'd need to win a lot more than £50k to be able to afford to do that though, and I'm pretty sure New York is already full to the brim with aspiring writers, it doesn't need one more – especially not one who has spent the last year writing advertorials.

'I can't believe you're cooking,' I say. 'You never cooked.'

'Yeah, I move into a city full of incredible restaurants and I decide I want to learn to cook,' he says with a laugh and a shrug. 'My hours are so crazy sometimes. If I hadn't learned to cook, I either would have lived on takeout or instant ramen noodles.'

'I want to hear all about your work,' I insist.

'Well, let me plate up this food, and I'll tell you everything, how's that sound?'

'Perfect,' I reply.

As Simon does his thing in the kitchen, I walk across the living room. As I do, I take the smallest possible sip of my drink, testing the waters to see if my body will allow alcohol inside it after my last ordeal. Thankfully it is fine.

Simon's place is so effortlessly stylish. It isn't huge, but it's in a great location. I can't even imagine how much it must cost to live here, on the edge of Central Park, with the view he has, but I don't need much of an imagination to know that I could never afford it. It's a cute space, but he's done so much with it. He has bookshelves built into alcoves, a kind of funky, modern sofa that seems like it can be rearranged with minimal effort, to create different shapes, depending on how you want it. The room is full of beautiful art, interesting sculptures, fancy rugs, and, of course, lots and lots of photos. I take a little time to look over them. I can spot Simon's snaps a mile off – all portraits of models.

'OK, here we go, get it while it's hot,' Simon says. 'I hope you like Thai food.'

'I absolutely love it,' I reply, having never had Thai food in my life.

I head over to the dining table, where two beautiful plates of food wait for us. Delicious-looking, perfectly formed domes of rice, with all sorts of colours and textures peeping out from inside.

'This looks amazing,' I say. 'What's in it?'

'Beef, egg-fried rice, peppers, onions, oyster sauce, chicken stock… you're not about to tell me that you're vegetarian now, are you?'

I laugh. 'Nope, still eating almost indiscriminately,' I say.

'Glad to hear it,' he replies. 'Dig in.'

'After this holiday, I need to go on a diet,' I say. 'I ate so much on the cruise, I feel like I'm bursting out of my dress.'

'You look incredible,' he assures me. 'I actually thought you'd lost weight.'

Wow, even if it isn't true, Simon sure is saying all of the right things.

'So, you've been on a cruise?' he asks.

'Yes...' I laugh nervously. 'With my parents and my friend Eli. My dad booked it for us, but it turned out to be a cruise aimed at the over-55s.'

'Oh wow, what was that like?' he asks. I can tell that he's amused, but he is politely holding his smile back a little, I can see the corners of his mouth twitching though.

I tell Simon all about my time on board the Silverline cruise. Well, almost all about it, I leave out all of the stuff about Josh, and I absolutely leave out all the bits where I embarrassed myself. Instead I tell him about the ship, how big it was, all of the cool things to do on board, all of the things I would have previously dismissed as uncool which I'm now quite fond of, like water aerobics (the first time was great) and I even grew to love shuffleboard, I just need to get better at it.

'Wow, it really sounds like you made the best of it,' Simon says. 'You've always had that ability, to see the best in bad situations, to see the glass as half full.'

'I try my best,' I say. I'm not sure being positive comes to me as easily as it used to any more. 'Hey, you said you would tell me about your work.'

'I did. I'm a photographer for *Baci* magazine – mostly high-profile celebrity portraits. Not just musicians, actors, TV personalities, and models, the magazine has had a major overhaul, it's arty now. I get to photograph politicians, inventors, activists. It's fantastic to meet so many incredible people, they are really shaping who I am. I met Gabrijela Martinić, the climate change activist, have you heard of her?'

'I have,' I say. She's all over the news at the moment.

Absolutely stunning blonde twenty-something, even more beautiful on the inside. Every time I hear about her, it makes me want to be a better person.

'Her work is just so important – so incredible. She convinced me to take an extended break from work to join her group, removing plastic from the ocean. I haven't been back long, actually. Work were happy for me to take the time off because Gabrijela is a brilliant artist too. She's using the plastic we retrieved to create art, which I will be photographing for a magazine exclusive. I'm going to shoot her with her creations, I can't wait to see them.'

'Wow, that's amazing,' I admit. 'It sounds like the perfect job for you.'

'It really is,' he says. 'I am combining all of my passions, I'm changing the world – well, trying to.'

Simon gives me a warm, friendly smile. He really seems like he's grown as a person, from someone quite superficial and selfish to someone who is less hung up on the material things, who cares about the world.

'What about you?' he asks. 'How's the writing going?'

'I am also taking an extended break from work,' I tell him. Initially it seems like an OK thing to say, given that he has just done the same, but as my brain catches up with my mouth, it's hardly comparable, is it? He took time off to remove plastic from the ocean, to save animals and the planet. I quit my job on a whim before going on holiday. I wonder what kind of carbon footprint a week-long five-star cruise, plus a week in New York getting taxis from A–B because I'm too scared to navigate the subway, before a flight back to the UK leaves? A really bloody big one, I would guess.

'Oh really? How come?' he asks curiously.

Telling the truth, or even part of the truth, is going to make me look pathetic, isn't it?

'I was working as a journalist...'

Which is true.

'... But I wasn't happy with the work...'

Also true.

'... There were some moral issues that didn't sit well with me...'

Well, writing advertorials and passing them off as unbiased editorial opinion isn't right, is it?

'... And I couldn't take it any more. I had to quit immediately. My plan is to look for a new job – one where I can sleep at night. In the meantime, I thought it might be nice to spoil my mum and dad with a holiday.'

OK, so the truth might be harder to spot in that last part, but there is some in there.

'That's so sweet of you, Rosie,' he says. 'You've always been such a sweetheart. So, no ideas about what you want to do next?'

'I definitely want to keep writing,' I tell him. 'I do like working in journalism, I just want to be actually writing, not rewriting what people tell me I have to, whether I believe it or not.'

'We are always looking for new voices at *Baci*,' he says. 'You know I would put in a good word for you.'

'What, here in New York?' I ask.

'Yeah, if you ever fancied a change of scenery, I could hook you up.'

'Oh my God, Simon, you have no idea how much I would love that... I'm not sure I could relocate though.'

'Something to think about,' he says as he clears our plates. 'Dessert?'

'Yes please,' I practically groan. 'Dinner was amazing, thank you.'

'You're very welcome,' he replies. 'It's just so great to see you, for years I've thought about talking to you...'

Simon places a ramekin of something that looks and smells like a rich chocolate ganache in front of me. A couple of chocolate chip cookies are sitting on a plate next to it. I can feel my taste buds actively preparing for me to eat it, it looks so, so good.

'Chocolate still your favourite thing?' he asks me.

'Absolutely,' I reply.

'Well, dig in,' he says. 'The cookies should still be warm.'

Oh my God, they are. They're so warm and soft and delicious.

'So you're an amazing photojournalist, a philanthropist, an incredible chef... anything else to report?' I ask curiously.

'You make me sound far better than I am,' he says. 'I'm just one man trying to make the world a better place.'

For a moment, I wonder if Simon is as humble as he seems. When I went out with him he was nothing like this. He was selfish, he hung around with models, he liked to stay out late, he spent all of his money on designer clothes... New York has clearly been a positive influence on him. Perhaps sometimes you need to take yourself out of your hometown, and your small-hometown mentality, and look at the bigger picture from a different part of the world. Maybe it really would do me good to take a job somewhere else. I'm not sure I could move too far away from my parents though, as crazy as they make me, I'd miss them.

'I know I keep saying it, but I still can't believe you're here in front of me,' he says again. 'Such a surprise – an amazing surprise, but a huge surprise.'

'You had no idea I might get in touch?' I ask.

'None at all,' he says. 'After the way things ended... '

'So this is completely out of the blue,' I say to myself. Simon didn't send the flowers either then.

'Definitely,' he says. 'I didn't think you'd ever speak to me again, I—'

'Simon, I'm just going to be honest with you,' I start, before polishing off another cookie. 'People really need to be more honest, it will save a lot of time and effort and misunderstandings and running around town looking people up...'

I realise that won't make too much sense to him. I take a deep breath.

'I was on TV recently. On a quiz show. Things didn't go well... I won, but it was so embarrassing, and it actually went viral, so it's proving quite hard to ignore.'

'Wow, really?' he says. 'I'm on a social media cleanse and only responding to work emails, otherwise I might have seen it.'

'Trust me, if you haven't seen it, you don't want to. Anyway, it was so messy, that's mostly what forced me to quit my job – I did want to quit, but it was the fallout from the TV show that made me pull the trigger – and it's why I went to stay with my parents and how I ended up going on holiday with them... But, before I left, I got this bunch of flowers delivered to my flat, and they were clearly from an ex, and I really thought they were from you...'

'Oh,' he says. 'Well, they weren't from me, I'm sorry to say. I wish they had been. I mean, if anyone should send you flowers, it should be me, the way things ended...'

'We both messed up in the end,' I reassure him. 'I was being a crazy bitch, I was on your case 24-7, I was convinced that I couldn't trust you, I was spying on you... I needed stopping. Anyway, I worked through my issues and I'm a better person for it.'

'I'm really glad to hear that,' he says. 'I still don't think I should have gone as hard as I did but... well, I've matured too.'

'Let's just forget about it, OK?' I say. 'It's water under the bridge. It's just nice to see you, and to catch up.'

'Shall we go sit on the couch?' he asks.

It's so weird, hearing him talk with an American accent. Mostly it reminds me of Josh and his faux-Canadian accent, which annoys me. Why am I thinking of Josh right now? I doubt he was thinking of me, when it was me who was waiting to see if he would come back for me. And, spoiler alert, he never did, and what he's doing now doesn't count because his latest decision absolutely isn't for my benefit.

'Yes, sure,' I say.

'I'll top our glasses up and join you,' he suggests.

I make myself comfortable on Simon's grey U-shaped sofa. Well, comfortable-ish. I'm still holding my back straight and my tummy in, after all. I'd love nothing more than to just let it all out, exhale, slump down, curl up in a ball and maybe see if there are any more of those cookies, and if I can get a cup of tea to go with them, but I can't stop myself from still trying to impress him – even more so now that I've confessed my live-TV epic-fail drama.

Simon hands me my glass and sits down next to me. He reaches for a remote control that he uses to turn the music up at a little. It's funky, ambient background music. He uses another remote control to turn the lights down a little.

'Much better,' he says. 'Man, I can't get over how good you look. I don't remember you being such a feisty dresser.'

'We've both changed,' I tell him, nodding towards his own look.

Although I do wonder how much Simon has actually changed. This looks like a bachelor pad to me, and it's hard to believe that someone so seemingly perfect could still be single.

'That's New York,' he tells me. 'I am fully embracing my inner creative here. I travelled all over the world, before ending up here. I love it. Have you thought any more about relocating?'

'Since... since dinner?' I ask. 'Not really. It's a big thing.'

'It's a leap,' he says. 'But we have to take leaps in life.'

'I suppose we do,' I reply. 'It's just that, recently, all my leaps feel more like me falling into shark-infested waters full of sharp rocks.'

Simon laughs. 'You've always been so funny. So funny and so sexy and...' Simon leans forward and takes my hand, his face just inches from mine now. 'You don't know who sent you those flowers, do you?' he asks me.

'I don't... I thought it was you, but if it wasn't, then I don't know who they could be from.'

'Don't you find that rather strange?' he asks me.

'Oh, for sure,' I reply. 'It's been driving me crazy.'

'I recently asked the universe to send me something good – something amazing – and, well, you have turned up, seemingly sent here by a sign that you received, a sign that wasn't from me but has led you to me...'

'Right...'

'Doesn't it seem like it was meant to be?' he asks me.

'Doesn't everything, if you look at in the light that you want to?' I ask him.

'Now, that doesn't sound like the optimistic Rosie I knew,'

Simon replies. 'But, do you know what, maybe this is a better version of you, a more realistic one, one more equipped for dealing with the harsh realities of life.'

'Maybe,' I reply.

'You're just... you're right here, on my couch, you came all this way to see me... that sounds like fate to me. You are everything I want.'

Well, on paper, Simon is everything that I want too. He seems like a great person with a job that he loves, he cares about the planet, he sounds like he's matured a lot, he sure is easy on the eyes, and he seems to be offering me a brand new start in New York, a city I've always fantasised about living in... can you imagine, if I could live in New York, be a writer in New York! With my hot photographer boyfriend, too.

'This just feels so right to me, doesn't it feel right to you?' he asks me.

'It feels very fast,' I tell him.

'Let me show you how right it is,' he insists.

Simon kisses me. It's passionate, with a few fancy tricks he has obviously learned since we were together. It's a good kiss, on paper, I'm just not sure it feels right...

'Wait,' I say, as I pull away. 'Can we just slow things down a bit, please?'

Simon runs a hand through his hair.

God, I feel like such a square. There is a gorgeous man trying to kiss my face off, offering me the life I have always dreamed of, and I just cannot make myself go through with it. What is wrong with me?

'I know what this is,' he says. 'This is the universe testing me... it brought me the good thing that I want, that I asked for... I just need to restore balance.'

'What do you mean?' I ask curiously. Simon didn't used to

believe in the universe actively doing things, meddling in people's lives, bringing them the things they want like Santa after checking his naughty or nice list.

'You were so honest with me, telling me what has happened to you recently and what brought you here,' he starts. 'I need to be honest with you, that's what is stopping us from moving forwards.'

'OK...'

'I *was* cheating on you,' he says. 'When we were together. You were right. I did the phone thing as a test, to see how on to me you actually were... and when I realised you had me rumbled, well, there was nothing else I could do... If I had confessed, you would have dumped me, so it was just easier to go out fighting. But I was young, and immature, and I've learned so much about how to treat women since then. I'm a different person.'

I just stare at him for a second, as my brain tries to process everything he has just said.

'And, full disclosure, I am sort of seeing someone right now – well, a couple of people – but I'm going to call them up immediately and tell them that it is over, because you are back in my life and everything happens for a reason, right? I've learned my lesson; I'm getting a second chance. My relationships all feel so empty, I've been looking for something more, something deeper. No more models, I need someone for my soul.'

I laugh. It's a sort of small chuckle that builds up into to something wilder, something more menacing. 'You were cheating on me,' I say. 'Josh knew you were, I knew you were... I let you make me think I was crazy.'

'Who is Josh?' he asks as his eyes narrow.

'He's the person who fixed me, after you broke me,' I tell him. 'You're never going to get the chance to do it again.'

'Rosie, wait, I had to tell you the truth,' he says. 'So that we could move forwards.'

'I came here for a catch-up and to see if the flowers were from you,' I remind him. 'Now you're trying to stick your tongue down my throat and get me to move to New York – you're off your head. And you haven't changed at all, you're still a poser, you're just striking a different pose, this wholesome man of the people who wants to change the world, and yet you still kissed me just now, knowing that you're seeing someone else? Or a couple of someone elses? Oh no. No, no, no. I'm out of here.'

'Rosie, please don't leave,' he says as he follows me to the door. 'Let's talk about this?'

'Nope,' I say, and it's the last thing I say to him before I march out of the door.

I was so convinced, so, *so* convinced, that my future might be lurking in my past somewhere. But, apparently, no one sent me those flowers. I've been chasing my tail, thinking I was on some quest to getting my life back on track, and all I've done is double back on myself before wandering even further off course. I feel like such an idiot, but, even worse than that, I feel so guilty about Josh. He was right about Simon and he knew it. And things were so great between us and I actively left him to come and see this tosser, letting Josh think that I would rather spend time with Simon than him. I have screwed things up with one of the only people to ever really care about me. And there's no Rosie Outlook to put a positive spin on that one.

33

There is something so amazing about this city, the way it brings people together from all over the world.

The hotel had a breakfast buffet, so, when we went to get something to eat this morning, it was interesting to meet the other residents of the hotel. It seemed like almost everyone was a tourist, from all over the world, which I liked. Immediately it felt like we were this weird little community, all speaking different languages, who briefly united to share tables for breakfast and to try and work out how the bagel-toasting machine worked.

Now we're back upstairs. Eli and I are in my mum and dad's room with them, sitting on their bed watching TV while we figure out what we should do today. So far, I have refused to talk about what happened with Simon last night. To be honest, other than kicking myself for coming here at all, I haven't dwelled on what happened with him. He's history and he's staying that way.

'Can't we have a day to take a breather?' my dad asks. 'Just to find our feet and relax.'

'I don't want to sit in this room all day,' I say, my patience wearing thin. 'And if I have to watch another second of *Family Feud,* we're going to have a family feud of our own.'

I swear to God, the only thing on TV right now is *Family Feud* or Harry Potter movies.

'Come on, sis,' Eli says quietly. 'It's OK. We can all do something.'

'We could go for lunch somewhere?' I say.

'I did see somewhere outside that advertised New York's best pizza,' my dad says.

'I'm pretty sure they all say that, Tim,' Eli replies. 'But one of them has to be right, and I'm willing to try and figure out which one it is.'

'It's been a while since breakfast,' my mum reasons. 'I could eat. We can go there and plan what we're going to do this week? And it would be nice to take a walk.'

'Yes, great, let's do it,' I say, jumping to my feet. All I want to do it get outside.

'Still not want to talk about it?' Eli asks at a volume only I can hear as we make our way out of the room.

'Still don't want to talk about it,' I confirm.

The first thing we do is head to Central Park for a stroll. It's gorgeous, and it really does feel like being in a movie. I would be waiting for my meet-cute, were I not terrified of bumping into Simon. I know, the chances are slim, it's just with him living on the edge of the park, maybe he comes over here to do yoga and ask the universe to help him stop being an arsehole? I haven't heard anything from him since last night (not that I would want to, because he can't possibly say anything to fix this) which just goes to show how insincere he was being.

After a nice walk, and a cold $8 churro, we finally make it

out of the park at the other side, having not bumped into Simon thankfully, ready to begin our quest to find New York's actual best pizza.

After passing a few places, we happen upon a restaurant called Mario's. It looks so authentically Italian, and everyone inside has a strong, New York Italian accent, which we take as a definite sign of authenticity. Everything is green, white and red. The furniture, the table clothes, the uniforms – even the picture frames on the walls are a mixture of green, white and red. The pictures inside them are all of celebrities who have dined here. They are never huge celebrities, are they? Still, it's a cool idea.

We sit down and order a couple of pizzas. When they arrive, the slices are bigger than our faces. I'm so happy, I could cry.

'So, fair enough, this might be the only New York pizza I've tried,' I start, 'but I'm happy to sign off on this being New York's best pizza, it's incredible.'

'Oh, it's so good,' Eli enthuses. 'We don't need to eat anywhere else the whole time we're here.'

'Thank you so much for bringing us here,' my mum says. 'To New York, not just for pizza.'

'Yes, thanks, love,' my dad says. 'I know we're only halfway through the holiday, but I'm having such a fantastic time, and it's all thanks to you.'

It takes all my effort not to cry. They seem so happy, and it's so sweet.

'Most of all though,' my mum starts, 'it's just so nice to spend time with you again – with both of you – but, with Rosie, it feels like we hardly see you these days, and I do worry about you, living alone.'

'Can I move back in with you please?' I blurt.

'What?' my mum replies.

'Can I move back in with you? Just for a bit, until I sort my life out. I just... it's been so great to spend time with you too, and I don't want to be alone.'

'Well, of course you can,' my mum says. 'You can live with us forever if you like.' I'm pretty sure she means it. 'Gosh, this is the best holiday ever. Now I'm excited to plan things, and I'm even more excited about when we get back home, having someone to talk to, someone to watch *Bake Off* with.'

'You've had me all this time,' my dad points out.

'Yes, but you don't talk, and all you do during *Bake Off* is complain about how you don't like Paul Hollywood.'

'Such a crush on Paul Hollywood,' Eli says, biting his lip.

'Don't we all,' my mum replies.

'That's why I don't like him,' my dad tells me with a smile.

'So, where are we going while we are here?' my mum asks. 'Rosie, where do you want to go?'

'To name a few places I'd love to visit – so we can work out what is possible – the Met, the Guggenheim, the Museum of Modern Art...'

'Are these all museums?' my dad whines.

I ignore his uncultured complaining and continue. 'I'd love to go to the Strand bookstore, and Chelsea Market. I want to visit all of the cool TV and movie locations.'

'Not seeing Simon again then?' my mum asks curiously.

I've kept a dignified silence since I got back from dinner with Simon. I don't suppose dignity has ever been my strong point though, has it?

'I sincerely hope I never see Simon again,' I tell them.

'It didn't go well then?' my dad says. 'Do you want me to have a word with him?'

I'm touched that my dad is willing to do this in theory

although, in practice, I'm not sure how intimidating my daddy would be.

'I just want to forget he exists,' I say softly.

'Rosie, let's go and order milkshakes,' Eli suggests. 'That will cheer you up.'

I move my head from side to side thoughtfully. It might.

'OK, come on, what happened?' he asks once we're alone.

'Honestly, Eli, at first, he seemed amazing, like a dream come true.'

'And then what happened?' he asks.

'Then he tried to kiss me. And he's some sort of cosmic-ordering hippy type now, he thinks I was sent to him because we were supposed to be together... and when I didn't seem into it, he thought that was the universe telling him that he needed to clear the air with me.'

'The super hot ones are always super crazy,' Eli says with a sigh. It sounds like he has been burned before. 'It's always the way.'

'So, get this, he tells me that he *was* cheating on me when we were together!'

'Well, we knew that one, didn't we? That isn't exactly a spoiler.'

'How did we know that? We didn't know that.'

'Well, I knew it. And Josh knew it. It was blaringly obvious. I thought you did too, I thought you were just making excuses for him. It sounds to me like he worked you so hard back in the day, he left you doubting yourself, convinced you were wrong – that's how cheaters work, that's how they get away with it.'

'Well, he does all that and then tells me that he's going to tell the girls he is seeing that it is over, so, even if you could make a case for him having matured and grown into a better person, he's still a cheater.'

'A cheater never changes its spots,' Eli reminds me.

'Wait, so, if you were so sure that Simon was a bad egg, then why did you encourage me to go and see him?'

'At first, when you showed me a picture of him and told me about him, he sounded amazing, and you sounded like you wanted a second chance from him, and I love you, you deserve one. But as I learned more about him from you, and from Josh, it became obvious that Simon was a dick. And Josh is so obviously the one for you. Come on, you know it. Don't get caught up in who quit their job for whom and when. You're being handed a dorky life vest, don't try and figure out where it's coming from, just put it on. So, when you sent him packing yesterday morning, I knew you were making a mistake by going to see Simon... but I knew that you needed to figure it out for yourself.'

'You're like my fairy godmother,' I tell him.

'I'm pretty sure you calling me that is a hate crime,' he replies with a smile. 'Now that you've seen sense, can we please just figure out how we get Josh back on side?'

'It's funny, I was almost judging him for moving back in with his mum yesterday, now I'm doing the same.'

'So, you're going to be living in the same town,' Eli points out. 'Same town as me too.'

'Naturally I'm hoping we'll be best friends,' I tell him.

'We already are,' he points out. 'Now, Josh...'

I should never have left Josh on the ship the way I did. I don't know if I was scared about falling for him again, worrying about the future, or what, but it's easy to see now that it was the wrong thing to do. I have to find him and make things right. Whether he sent the flowers or not, he's the person I should be with.

'I think I might have an idea,' I say. 'But you might be a bit disappointed.'

'Well, in that case, let me get this good news out of the way before I fall out with you,' he jokes. 'I was going to save this for after the holiday, when you've got the post-holiday blues, but I'm going to tell you now instead: I've got you a job.'

'You've got me a job?' I repeat back to him as a question.

'I do,' he says. 'Have you heard of Viralist?'

'Of course I have,' I reply. 'Super cool, contemporary news website – news, lifestyle, humour.'

'Yeah, that's the one. Well, I got you a job writing for them.'

I laugh.

'No, you didn't.'

'Yes, I did,' he replies.

'How?'

'I'm an image consultant,' he reminds me. 'I worked with your image, made it your brand, got you a gig with them off the back of your TV blunder – they love a viral star, and you're one who can write. They want you to write for their love and lifestyle section. You'll probably have to do an interview, but it's just a formality.'

'Am I qualified to write about love?' I ask with an awkward laugh.

'No, but you're about to fix that,' Eli reminds me. 'So, will you take the job? It's at their offices in Manchester, it really is the perfect gig for you.'

'Of course I'll take it,' I say quickly. 'Thank you, thank you so much.' I throw my arms around him and plant a big smacker on his cheek.

'You're welcome,' he says. 'Now, tell me your plan.'

As I start to explain exactly how I'm going to make things right with Josh, I can't help but feel fortunate to have Eli and my parents in my life. Even if Josh tells me to do one, I know that these guys will always have my back. Finding romantic love would be nice, of course it would, but the love that these guys have for me is something else. Anything else is just a bonus.

34

When you arrive in New York City, if you are anything like me, you will have this long list of things you want to do and places you want to visit. My list was overflowing with museums, shops, landmarks, movie and TV filming locations, restaurants – I wanted to pack so, so much into this week. One thing you quickly realise is that, no matter how hard it would be to try and whittle that list down, you are going to have to come to terms with the fact that you cannot possibly do everything, especially not in one week. You would need to visit New York for a long time, or multiple times, to fit everything in.

Still, even if you only have a week here, there is plenty you can squeeze in. Unfortunately for me, all I will be able to say about my holiday to New York is that I took a trip to Central Park, caught a fleeting glimpse at the Empire State Building, and ate (probably) New York's best pizza. The reason for this is because I am heading home. Yes, little more than twenty-four hours after I arrived in New York, I was packing my bags to head home again.

I insisted that my mum, dad and Eli stick around and finish their holiday and then catch our booked flights back to England, not that they took much persuading. Well, my mum and dad didn't. Eli, on the other hand would not be put off going home early with me. He said that we had started this journey together and that we were going to finish it together, and that we would have plenty of opportunities to visit New York again in the future. I told him that he was crazy, not just for abandoning the holiday, but for agreeing to travel back with me. I mean, who wants to spend another seven days at sea unless they absolutely have to?

It was touch and go, and we almost didn't make it, but we managed to book ourselves a cabin on the Silverline cruise, from New York, back to Liverpool. We bought it from the on-site Silverline office where the oh-so helpful employee kept trying to put us off, treating us like we were idiots, explaining that this was a cruise aimed at much older clientele and that we might be happier doing something else. It took a lot of explaining and insisting before we were sorted. We practically ran towards the ship check-in area – and it really was like a scene out of *Titanic*. Yep, after a solid seven days of *Titanic* references, I get to spend another seven days making even more.

So now, here we are, on the Silverline cruise, sitting at our dinner table in our formal wear, waiting for our big plan to play out. I say big plan, it's more of a rehashing of the old one.

We've nearly finished eating. This time, our tablemates are rather tame, compared to our previous voyage. There is married couple, Rob and Pamela, who are cruising to celebrate their retirement, twin ladies, Eleanor and Elizabeth, who have been going on holidays together their entire lives (they are in their eighties now) and then there is Mrs Rice – I don't know her first name because she never gave us it – and next to her is an empty chair. We didn't really get into it, because she very clearly didn't want to talk about it, but it sounds like her husband must have died at some point between them booking the cruise and her being here today. It must have taken guts for her to come alone. People always seem much stronger than you think you can be yourself, don't they? Mrs Rice is probably well into her eighties, so she and her husband must have grown old together. It's a shame they didn't get to take this trip like they had planned, but life rarely cares about your plans, does it? I'm just so amazed she's here and living her life still. We could all learn a lot from Mrs Rice.

'Is it weird that I miss Colin and Clive?' I whisper to Eli. 'Even Linda and Karen. They were all such characters.'

'These guys do seem quite normal, don't they? It's very disconcerting.'

'What I'd give to hear a weird anecdote about someone falling into the ocean while having sex,' I joke.

'I'm going to hazard a guess this trip feels a lot longer than the first one.'

'It depends how tonight goes,' I say. 'I'm sure André will be pleased to see you, to spend a bit more time with you.'

'I'm sure he will,' Eli says. 'He messaged me earlier, saying he was looking forward to the next time we saw each other. We didn't make any plans or anything, we just said that we would keep in touch, and see each other again. Funny how things work out, isn't it?'

'Don't start banging on about the universe course-correcting us, please,' I insist. 'I'll throw up my salmon.'

'Just make sure it isn't in the pool,' he teases. 'You finished your dessert?'

I tilt my empty plate for Eli to see. 'You know I have.'

'OK, well, we're missing the show, so come on, let's go,' he insists, jumping to his feet.

'We're going to catch the show,' I tell the table. 'Would anyone like to join us?'

Everyone just kind of stares at me, like I've just proposed something weird.

'OK, see ya,' I say awkwardly as I follow Eli.

'You know how we assumed that on cruises you buddied up with your tablemates, and that's why we kept hanging around with Colin, Clive, Linda and Karen?'

'Yeah?'

'Well, it turns out that's not the done thing, I guess they just liked us – I think we might have liked them.'

Eli just laughs. 'I, for one, will never forget their stories about the oil industry, I only wish they had told us more,' Eli says sarcastically. 'Now, come on, pick up the pace, the show will have already started.'

'I thought the idea was to slink in late like last time.'

We are actually redoing day one of our cruise down to the last detail. We were kind of late getting on board: Eli complained all the way through the safety drill (although I don't think that was to recreate last time, I think he just hated wearing the dorky life vest for an extended period of time while not being in any immediate danger of drowning), we are wearing the same outfits and now we're rushing to catch Josh's set. We're a little later than last time (I remember him telling me that his sets rarely differed). I know this because he's well into his rendition of 'Feeling Good' already.

'Quick, behind the pillar,' Eli says.

Now we're in position, hiding behind a pillar in the bar, just like we did that first time I saw him again, when I lurked here and stared at him, marvelling at how amazing he looked and how good he sounded. Today is no exception, only somehow he looks even more attractive to me. I suppose, having spent the past week with him, rediscovering our connection, reigniting our flame, I've completely fallen for him all over again. He's such an amazing man, why would I get so hung up on why he was giving up ship life to move back to Manchester when all I should have been doing was thanking my lucky stars that he was?

There's something about his performance this time... He would always give it his all, but I don't know, it's like he's found a little something extra to throw into it. Perhaps because it's his last cruise, he's just making the most of it. He really is such an amazing singer, even if he moves back home, he should never give up on doing what he loves, not when he's so good at it.

'Thanks, everyone, thank you,' Josh tells his applauding audience in that faux-Canadian accent I have missed more than I ever thought I would. 'I can see a few faces I think I might have seen before, a few of my favourite fans sitting in the audience who I think know that I'm about to see if anyone wants to dance with me... but what none of you will know, and I'm sad to tell you, is that this is my last voyage singing on the ship.'

A few gasps echo around the room.

'I know, you're all gonna miss me, but I'm sure someone even better will be taking my place and, tonight, the show must go on, so...'

Josh takes a moment to compose himself.

'So, this next song is called "Save The Last Dance For Me". For the instrumental, I like to select a lovely lady from the audience for a twirl on the dance floor. So, for the last time, if you fancy a dance...'

As always, the regulars (different regulars to last time, I suppose) and lots of other eager women make their way to the dance floor, some bring their husbands – I imagine to dance with, rather than to swap for the next best thing to the real Michael Bublé.

Josh reaches that point in the song where he hops down from the stage, ready to find a lucky lady to dance with him.

'Ready to take the leap?' Eli asks me.

'Shove me like you love me,' I demand.

I feel that force behind me again, that well-intentioned shove by my best friend, sending me flying into the arms of the man I'm supposed to be with.

The last time this happened, ever the professional, Josh barely acknowledged that he recognised me, so much so that I did wonder if there was a chance he might not have. This time though... this time he catches me in his arms, but instead of dancing with me he just stares at me. This is not how I wanted this to go at all.

'I'm sorry,' I whisper to him.

After a few seconds of staring at me, Josh snaps back into action, being his usually bubble Bublé self, dancing with me like he's supposed to. He's so professional, almost too professional. I don't feel like he's connecting with me, I just feel like a part of his set. He lets go of me as soon as he can before hopping back onto the stage to finish the song.

I slink back over to Eli.

'I'm not sure that went well,' I tell him.

'I don't know,' Eli says. 'You know how professional he is, he's probably just playing things by the book, sticking to the script.'

'Thank you,' Josh tells the crowd. 'Now it's time for "It's a Beautiful Day" – actually, no, just a second.'

Josh turns to his backing band before stepping back up to his microphone.

'Tell you what, we're going to do something a little different, this is "Cry Me a River",' he says.

'You were saying...' I say to Eli. 'That isn't just going off script, that has to be a blatant dig at me, right?'

'I mean...'

'Oh, come on, Eli, you don't have to sugarcoat it – "Cry Me a River"? Just listen to the lyrics. This is the song you sing to a grovelling ex who comes crawling back into your life after fucking you over. It's the song that tells them to take a hike.'

'Who knew Michael Bublé music could do so much?' Eli marvels. 'Amazing.'

'Oh, yeah, he's a modern-day Sinatra,' I reply. 'Can we just get out of here please?'

'Sure,' he replies.

We leave just as shiftily as we arrived, only this time failure follows me out the door.

'I really thought that was going to work,' Eli says. 'Like a fresh start.'

'Me too,' I say. 'At least that was the plan. How many chances do people get though?'

'Two,' Eli tells me. 'Everyone gets a second chance. You've given us all a second chance. Me, Josh, even that tool Simon, who isn't actually that sexy now you've shown me him with that stupid hair.'

'Thanks, buddy,' I say. 'You always say the right things.'

What Eli is saying might sound good, but I'm not sure he's right about this one. Well, he's right about Simon's hair – now that I've had time to process it, I can confirm that only Chris

Hemsworth should have hair like Chris Hemsworth – but not about Josh. There's no way he's going to give me a second chance, and now I have to spend seven days at sea with him. So much for taking a leap, all I want to do is leap off the side of the ship and head back to New York.

35

'That screen is the single most depressing thing on this ship,' Eli says. 'And I ate dinner next to a chair intended for a man who died.'

'It's supposed to make the room seem bigger or better or less claustrophobic or something,' I say.

I'm lying on a double bed with Eli next to me, staring at our virtual balcony.

'I hate it too,' I tell him.

'Oh, how the mighty have fallen,' Eli says. 'Suite today, gone tomorrow. I hope I'm never poor again.'

'Easy come, easy go,' I say. 'My prize money wasn't much; I need to be careful with what is left.'

'I would have booked us a suite,' he says.

'I know, that's why I didn't tell you I was booking this,' I tell him.

Eli lies flat on his back.

'I feel like I'm in the ocean,' he points out. 'Like I'm Rose, on that door, floating on the water. I can feel every movement.'

'That's because we're in the cheap seats, buddy. God, you've changed.'

'I haven't changed, I've just... upgraded,' he reasons. 'I'd sleep in the boiler room for you.'

'Are you making *Titanic* references to cheer me up?' I ask him with a smile.

'Maybe,' he replies. 'Reckon we could watch it on that screen instead of staring at a black wall? It wasn't so bad during the day, but, God, at night, it's just nothing.'

'So was our actual balcony,' I remind him.

'But it was real, in a big room' he counters.

'And how would we watch movies on a vertical screen?'

'We can lie on our sides?' he suggests. 'Or just wait for this thing to go full *Poseidon Adventure* like Colin warned.'

'I'm not sure Colin knew what he was talking about,' I point out. 'I'd probably just watch something on your laptop.'

Eli snatches it up from next to the bed and fires up Netflix.

'Have you been watching weird stuff on my Netflix account?' he asks me accusingly.

'You said I could use it,' I remind him.

'I did, but not for weird stuff. If I ever make a mistake or I'm wrongly accused of a crime, someone at *The Daily Scoop* is going to publish a list of all the weird shit I supposedly watched on Netflix and it's going to make me look guilty.'

'I reckon you will be guilty,' I tell him. 'I've been to your apartment; it couldn't be more Patrick Bateman unless you had newspaper on the floor and an axe in your hand.'

'Why do I take that as a compliment?' he asks me with a smile.

'Because... I rest my case.'

There's a knock at the door.

'Fuck, that's it, they've come to tell us we're sinking,' Eli jokes – at least I think he's joking.

'I imagine they would have a more modern system than knocking on the door,' I tell him as I hop up to answer it. 'Oh, hi,' I say.

'Who is it?' Eli calls.

'Come in,' I say, stepping to one side for André.

Eli is lying flat on the bed, his laptop on his tummy. He looks up without moving anything but his eyeballs. As soon as he sees that it is André he jumps to his feet.

'Oh, hey, hi, hello,' he babbles. 'I was going to come and find you tomorrow – I'm not stalking you, she's stalking Josh.'

'You're always so quick to throw me under the bus when men are involved,' I tell him. 'I'll leave you guys to chat.'

'Don't be daft,' Eli says. 'You stay here, we'll go.'

'Actually, there's someone waiting outside who wants a word with you,' André says to me, nodding towards the door.

'Oh, OK,' I say. 'I'll head out then. Eli, you can stay here, look out of the balcony.'

'I should have Rock, Paper, Scissors'd you for it,' he calls after me. 'Have fun, you'll be fine.'

Outside in the corridor, Josh is waiting for me, still in his fake Bublé get-up.

'You want to go and get a cup of tea?' he asks me.

'Sure,' I reply.

We walk in awkward silence for a few steps before both clumsily trying to break it at the same time.

'Sorry, you go first,' he insists.

'I was just saying, I have a virtual balcony this time,' I tell him. It seems like a stupid thing to say now. 'You were right, they're kind of dumb, nothing like the real thing.'

'The real thing is always better,' he says. 'That's another

reason I wanted to give up this gig. I'll only ever be the virtual balcony equivalent of the real Michael Bublé. It's one of a bunch of reasons I wanted to give it up... I'm sorry that you weren't one of them, but you kind of were. I knew that I didn't want this life any more, I missed having someone, I missed having you, but I didn't think I'd ever get to see you again...'

I don't think Josh was expecting to get into it with me so quickly, but it's just pouring out of him.

'It was stupid of me to expect anything from you,' I tell him. 'You'd already given up your job, how were you supposed to go back in time and give it up for me? And I would never ask you to.'

'I know,' he says. 'Leaving you was one of the hardest things I have ever done because, the more you encouraged me to leave, the more I wanted to stay with you.'

'Let's not get caught up in the past,' I tell him. 'I've spent a lot of time down memory lane recently and I don't like it.'

'OK,' he says as we approach the ship's twenty-four-hour cafe. 'But I just want you to know that when I came to see you the other night, I had no intentions. I didn't even consider anything happening between us, and when it did, it didn't even cross my mind that we would pick up where we left off.'

'I realise that now,' I say. 'At the time, I think it just made me so mad, to think that was what you were thinking; it just made me want a bit of space.'

'Tea?' Josh asks.

'Yes please,' I say.

I find us a seat in a cosy corner while Josh gets our drinks. He soon catches up with me, with two teacups in hand.

'How was New York?' he asks curiously.

'Well, I understand what a "New York minute" is now,' I tell him. 'I wasn't there for very long, before I realised I needed to chase after you. And I know that we're heading in the same direction, I was just supposed to be a few days behind you, but I couldn't wait. I needed to take a leap, make a big gesture. And look how well that went.'

Josh smiles.

'"Cry Me a River"? Seriously?' I say.

'I was just playing hard to get,' he replies. 'But, seriously, I think I was upset that you bailed on me when things were seeming great again, I was hurt, then you were back and I suppose, like you, I was just being stubborn.'

'Can we just forget the past, please? It doesn't matter what happened years ago and who should have said or done what. Lord knows, I replay the past in my mind all the time – wondering how I could have said things differently or acted differently in certain situations. I'm here now because I didn't want you to be the thing I kick myself over in five years' time, every time I close my eyes to try and sleep.'

'I appreciate the big gesture,' he replies. 'Did you see Simon?'

'I did. He's still a major douchebag – perhaps an even bigger one. He finally confessed to cheating on me though. Do you know what? I feel lighter for hearing it.'

'Well that's good,' he says.

'Yep,' I reply.

Things go a little quiet again.

'I know you were saying that you didn't expect things to go back to how they were, but you know you said you were moving back in with your mum? Well, I'm moving back in with my parents too, so it really will be like old times.'

'Wow, that is weird,' he says. 'It's like we're both going back to square one.'

'Sometimes I think you need to,' I reply. 'Eli has got me a new job, so I'm excited to start that.'

'We swapped details before you guys left the first time, he said he would help me find a new singing gig – better than the job I've lined up for myself singing at a hotel in Manchester a few nights a week. He told me he had dated someone from Universal Music who he could get to listen to my original stuff, but I don't know if that was just a ploy to keep us in touch via him?'

'Or just so that he could have your number,' I joke. 'But, no, that sounds like my Eli. It would be so like him to date a record exec, and he's so, so generous. He just wants to help the people he cares about.'

'I don't know him all that well, but I suppose it does sound just like him,' Josh says with a smile.

I sigh. 'What a mess, huh?'

'We're cleaning it up,' he points out. 'So... what now?'

'I could hit you with a line I heard somewhere... I love you, I should have never let you go; I want you back – did you send me those flowers?'

'I didn't,' he says. 'Honestly, I didn't.'

'Damn, no one will own up to them,' I reply. 'Anyway... I could say that to you... but that would be such a movie ending, wouldn't it? We're not at the end, we're right back at the beginning. Why don't we hang out and just... see what happens? That way there is no pressure on anyone. If anyone wants to take any jobs on the other side of the world, no big deal, no one was expecting otherwise.'

'If that's what you want, that's fine by me. I'm not taking any more jobs abroad, it's not what I want. But I don't need to tell you, I need to show you.'

'OK,' I say with a smile.

'Now would be a really good time to sing "Home",' he points out.

'Please don't,' I say with a laugh.

'OK... can I kiss you then?'

'Definitely,' I reply.

And just like that, we have our new first kiss, in the corner of an otherwise empty café on a cruise ship, somewhere in the Atlantic.

'Listen, I don't want to sound presumptuous,' I start when we eventually pull apart. 'But can I sleep with you tonight? I'm pretty sure Eli and André will be destroying my cabin. Honestly, without the threat of falling over a real balcony, I dread to think about what they'll be doing.'

'There's an urban legend about someone falling over their balcony,' Josh starts.

'Oh, God, I've heard it.'

'All the more reason I can't wait to get back on dry land,' he jokes. 'And, yes, you can stay with me tonight.'

Josh wraps an arm around me, so I cuddle up into him and rest my head on his chest.

It was such a rush, to book a cabin to travel back in, but the second I did it, I started to feel anxious about another seven days at sea. Now that I'm with Josh, I don't mind it at all. I get to spend a week properly enjoying the cruise, sort of like a do-over, and then Josh and I get to do the same once we're back home, no expectations, no old scores to settle, just starting again and seeing what happens. And I can't wait to find out what does.

36

People normally feel blue when they get back from holiday, don't they? Transitioning from relaxing, fun, exciting days, back to the boring day-to-day of life. For me, I'm kind of glad that my holiday is over, because all I want to do is get on with my fresh start.

I don't mind that I'm heading back to my flat alone, because it's only to pack my things. I know that I have a cool new job waiting for me, so I'm not worrying about going back to work. I have Eli now, who is even better than the best friend I always dreamed of having. And then there's Josh... Josh who I am just going to see how things go with, but who I cannot wait to spend more time with. We're not picking up where we left off, we're going back to where we started. Maybe we can get it right this time around? I really hope so.

The first thing I notice as I approach my flat door is the dead bunch of flowers sitting on the doormat waiting for me. They were beautiful – I imagine. They're all brown and dried up now. They must have been here since, well, maybe a day or two after the last bunch arrived.

I pick them up and take them inside with me, placing them down next to the other bunch, which are also dead. They're similar-looking bunches, which makes me think they came from the same place.

I take out the card and see what it says.

'Thanks for giving me a second chance. I love you.'

My eyes widen as I read the words. These flowers obviously arrived weeks ago, so... they were never meant for me? It seems like someone has been sending flowers to the wrong address and whoever the first bunch was for took the sender back, so they sent a follow-up bunch, which also came to me in error...

Have I been running around on a wild goose chase, stalking my exes, putting myself in excruciatingly embarrassing circumstances, all because of a bunch of flowers that I received by accident?

I mean, it's a good accident, I suppose. If they hadn't come to me, I wouldn't have looked up Josh, or Eli for that matter, and I wouldn't be in the amazing situation I'm in now.

Oh, no, don't give me that, this isn't fate, or the universe or any of that nonsense. These flowers weren't sent to me in a magical act of course correction. And it isn't me finally having good luck either. Just an incredible coincidence that got my life back on the right track.

It might be my Rosie Outlook talking, but maybe sometimes things just do work out because they do? It just goes to show, you really never know what's going to happen, and you should always take chances. Imagine if I hadn't gone to that TV show recording, I'd still be lonely, doing a job I hated, maybe still dating Dinosaur Dave, because I'd just come to accept a comfortable level of boring. Always take chances, and even if they don't work out, take new ones. You never know what's waiting around the corner that will completely change your life.

ACKNOWLEDGMENTS

A massive thank you to my editor, Nia, to Sue, and to the rest of the Boldwood Books team for all of their hard work on this book.

Huge thanks to everyone who has taken the time to read and review my books. I really hope you enjoy this one too.

Extra special thanks to the people who I couldn't have got through this year without. Thanks to Kim and Aud for all of their love and support. Thanks to James and Joey, for all the tech support, and for keeping me in stitches and synonyms, depending on which one I needed.

Special thanks to Bambi and Teddie, who I will never forget.

Finally, thank you so much to my fiancé, Joe, for every single thing he does for me. This year would have been impossible without you. I can't wait to marry you.

MORE FROM PORTIA MACINTOSH

We hope you enjoyed reading *My Great Ex-Scape*. If you did, please leave a review.

If you'd like to gift a copy, this book is also available as a paperback, digital audio download and audiobook CD.

Sign up to Portia MacIntosh's mailing list for news, competitions and updates on future books.

http://bit.ly/PortiaMacIntoshNewsletter

ABOUT THE AUTHOR

Portia MacIntosh is a bestselling romantic comedy author of 12 novels, including *It's Not You, It's Them* and *Honeymoon For One*. Previously a music journalist, Portia writes hilarious stories, drawing on her real life experiences.

Follow Portia MacIntosh on social media here:

 facebook.com/portia.macintosh.3

 twitter.com/PortiaMacIntosh

 instagram.com/portiamacintoshauthor

ABOUT BOLDWOOD BOOKS

Boldwood Books is a fiction publishing company seeking out the best stories from around the world.

Find out more at www.boldwoodbooks.com

Sign up to the Book and Tonic newsletter for news, offers and competitions from Boldwood Books!

http://www.bit.ly/bookandtonic

We'd love to hear from you, follow us on social media:

 facebook.com/BookandTonic

 twitter.com/BoldwoodBooks

 instagram.com/BookandTonic